THE HARD TRUTH

A HIDDEN TRUTHS NOVEL

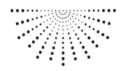

BRITTNEY SAHIN

EMKO MEDIA

THE HARD TRUTH

By: Brittney Sahin

Published by: EmKo Media, LLC

Copyright © 2016 EmKo Media, LLC

Second Edition © 2018

Previously titled: ***Buried Lies***

This book is an original publication of Brittney Sahin.

Editor: Sarah Norton, Chief Editor, WordsRU.com

Cover Designer: Mayhem Cover Designs /Istock/Deposit photos -licenses

Paperback ISBN: 9781719963060

❀ Created with Vellum

1

CONNOR

Ciudad Juárez, Mexico

The aluminum alloy of the Sig P220 cooled my sweaty palms as I attached the silencer. What had I gotten myself into this time?

I rubbed the butt of the gun against my forehead and leaned up against the splintered stable door. The firearm dropped to my side as hooves stomped behind me. The smell of horse manure slammed hard and fast into my nostrils, settling in my throat.

I needed to get out of there, if not for the damn odor . . .

Shit. Something was moving outside.

I edged closer to the door and peeked through a baseball-sized hole with ragged, singed edges.

The men were tall, tan, and resembling villains from some cliché Western. They stood across the courtyard by the house. Each had a hand resting near a weapon holstered at the hip. They were waiting.

Waiting for what? Me?

They weren't supposed to be there—not in the back. I'd spent the last two days studying aerial footage of the home, and there had only been guards at the front of the house. Why the hell were they in the back now? And why was the courtyard lit up like some Goddamn Christmas tree? I had planned to use the darkness as my cover, but now I needed a new strategy and fast.

I ignored the buzzing of the smartphone against my leg as the sound of the neighing horse gave me an idea. It probably wasn't the best of ideas, but it would have to do. Stepping back, I sucked in a breath and swung open the door to the stable.

The horse angled its head, and a pair of black glossy orbs studied me as the beast pounded its right hoof in the dirt. I jumped out of the way just as he leaped forward and pummeled the barn door head first, busting it wide open.

"Maldición," one of the guards cursed, reaching for his weapon.

The two guards chased after the mustang as it wheeled around the courtyard, raising its front legs up in the air as it cried.

It was now or never.

I darted through the broken door with my gun aimed at the first guard. My bullet stung him in the shoulder, and his pistol clattered to the ground. He dove away from the charging mustang as his tongue spewed forth several more curses.

The other guards' eyes locked onto me as the sound of death whistled past my ear. The bullet careened off the statue of an angel that stood just outside the barn.

An angel? Really?

The magazine of my weapon sprang, popping forth a new round into the chamber. My finger light on the trigger, I fired off another shot as the second guard began retreating to the house.

My bullet pierced him in the hand, and an explosion of red rained as he stumbled.

My combat boots carried me fast through the rest of the large courtyard, and I barely felt the guns' recoil as I squeezed off two more perfect shots, which struck each man once in the leg. It would have been easy to kill them, but I prefer to leave God as the judge, jury, and executioner . . . well, at least the executioner.

The people in the house must have heard the shouting of the guards, as well as the damn screams of the horse. With my back pressed to the house beside the back door, I pushed away the noise of the mustang and the groans of the injured guards.

A shuffle of steps . . . only one guard? There had to be more than one. At least two or three inside.

The rickety old door creaked open as my ears registered the familiar sound of a safety being removed.

I whipped around in front of the door and blocked the man's gun with my forearm. My assailant's gun clanked on the floor as I gripped his arm and twisted it behind his back. His clothes reeked of cigar smoke, the cheap kind—definitely not Cubans. They were probably new to this game.

"Where's the girl?" I asked as another man appeared at the other end of the hall.

The man charged, and I lifted my arm and shot him in the chest.

Now that he was no longer a threat, I shoved the man before me to his knees and leaned forward, my face inches from his, my weapon pressed against his sweat-slicked temple. "Where's Lydia?" I gritted my teeth, adding a bit of a snarl. There had to be one more man in the house, and he was probably with the girl.

"Call out to your friend and tell him you took care of me."

Did he understand me? The same line in Spanish slipped fast from my lips.

He shook his head before reaching into his pocket and revealed a knife. The silver blade flashed toward my face, but I shifted to the side, just avoiding the cut, and smacked the butt of the gun against his skull.

I stepped around his crumpled body and strode down the hall. The vibration in my pocket alerted me to another call. Perhaps I should have powered down my phone . . . but that would introduce its own risks. If someone got the drop on me, at least my government pals would be able to track my phone.

"Hello?" A young girl's voice. "Help! There's one more . . ."

At the end of the hall, I peered around the corner to my right. A tall, lithe man stood beside the girl. Her shoulders slumped forward with her head hung down. She was unconscious.

"Drop your gun," the man warned as he gripped her by the hair and yanked her head back, holding a knife to her throat.

With no time to think I blasted a round from my weapon. Something told me the world wouldn't miss this asshole.

But I didn't kill him—I didn't need to. Although damned if I wanted to after seeing the girl unconscious.

The bullet grazed the man's neck, forcing him to drop the knife and apply pressure to the wound at his throat.

"Back away from her."

He mumbled, "I'm not paid enough for this," as he sank to the floor.

"Cuff yourself." I chucked a pair of handcuffs in his direction.

His lips curved and twisted into an ugly scowl, but he followed my command quickly. He rushed his cuffed hands back to his throat to help control the bleeding.

I hurried to release the girl from her restraints, not knowing how long it would be until the men from the courtyard came barreling in. Or, perhaps, the real man in charge.

The girl was light in my arms. Aside from the recent blow, she appeared to have been unharmed.

"Tell your boss that if he ever plans on kidnapping another American in Mexico, I'll send ten men just like me down here to deal with him."

* * *

"THANK GOD," LYDIA'S MOTHER CRIED.

A smile tugged at my lips as she wrapped her arms around her daughter in a warm embrace. "These people are animals. They'll go after anyone for money, but they don't always stick to the deal."

I grimaced at the thought of what might have happened to the girl if I hadn't gotten to the house in time. If I had a daughter . . . damn, I couldn't even imagine. I'd be one of the fathers who stand in the door with a shotgun in hand when my daughter went on a date.

What in the hell was I thinking? I would never marry. Never have a daughter.

"I don't know how to thank you." With a shaky hand, the girl's father held out a check. There was an absurdly large number written on it.

"I don't want your money."

"But you did a job for us, a job the police couldn't even do." He exhaled a deep breath. "When I called Michael for help, I wasn't expecting a handout. I'd pay anything to get my daughter back. Thank God he was willing to help out an old veteran like me, even though he was on his honeymoon." He set the check on the kitchen table and rubbed the nape of his neck. "I—I just can't believe they came after us. After my precious Lydia." He looked over at his wife, who cradled their daughter in her arms.

Sadness snaked its way up inside me. I wasn't sure why—this had all ended well. "Sir," I started before clearing my throat, "I think you should consider coming back to the States. The situation down here in Mexico is getting worse. I understand your wife has family here and all."

The man held up his hand. "Of course. We're leaving immediately."

"Well, good luck to you, sir." My phone vibrated in my pocket as I made my way over to the mother and daughter. "Are you okay?" I asked, placing my hand on her shoulder. "You're one strong girl. You know that, right?"

She wiped away the tears from her cheeks and flung her arms around my neck. "Thank you," she cried into my ear.

I allowed myself a brief feeling of relief. "Stay safe." I tried to ignore the strange swell of emotion in my chest. "Goodbye."

On the way back to my rental car, I shoved my hand into my pocket to see who was calling.

An unknown number.

"Hello?"

"Connor?"

As the engine purred to life, my hand fell from the keys and onto my lap. "Mason? Mason, is that you? Are you okay?" Worry seized my body as my face grew taut with concern. Images of my own time in Afghanistan flashed into my head: IEDs, shrapnel, terrorists . . . had something happened to my kid brother? "Mason?"

Static.

"Mason, what's wrong?"

"Shit, Connor. I've been calling . . ." Interference. "I'm about to board . . . back to the States."

Did I hear him right? "Are you hurt? Why are you leaving? What's wrong?"

"I'm okay, but . . ."

"What?" Panic strangled my nerves. Something wasn't right.

"No one could reach . . ."

"What? You're breaking up. I'm losing you."

"Dad's dead."

2
OLIVIA

THE SOUND OF HIS VOICE INSTANTLY GAVE ME THE CHILLS. "Olivia?"

"Oh jeez, what does he want?" Claire took a sip of coffee from her oversized, hot pink mug.

I rolled my eyes and squirmed in my office chair, trying to get comfortable. "How did your date go with him, anyway?"

She shifted in her four-inch leopard print heels and continued to chew on her lip without making eye contact—I knew what she was going to say.

Claire set her cup on my desk. Her young, porcelain skin assumed a barely-there frown. "Um. He's a total asshole. It wasn't even a date. It was an 'I want to screw you' kind of thing." She pulled on the strands of her raven black hair and squinted at me.

Thoughts of pounding our boss in the face with my killer right hook shot into my mind. The cheap plastic arms on my chair melded with my palms as I gripped them in a frantic attempt to keep my thoughts to myself. It was even harder than usual not to say more than I should about the jackass of a boss we worked for. "Claire."

Even with her shoulders slumped forward, she was incredibly

tall. Why was she a secretary when she should've been a model? She had crazy long legs and a bust size that should be X-rated.

"We skipped dinner and went straight to his place." She looked at me with hooded eyes. Ugh, why him? Anyone but him.

I must have lost my poker face, because she said, "Don't give me that look, Liv. I couldn't help it. He's just so damn hot." She fanned her face with her free hand and rolled her shoulders back. "I know you don't like him, but it was just sex."

"Okay." I stood up and reached for my tablet.

"He totally looks just like this super sexy DJ I have the hots for, who spins at The Phoenix. You know the one I'm talking about, right?"

"Um . . ." My mouth parted as I waited for her to continue, knowing that I probably didn't want to hear what else she had to say.

"And Declan's kind of kinky," she whispered. "Into all that *Fifty Shades* stuff . . . and you know how I have a thing for bad boys." She sat in my vacant chair and sipped her coffee.

"He's not a good guy, Claire."

"Shit. I know, and I resisted his approaches for the last two months that I've worked here . . . but I'm weak."

Something in my chest physically hurt to hear her talk. "I wish you would stay away from him. I don't want to see you get hurt." That was all I could say. "Be right back." My lips puckered sourly as I left my cubicle, and a tingling coursed through my body as disgust swallowed me whole.

I wish I understood why men like him existed, not to mention why women are attracted to them.

"Come in," he ordered when I tapped on his door. "What took you so long?" Declan Reid, owner and CEO of Reid Enterprises, was the same age as me. Twenty-freaking-nine. His father had retired three years ago and left Declan his failing portfolio of businesses. Somehow, the inexperienced young owner had managed to turn everything around. It didn't impress me, though—not with what I knew.

Declan turned away from his wall of windows and sipped his coffee, and I indulged in a mental image of his coffee spilling and burning his chest as I stepped inside what I had nicknamed Lucifer's Den. "Just wrapping up a discussion with Claire." I cleared my throat and sat in the bright red leather chair in front of his desk. Red—the devil's color. How perfect.

I set my tablet on his silver desk, which was massive and had no drawers. "What can I do for you?" The sound of my overly pleasant voice was enough to make me nauseous.

Declan remained standing in front of the windows, which overlooked the water. Our office sat near the docks, as the majority of the business was handled overseas, and cargo shipments were made on a daily basis. "How would you feel about a promotion?"

My shoulders arched back as my attention focused on his black dress shirt.

"What?"

He squinted down at my black heels. Then his eyes wandered up over my calf muscles to the hem of my modest, black pencil skirt.

What sinister thoughts were going on in his head?

I bit back my desire to curse at him as his heated stare settled on my chest, which wasn't even exposed. He'd just imagined me naked, hadn't he?

I hated that Declan was so good-looking, with his spiky black hair and haunting brown eyes. He was fit and strong, but not muscle bound, and he had black ink on his forearms, which I noticed whenever he rolled his sleeves to his elbows.

My hand slipped up to my chest, double checking the buttons on my blouse.

"Mr. Reid?"

He approached his desk and set his coffee down before sliding into the nearby leather chair. A quick image of red leather and whips popped into my head as I remembered what Claire had said.

"Olivia, you've been a valuable asset here at the office, but I think I'd prefer to offer you a different position—one outside of Reid Enterprises. Or at least, outside of this building."

"What did you have in mind?" I rolled my tongue over my front teeth as I considered the implications. I didn't mean for it to come across as sexual, but it must have because he narrowed his eyes on my face. His attention pinned to my mouth.

"I'd like you to work for me as my personal assistant," he said after shaking his head a bit. "It'd be more of a nights and weekends kind of deal. I want someone who can help me with the nightclubs and restaurants I own."

Oh wow.

"Olivia, I need someone I can trust, someone always by my side. But the job will require a lot of hours, as well as travel. I'm opening a new club in Vegas soon, and I'd need you there with me. We'd probably go to Vegas a lot." His lips quirked into a quick smile but faded as he stood up. "I respect you, Olivia. You're not like most of the women who work here."

Yeah, I'm almost thirty. I cover my cleavage. And, oh yeah, I don't want to sleep with you.

"I know I have a certain reputation at the office." He rubbed the nape of his neck. "And it's not that I'm not attracted to you." He grinned, exposing his bright, almost too-perfect, teeth. "You're by far the sexiest woman here, in fact. But I need to exercise restraint when it comes to you because I see big things for your future." He walked around behind his desk and took a seat in the leather chair, which looked so much more comfortable than the tiny red one on which I was perched.

"What are you trying to say?"

"My goal is to groom you to run one of my nightclubs someday. Maybe even more than one. Business is booming for me, but it's exhausting to directly manage my manufacturing companies as well as my entertainment ones. It'd be nice to bring you up in the ranks so that you could help me out."

"Are you serious?" I couldn't believe it. Not really.

He nodded. "You have an MBA—you shouldn't be wasting your time as an admin." He scratched his chin and tilted his head. "I have no idea why you took the job to begin with, but I'm glad you did. I have greater plans for you."

"I don't know what to say, Mr. Reid." I *did* know what to say, but I figured I should act meek. Maybe bat my eyelashes a few times for added measure.

"Say you'll start now. And stop calling me Mr. Reid. From here on, I'm just Declan to you." He reached into his desk drawer. "Here."

I reached out and caught the set of keys he tossed my way.

"One is a key to my club, The Phoenix, and the other is to your company car. I hope you don't mind driving an Audi?"

Was that supposed to impress or excite me? "Wow. I'm a little shocked by this." I stood up and set the keys on top of my tablet. Fortunately, after the last eight months, I'd mastered the level of flattery required to impress such a narcissist.

"You can go ahead and pack up your desk. You won't be reporting here anymore. I have an office set up for you at The Phoenix." He looked pleased with himself as he leaned back in his seat.

"Thank you," I bit out.

"Be at the club at eight. We'll have a briefing to discuss your new roles and responsibilities before we open." Declan glanced down at his ringing cell and waved me away with his hand.

"Well, what did he want?" Claire asked as soon as I returned to my cubicle.

"Don't you ever work?" I motioned for her to get out of my seat.

"Did he mention me?"

"No, Claire." Clearly she didn't intend to heed my earlier advice. "He offered me a new job."

"What?" she gasped. "Really?"

"Yeah."

"Wow. What job?"

"His personal assistant. I guess I'll be helping him with his nightclubs."

Something that sounded like a squeak escaped her lips. "Oh my God. I'm so jealous. Can you get me on the guest list for a VIP booth at The Phoenix this weekend?"

"Um. Sure."

As I sat down at my desk, the red logo of Reid Enterprises swirled across the screen of my computer, ricocheting against a black backdrop. For the first time in eight months of working at Reid, a bubble of hope swelled inside of me.

3

CONNOR

"I STILL CAN'T BELIEVE HE DIED OF A HEART ATTACK." MASON scrubbed a hand over his jaw. "I mean, I know he had heart issues in the past, but I just didn't expect this."

"Technically he died of a stroke to the brain," my dear old mom chimed in.

I stood in the doorway to the lawyer's office, not overly enthusiastic to hear my father's will. "Why are you here?" I snapped at her. "And why are we having this meeting right after the funeral?"

My mother looked up at me from her seat. She ran a hand through her auburn hair and wet her red lips. Really, Mom? Fire engine red? At least she had managed to wear black. I'd half expected her to show up in glitter and feathers.

"I have to get back to Scottsdale today. Jerry has an important golf tournament." She pressed a hand to her chest as the lawyer cleared his throat behind me. I stepped aside and allowed the lawyer entrance to his office.

"You shouldn't even be in this meeting. You really think he put you in his will?" I tried not to laugh at the absurdity of my hard-ass father leaving anything to my mother, who was now his ex-wife—

13

the woman who gave up custody of my brother and me in exchange for the yacht and a home in Aspen. Well, maybe that wasn't quite what happened, but it was pretty damn close.

She ignored me and directed her attention toward Mason, who was a lot less jaded than me. He didn't know what I knew about our parents, however. He didn't have the privilege to see how ugly they could be.

Guilt pulled at me as I fought the continued urge I had to be angry with my father. The man was gone—there was nothing left to say.

"How are you feeling, sweetie?" My mom rested her hand on my brother's shoulder, but his attention was still on me.

"Let's just get this over with." He gestured for me to join them.

"I'll stand." God, I didn't want to be there. Even if my father put me in his will, I didn't want anything from him.

"Connor? Mason?" The lawyer perched his black rimmed glasses on his nose and slid two envelopes in Mason's direction. "A man dropped these letters off the day after your father passed away. He told me that your dad wanted you to have them."

Mason reached out and grasped the envelopes. "Take it," he urged, pushing his arm toward me. My name was written on the envelope in black capital letters.

I sighed and grabbed the letter, feeling the slight weight of it in my hand, then folded it in half and stuffed it in my back jeans pocket without more thought. I swallowed the lump in my throat, crossed my arms, and moved to the window, which overlooked 5th Avenue.

"Who delivered the letters?" Mason asked.

"I believe it was your father's personal driver," the lawyer responded.

"Tyson?" I turned back around. I hadn't seen Tyson in years. He was a good man, a former Marine. My father had hired him over twenty years ago, and Tyson had been with him ever since.

Where was he now? Who would he work for now that my father was gone? "Do you have a contact number for him?"

The lawyer looked at me. "I don't, but I'm sure your father's office will have his information."

I nodded and turned back to the window, making a mental note to call my father's secretary, Elsa. God, I hadn't seen her in years, either. How long had I been away?

Still not long enough . . .

"I really must get going. Perhaps you could go ahead and start?" My mother's voice grated on my ears. Was it wrong that my own mother got on my damn nerves?

"Yes, of course," the lawyer responded.

A guttural noise riveted my attention; my brother was clearing his throat.

With my back against the windows, I kept my arms crossed and focused on the cream carpet beneath my shoes. The lawyer began reading, but my mind was elsewhere, tuning him out.

"He what?"

My mother's shrill voice knocked me out of my daze. "What?"

"He left me nothing. After all those years—really?" She pushed to her feet, clutched her purse and bent over the desk. She snatched the file from the lawyer's hand.

"Mom." Mason grabbed the document and handed it back to the lawyer. "You need to get a grip."

"Easy for you to say—he left you and your brother everything." She did something ugly with her mouth. I don't even know what you'd call it. A scowl?

"Listen, I don't want whatever he left me." Everyone looked at me as their mouths edged open.

"Connor," Mason began, and I already knew my younger brother was about to lecture, "I need your help."

"Since your father's business was privately held, it looks like you two are in charge of everything." The lawyer stood up and removed his glasses, resting them on top of his paperwork. "Matthews Tech hovers around two billion dollars."

"Did you just say billion?" Mason pushed a hand through his dark brown hair. "Wow. I didn't think it was worth more than a few hundred million."

"It wasn't until last October when your father signed a two-billion-dollar contract with the Saudis." The lawyer reached for his tie and tugged. Did he hate wearing the noose of a tie as much as I did?

"As in Saudi Arabia? Where my troops are currently stationed?" Mason's brows pinched together as he stood.

"Aren't we missing the point here? He didn't leave anything," Mother dodged in. "Are you sure you haven't made a mistake?" She glanced down at the file.

I'll take bullets in Mexico over my mother's entitled attitude any day.

"Were you a part of the deal with the Saudis?" Mason asked.

"I wish." The lawyer chuckled somberly. "No, I just handle your father's personal assets."

Mason approached me, and I pushed away from the window. "So, you're going to help me run the company, right?"

My brother knew I was against everything my father stood for —did he think I would wear a suit and sit in board meetings all day? Hell, no. "You're kidding?"

Mason's silvery gray eyes appeared empty. Sad. We'd just lost our father, but I couldn't bring myself to shed a tear. What did that make me? Watching Mason stand over our father's casket at the funeral, his normally steely composure broken by sadness, had been as close as I came to crying.

I know that makes me a prick, but our father was a Grade A asshole.

"Connor." Mason rubbed the back of his neck. "You know I always wanted to take over Dad's company. But I still have almost six months left on my tour. Can you, at the very least, run the company for me until I'm back home?"

Fuck. How in the hell was I supposed to say no to that? Risk my brother worrying about the business while he's off fighting fundamentalists in the Middle East?

A whistling noise escaped my lips as I blew out a breath. "I don't know how to run a business. You know what I do, right?"

"Why don't you sign everything over to me, Connor? Jerry's a businessman; he can handle the business until Mason's back. And Mason and Jerry can run the company together." The wheels were spinning in my mother's head. "Everyone would be happy." She pressed a hand to my forearm.

My eyes locked on her hand, which looked like that of a thirty-year-old, rather than that of the sixty-five-year-old woman my mother was. What money could buy . . .

Mason immediately interjected with, "Hell no."

My mother's arm dropped to her side as she spun around to face him. "What do you mean, no?" She puckered her lips. "I'm your mother, Mason. Why wouldn't you want me to be involved?" she drawled.

Now where in the hell had she developed a Southern accent? We grew up in Manhattan, for Christ's sake. Mason ignored her, focusing on me, his eyes pleading.

"Mason, I don't have a clue about business, and college was a decade ago. I don't remember anything."

Ask me how to disassemble an automatic weapon—I'll do it for you in record time.

"Perhaps I should leave you alone to talk," the lawyer said on his way to the door.

Mason shifted his attention to me once again. "Connor, I need you." There was a rasp of desperation in his voice.

Six months. Could I run a billion-dollar business for six months without tanking the whole damn thing? Or losing my mind?

"I'll do it." My own words surprised me.

Mason flung his arms around me.

"Jeez." I stepped back from him. "Only until you're back. Then the company is all yours."

* * *

"You should've called me."

"You were on your honeymoon, dude. I wasn't about to get in the way of that." I reached for the tie around my neck and fidgeted with the knot, loosening it. "How do you do it, Michael? How do you wear these damn things?"

"Wear what?"

"A tie."

A light chuckle rose and fell. "Hi, Connor."

It was Michael's blushing new bride. "Hi, Kate. Sorry—I didn't know I was on speakerphone, or I would've said hi earlier."

"Connor?"

How did she manage to do that? Say only one word, my name, but pack it full of such emotion that it made the hair on my arms stand up. "Yes?" I leaned back in my seat and squeezed my eyes shut.

"Michael's right, you know. You should've called us. At the very least, you could have called us when we got back a week ago. Mason sent Michael an email saying to check on you. I can't believe we had to find out that way." Kate huffed.

"Hey, you're not allowed to be pissed at me. I get a pass, don't I? Since my pops passed."

"Stop joking around, Connor. You don't have to be that guy right now," Kate shot back, her voice ringing a blow of honesty I didn't want to deal with right now.

"I'm fine. Really."

I'd come to terms with my father's death. I just couldn't get myself into his office until this week.

"How does it feel to be rich?" Michael quipped, easing the tension, for which I was grateful. It had been six years since we'd both been in the Marines. God, time flew by.

I cleared my throat and opened my eyes. "Oh, it's fucking great. But the hours are shit." I moved closer to my desk and tapped a few keys. An email with a red exclamation point popped up. I really hated this. Emails. Seriously? I never would've thought this would become my life. How'd I go from bullets to board meetings? "Sorry, Kate." I try not to make it a habit of cursing around women, but sometimes I forget.

"Is there anything you need? Can we visit?" Kate's voice slipped through the line.

"No, I'm okay, but I'm swamped right now. I've only been in the office three days, and I'm ready to throw in the towel."

"Just hang in there. Your brother needs you." Michael, the voice of reason. Damn him.

"All right. I'd better get back to work. I'm sure I have some mind numbing meeting to attend to. I'll be in touch. Later." I hung up before they had a chance to respond. I didn't mean to come across like a dick, but I wasn't in the mood to discuss my feelings today. And I knew Kate—she'd find a way to peel back the layers, while I preferred to keep my skin thick.

I looked up to see Elsa, my father's secretary—well, now *my* secretary—tapping on the frame of my open office door. "Elsa, you don't need to knock. Come on in."

"I still haven't been able to get ahold of Tyson." She pushed a hand through her short white bob and took a seat in front of my desk.

"Are you okay?"

"Yes, sir. I'm just worried about Tyson." She removed her red framed glasses and shifted in her seat.

"Me, too. You've called his phone?"

She nodded.

"Has anyone checked his home?" I pushed to my feet and shoved my hands in my pockets.

"Yes—no answer. No one has seen him since your father passed away." Her voice cracked. How close had she been to my father?

"Do you need some time off, Elsa?" The thought had never crossed my mind before. Had she cried when I hadn't?

"I took some time off before you started."

"You sure you're okay?"

"Yes, but thank you for your concern."

"All right. Well, keep trying to reach Tyson. I don't need a personal driver, but I do miss him."

"Of course." She glanced down at her lap for a brief moment before looking back up. "You have a meeting with Lauren Tate now, the director of sales and operation. She just got back from Saudi Arabia this morning."

I'd lost count of how many people now worked for me and what their names were. I guess I needed to learn them and soon. "Sure. Send her in whenever." I sat back down and gave a slight nod to Elsa before she stood and left the room.

"Connor Matthews?"

An attractive brunette was standing in my doorway a few minutes later, wearing a figure-hugging, sleeveless black dress that revealed her long, toned legs. "Lindsey?" That had been her name, right? My mind was a garbled mess.

Her lips quirked at the edges as she approached my desk, her eyes studying me. "Lauren."

At least I had remembered it began with an L. "Hi, Lauren. Nice to meet you." I stood up and extended my hand. "You're so young." She couldn't be any older than twenty-five. "And in such a high up position . . ."

Her brows lifted as her lips parted.

"Shit." I pushed a hand through my hair, mussing it up. "I'm going to get myself sued or something, aren't I?"

She cracked a smile. Whew.

"I've seen pictures of you before. Your father showed me—"

"He did what?" I shook my head in disbelief. "He showed you pictures? Why the hell did he do that?"

I probably wasn't supposed to swear at work. Or check out her legs. I needed the HR department's number on speed dial.

She blushed a little, and her dark brown eyes focused on me with laser-like precision. "Your father was proud of you guys."

Her words reminded me of the envelope from the lawyer. I hadn't read my father's letter, which was still in the glove compartment of my Jeep. That's where I'd stashed it after the reading of the will. For a brief moment, I wondered what it said. *I'll read it, at some point*, I promised myself.

"You seem surprised." The way she said the word surprised, with both R's rolling a bit, I wondered if she was born somewhere else. If so, she didn't seem to like her accent. It was as if she went out of her way to over enunciate things.

"Lauren, I'd prefer not to talk about my father, if you don't mind."

Her forehead creased, but she didn't voice her thoughts. "We have a meeting tonight."

"Tonight?" I scratched my jaw, the stubble pricking my fingers. I had just shaved off my beard the other day, but damn did my facial hair grow fast. When I had showed up to the office on Monday in jeans, a T-shirt, and a full beard, the looks I got . . . well, I decided I'd better look the right part. And so I'd shaved, bought some suits, and have been trying to trick everyone into believing I actually belonged.

"We have a meeting with Declan Reid at The Phoenix."

"The Phoenix?" I shook my head. "Why do I have a meeting at a nightclub?" I reached for my coffee but noticed Lauren's gaze on my chest.

Did I have a stain? I looked down, adjusted my red tie, and checked my white dress shirt. Nope, everything looked good.

"Sorry, what was I saying?" She blew out a breath and forced a tight-lipped smile. "Your father was in the midst of a major business deal with Declan Reid. Did you want me to cancel?"

I thought about it for a moment, trying to filter through the barrage of facts in my brain. Had I heard of Declan Reid before? For some reason, the name sounded vaguely familiar. "No. I'll go." I couldn't help but picture my father at a club. The thought was almost funny enough to help me forgive him. Well, not really.

"Did my father always do his business at nightclubs?" I joked.

She smirked. "Declan owns The Phoenix and many other companies, but he preferred meeting with your father at his club and at night."

"In the Meatpacking district, right? I thought that place was on the verge of closing down years ago."

"It was, but Declan turned it around. It's always packed with models, actors, and trust fund babies. A great place to people watch."

"Sounds weird to meet at the club, but okay." I sipped my black coffee—the third of the day.

She stood up. "Meeting's at eleven. My car's in the shop. Mind picking me up?"

"Eleven?" Was she serious?

"Yeah." A smile teased her lips. "I'll text you my address. See you tonight."

I waited for her to leave, before I rested my elbows on my desk, and pressed my hands to my face. God, I was going to lose my mind if I kept at this much longer.

4
OLIVIA

Various shades of light ping-ponged off the walls in the club as the music poured through the speakers. The DJ waved his arms around, moving to his music. Whatever happened to the days when DJs spun vinyl?

Leaning against the bar closest to the dance floor, I shut my eyes and tried to seal out the sounds of the music I had once loved. I'd managed to avoid listening to it for almost ten years.

But it was hard to ignore the loud thumping base. The DJ was pulling off a unique blend of talent—Maroon 5 and Tiesto, maybe? God, did I want to dance. But not only was I working, I hadn't moved my feet to music since—

A sharp, stabbing pain pricked the walls of my chest, deflating me of the oxygen I desperately needed in the hot crowd. No, I couldn't think about that. I'd never survive this job if I let my memories haunt me every time I came into work.

It had been a little over three weeks since I began my new job with Declan. It was much better than being at the office, but I still didn't feel like I was getting anywhere.

"Olivia, can we talk?"

It was Declan. "Sure." I followed him out of the main room of the club, down a long hallway, and into his private and absurdly lavish office. I'm not sure if Declan thought he was Hugh Hefner, but there were two women in his office, decorative fixtures in tight, revealing getups. Then there were the two metal cages he had set up in the corners of his office. Did this place turn into some kind of DOM club after hours?

My skin flushed, like it always did, every time I walked across the red carpet and past his two, um, ladies to sit in front of his desk.

It was all just very . . . odd.

I cleared my throat and tried to focus.

"Veronica. Summer. We need some privacy." Declan slid into the seat behind his modern black desk, and the two women sauntered out of the room in their death trap heels. The one called Summer pulled the door closed.

"I have a meeting tonight." Declan lifted his iPhone from the desk and used his thumb to unlock it. "There's a big deal I've been working on, which pertains to Reid Enterprises, but we usually meet here instead." He tapped at his smartphone and slid it away before focusing his dark eyes on mine.

"Okay." What was he expecting me to say?

"I need you to sign something."

I reached for the paper he slid across the desk. A non-disclosure agreement. "What is this about?"

"Anything you may hear at this meeting must never be shared with anyone. The information is sensitive. Classified, even." He leaned back in his leather chair and clasped his hands against his chest.

"I would never share anything about my job, anyway."

"Of course not. Nevertheless, I need you to sign this."

"Sure," I managed and grabbed a pen from his desk. "Who are you meeting?"

He scratched the back of his head and narrowed his eyes at me. "Actually, the man I was working with died of a heart attack a few weeks ago." There was a slight pause and a twitch to his lips. "I'll be meeting his successor tonight."

"Oh. Okay. Well, is there anything I need to do to help prepare for the meeting?" I fiddled with the pen in my hand.

"No." He reached for the paper I'd signed. "You probably won't be in on the meeting, actually. You could serve us drinks, though."

I dropped the pen and shot him a look. "So, why did I need to sign—"

He held up his hand, stopping me. "In case you overhear anything. Or, if the deal is resumed, as I hope it is, I might bring you in. Just covering my bases."

"Sounds good."

"You've been dying to ask me about those for weeks." A smile skirted his lips. "Go ahead."

I must have squinted in some lame attempt to act like I had no idea what he was talking about. "I'm sorry, what?" I stood.

He glanced over his shoulder at one of the metal cages. "You sure you don't want to ask?" His eyes were back on me, assessing me.

"Nope, I'm good. Let me know if you need me for your meeting."

"Have Bobby make three gin and tonics. The meeting starts in five minutes." He smoothed a hand over his black dress shirt.

"Of course."

I left the office, walked down the hall, and made my way to the main bar on the ground floor. It was massive in size with a sleek wall of glass behind it, allowing the light in the room to reflect off it. "Hey, Bobby. Boss needs three gin and tonics," I hollered over the noise as I pressed my hands on the sticky counter.

"You're looking good tonight." Bobby's brown eyes focused on me as he poured the gin.

He was always flirting, even though he was probably two or

three years younger. I wondered how much those years mattered, now that I was one year away from thirty.

I shifted uncomfortably in my heels and rubbed my neck, trying to ease my tension.

"Are we on for tomorrow?" He placed the drinks on a tray.

"Yeah. See you at eight?"

"Make it ten. I need my sleep. I work until four, unlike you."

"Nine," I negotiated and grabbed the tray. I turned away from the bar, and my heart started pounding hard in my chest. The tray slipped from my hands and crashed to the floor.

I stood stupidly, just staring. My lips parted, my hands still outstretched. I couldn't take my eyes off him.

A fist of pain clawed at my chest.

"Liv?" Bobby came around from behind the bar and knelt down to pick up the broken glass.

I barely noticed the splash of cold, sticky alcohol that had run over my high heels.

"Olivia? You okay?" Bobby stood in front of me now, blocking . . . him. HIM. Oh my God. This couldn't be happening.

And then he saw me. His eyes narrowed in, and a look of shock —no, dread—curled its way over his face.

"Olivia? Talk to me." Bobby was snapping his fingers in front of my face.

I shook my head. "What?" I shifted my attention to Bobby. "Yeah, I just—I don't know what happened." I kneeled down to help clean the mess before any of the customers slipped.

A pair of black loafers stopped in front of me. I pulled my gaze up the dark denim jeans to the trim waist and up to the hard chest —a chest I'd touched so many times before.

His hand was on my arm. He was helping me up.

No. Goddamn him. No.

I sucked in a breath as I lurched back to my feet, but his hand was still placed on my arm, like it had any business there . . .

"Olivia."

God, the sound of my name on his lips still had the same old effect. Chills and heat all at the same time. I swallowed, pulled my arm away, and forced myself to look up into his soft green eyes.

"Connor."

He raked a hand through his freaking perfect brown hair—as always, it had that sweet, just-fucked look. Damn him. He focused on my lips for a moment and drifted back up to meet my eyes.

"Hi, I'm Lauren."

I hadn't even noticed the woman standing next to him. "Hi."

"You two know each other?" The woman glanced in Connor's direction.

No sound escaped his lips. A flash of a memory pushed forth in my mind—his mouth on my neck, trailing kisses down my body. Heat shot between my legs.

No. No. No. This couldn't be happening.

"Um," I finally forced out a word, but I wasn't sure what I said. Was it English?

Since Connor seemed to have no intention of speaking, and I was tongue-tied, the brunette to his left spoke up. "Do you work here?"

I think I moved my head up and down, but I couldn't be sure. I still couldn't take my eyes off Connor, and he had yet to rip his heated gaze from my face.

"We have a meeting with Declan."

Her words had me snapping my attention in her direction. "Oh. Okay." Oh my God, that must mean . . . "Did your father—"

"Yes," was all he afforded me, and his mouth tightened.

"So, you're running the company now?"

He nodded. Clearly he had no desire to talk, which suited me just fine. I didn't want to talk to him, either. "Follow me. Mr. Reid's expecting you." I turned my back, but I could feel his eyes on me.

When I showed him to Declan's office, the two blonde playboy wannabes shifted their attention to him with the fury of hungry tigers. Had they both just wet their lips?

Connor didn't seem to notice. He was still looking at me.

"I'll just get you all something to drink." I stole one last glance at Connor out of the corner of my eye and moved past him to the doorway.

On the other side, I shut the door and leaned forward, pressing my hands against my bare knees. I couldn't breathe. Memories came hurtling back at me until I thought I might throw up.

5

CONNOR

Ten years. It had been ten years since I'd seen Olivia. She was one of the reasons—hell, the main reason—I detested New York. And there she was, looking better than I ever remembered.

How in the hell was I supposed to sit through a business meeting after having seen her? No—I needed to get out of there.

But if I rescheduled, I'd probably have to see her again.

"You okay, Connor?"

Lauren was staring at me. It didn't take a genius to see the wall of tension in the room.

As I beat back the burning sensation that had crept into my chest, the man diverted my attention to the two half-naked women in the room.

"Ladies?" He cocked his head, and they started for the exit.

Declan was probably trying to communicate something with their presence, but I really couldn't have cared less.

"I'm Connor Matthews." I forced myself to get a grip and shook the man's hand.

"Declan Reid. Nice to meet you." Declan paused and cleared his throat. "My condolences about your father. He was a good man."

My hand dropped to my side, and I studied the man before me. He wasn't what I was expecting. He was young—probably younger than me. And there was an edginess to him, to his rocker-dark hair and the slim line of makeup beneath his eyes. I couldn't imagine my father sitting in this office.

"Hi, Declan, good to see you again." Lauren reached for his hand. "Oh shit," she moaned. "I left my clutch in your Jeep."

"I'll get it," I volunteered.

She placed her hand on top of mine. "No, you stay. The valet can just pull up your Jeep for me. No biggie."

"Okay." I handed her my valet ticket as Declan motioned for me to have a seat in front of the desk. He took a seat next to me as Lauren clicked the door closed behind her.

"Thank you for meeting with me, especially given the circumstances," Declan said.

I nodded and heard the door opening.

It was her. It was Olivia. My pulse quickened.

"Come on in," Declan called as she stood inside the door frame, holding a tray.

Was Olivia really working for this guy? It was a far stretch from what she had planned in college. What had her life been like for the last ten years?

I looked away. I had to focus on something else—anything else.

Were those cages?

"Your drinks, Declan."

I fought like hell not to steal a look at her legs as she walked past, but the temptation was too damn hard. The memory of her legs wrapped around my hips—God, we had been so young.

She placed the drinks on the desk and ran a hand through her long chocolate brown hair. Her hair had been as soft and fine as silk. The feel of her hair on my fingers as I kissed her . . . *shit.*

I swallowed as my eyes met hers—they still had the same flecks of gold among the green.

"Do you need anything else?" Olivia focused on Declan.

"This is Connor Matthews." Declan tipped his head in my direction.

She took a step closer to me, and I could smell her sweet perfume. "Hi. I'm Olivia Taylor."

Taylor? Was that a married name? I didn't see a ring. Maybe she was divorced.

"Hi," I managed as I took her hand and released it just as fast.

She stepped back and bumped into the desk. Her cheeks reddened slightly beneath her bronzed skin.

Declan's eyes became thin slits on Olivia. "Do you know each other?"

Did she want him to know? I'd let her take the lead on this, but it would come out at some point. She had basically admitted to knowing me in front of Lauren, already.

"We both went to NYU. It's been awhile." She blew out a barely noticeable breath, but I noticed it . . . anything she did with her mouth was obvious to me. "Anything else?"

Clasping his hands on his lap, he shook his head no.

Once the door shut behind her, Declan said, "She's quite something, huh?" He crossed his leg over his knee. "So, I'm sure you have some questions."

That was an understatement. I had a lot of questions, but honestly, at the end of the day, I wasn't sure if I even cared who he was or what he did. The gig was short-term, after all. Perhaps I could get by without having to deal with him. But no—I was there for my brother. I wouldn't leave a wreck on his hands.

"You and I are very much alike. I took over my father's businesses a few years back. Unfortunately, Reid Enterprises was on the brink of bankruptcy. Everything from the factories to this very club was near closing."

I toyed with the black band on my watch. "And you turned it around?" I was doing my best to focus on what Declan was saying, but thoughts of Olivia kept infiltrating my brain.

Declan nodded. "It wasn't easy—I'll be honest. It required me to make some deals I wasn't a fan of, at first. But everything happens for a reason, and now look at me." He opened his arms, palms up, gesturing . . . to what? His office? What an incredible narcissist.

"You must be wondering about your father's business relationship with me." Declan rolled up his sleeves, exposing a black cross on one forearm and a skull on the other.

"Not really. I looked into your company—you guys bid on projects in the Middle East to help with the rebuilding efforts. The technology from our company would be of value to such projects, given our specialty in military-grade weapons design and manufacturing." I cleared my throat, and one of the cages caught my eye again. So weird. "I guess I'm just curious why you two would meet at your club and at night."

He stood and walked around behind his desk. "Not too long ago, your father was concerned for the future of his company. He was being outbid on defense contracts by the bigger guys, and he needed a big play to keep the company afloat. Matthews Tech is relatively a small fish in the game, but I have some influence in the Middle East, and so we began helping each other out. But our deals required some level of discretion if you will." He leaned forward to press his hands on the back of his leather chair. "How familiar are you with your father's business?"

Was this guy about to school me on my father's company? "I'm still learning," I admitted. "My brother will be taking over in five months. I'm just doing my best to keep the status quo until he takes the reins."

His lips quirked a little, but he didn't quite smile. "Totally understand. But, if you want to keep the business thriving, I'd suggest that you and I continue the relationship your father and I started."

And what kind of relationship was that? Before I had a chance to probe, I heard the sound of the door opening, and my heart lodged in my throat.

But it wasn't Olivia.

Lauren. Shit, I'd forgotten all about her.

"Miss me?" She moved with slow steps to where I sat.

Declan nodded at her and gestured to the drinks on his desk. She slipped the valet ticket into my hand before reaching for a glass.

I decided I could use a little something, as well. I swallowed a mouthful of the cocktail, and it sputtered in my throat.

"Do you like Vegas?" Declan also reached for his drink and perched himself on the edge of his desk.

Let's see: gambling, dancing, and gorgeous women. "Sure."

"I have a grand opening at one of my clubs out there this weekend. It's a replica of The Phoenix, but Vegas style. Would you two care to join me? We can talk business in more detail, and you can decide if you want to continue a relationship between Reid and Matthews Tech."

I rubbed my palms against my thighs. I expected board meetings and emails when I took over, not weekends in Vegas.

Lauren looked at me, her brown eyes widening with hope.

"Is it necessary to talk at a club?" I tried to hide the sneer that pulsed in my lip.

Declan shoved his hands in his pockets. "Your competition is watching every move you make, especially with the new technology you've just developed."

I wondered what new technology he meant. I still hadn't talked with the research and development department—I'd spent the last three days signing paperwork.

"It's in the best interest of your company to keep your competitors in the dark."

I swallowed the rest of my drink and set the empty glass on the desk as I stood. "I haven't been to Vegas in a while. I guess it would be good to get away."

Lauren quickly set her glass down and clapped her hands together.

"Why don't we get another drink? Put business on the backburner until this weekend. The entertainment will be starting soon," Declan suggested.

"Oh?"

"Come on. Follow me." Declan smiled at Lauren as he ushered us from the office.

She wet her red lips and ran her fingers through her dark hair. Was she flirting?

I suddenly realized that Olivia was out there somewhere. And God help me, I wasn't sure if I could handle seeing her again.

"You okay?" Lauren asked as we made our way back to the main dance area.

"Sure," I shouted over the booming music.

Declan stopped in front of the bar and pointed up to a pair of crystal chandeliers. "Had those specially imported from the Netherlands."

The spiral staircase off to the left of the bar was wrapped in LED lights, and there were twenty-foot bird wings suspended in the air above the bar.

"Can I get you something else to drink?" he asked.

"Just a Corona." Then again, Olivia was here. Maybe I needed something stronger. "Change that to a Jack and Coke."

Declan grinned and turned to the bartender. "Two Jack and Cokes and Lauren's usual."

So, Lauren was a regular.

"Can you escort them to a VIP booth?"

I turned around to see who Declan was talking to.

"Sure." Olivia looked at Lauren, offering her a small smile, which exposed only one of her dimples. "Follow me."

I sucked in a breath as I watched the sway of her hips beneath the blue fabric of her dress. The dress fell just above her knees, leaving enough to the imagination while also teasing me with her toned legs. Clearly she hadn't stopped working out. Even her shoulders and arms were sculpted and lean.

I forced my attention to the crowd and away from her ass. I didn't want to be attracted to her. It pissed me off that I hardened at the simple memory of her tight body pinned beneath me.

"Connor?" Lauren scooted on to the red leather booth, and a hint of lace from the top of her black thigh-highs was exposed.

I blinked a few times. Anything to help pull my mind from thoughts of Olivia.

I slid in next to her. "Are you joining us?" I forced myself to ask Olivia. I wanted her to say no as much as I wanted her to say yes. God, I was still hard. Was it noticeable? My gaze lingered on her mouth for a moment, and I heard a small cough behind me. Was Lauren jealous of Olivia? She should be. Lauren was hot, but Olivia was in a class of her own.

Olivia touched her collarbone but remained quiet. Clearly, this was as awkward for her as it was for me.

"What's your name again? I don't remember seeing you here before," Lauren said.

Olivia leaned forward a little to be heard. She was standing a few feet away like she was afraid to be in arm's reach. "I just started working at the club a few weeks ago," she answered. "I worked for Declan at Reid Enterprises before."

The music was starting to increase in volume, and I noticed the so-called entertainment walking out onto the stage, which was rising from the center of the dance floor as red lights lit the walkway and blasts of cryogenic smoke began to cloud the room.

Women and men dressed in black leather began performing acrobatic feats. Was this a circus? What happened to clubs where people listened to music and just danced?

"Can I get you anything before I leave?" So Olivia wasn't planning to stay.

"I'll take another drink." Lauren raised her half empty martini glass.

Even through the dim lighting, I could see Olivia was biting her lip.

"How about you? Anything else?" I glanced down at my hand, which held a nearly overflowing Jack and Coke. "I'm good. Thanks." How had Olivia wound up here instead of law school?

Olivia turned and walked through the crowd and clouds of smoke.

"Sit down, cowboy."

Cowboy? I smoothed a hand over my jaw and sat at the end of the booth. I didn't want to give Lauren any ideas. I wasn't sure about business protocol, but I was pretty sure it didn't involve screwing employees. And, despite her sex appeal, the woman rubbed me the wrong way.

She scooted a little closer. "What do you think?" She twirled a strand of her hair between her fingers and pressed her lips together.

"About?" I looked away from her and to the dancers on the stage.

"Declan." She placed her hand on my shoulder.

My instinctive flinch at her touch sent her scooting back.

"He's interesting." I didn't know what the hell to say. Clearly, she had some sort of . . . something . . . with the guy. And so had my father, apparently.

"Do you like the club?" Declan had come up behind us. He slid into the opposite side of the booth.

"The place is great," the lie slipped from my tongue.

God, I couldn't wait to get to a gym. Or maybe even a gun range.

I spotted Olivia at the bar across the room as the smoke began to settle. Her back was to me, and one of the bartenders was talking to her. "Can you excuse me for a moment? I think I need a stronger drink."

"I can get someone—" Declan started.

"I'm good. Thanks." I rose to my feet and moved through the crowd, Olivia still in my sights. Her hair was long, wavy, and had a wind-blown look to it, which reminded me of how her hair looked after one of our many days at the beach together.

She scratched the heel of her shoe against her calf muscle and began rubbing her neck. I scolded myself for imagining that it was my hands on her neck—massaging her.

"Can we talk?" I whispered in her ear as my hand rested on the small of her back.

She jerked from my touch and moved a few steps back. My hand dropped to my side. What the hell was I thinking, touching her?

"Connor." The way she said my name sounded like a warning.

I pressed my back up against the bar and noticed Declan observing me from across the room. "What are you doing working here?"

"Please." She moved a little closer. "Please don't talk about me with Declan."

"Why?" I'd had no plans to, but what was she trying to hide? "Are you married?"

"No, but please just don't mention anything to Declan, okay?"

My hand caught her wrist, and she pulled away again. Shit—what was wrong with me? I had some damn instinct to touch her, despite the anger that had consumed me for years. "Olivia, are you in trouble?"

She shook her head and glanced in Declan's direction. "If he asks anything, can you just say we hooked up once? Whatever you men say to each other . . . I don't know. Just not the truth, okay? I need this job, and I sort of fudged my resume to get it."

Lying again . . . Did anything change with her? I had to steel my nerves as my pulse began to quicken. The memories of our past pushed up into my throat, leaving a bad taste in my mouth.

I didn't say anything or get a new drink. I just turned away from her and started back for the VIP booth.

"Hey, there." A red tie had been flung around my neck by one of the dancers. Her glittered face was inches from mine as she pulled me closer. Great, this was all I needed . . .

I glanced at Olivia, who was still standing by the bar. Watching me.

Was she jealous? Did she think she had a right to be, after all these years?

I caught the tie with my hand and pulled myself free of the woman's hold. "Another time." I moved from the dance area and stopped next to Declan's booth.

"I think it's time for me to go. Lauren, do you need a ride?"

"Leaving already?" Her face went long as her lips curved into an exaggerated pout.

"Is there a problem with Olivia?" Declan asked.

"What? No." I shook my head. "I was an asshole to her in college. Just apologizing."

Of course, it was more like she needed to apologize to me. I couldn't believe I was lying for her.

"Women," Declan muttered and smirked. "I can give you a ride, Lauren." His hand rested on her thigh. Yet, her brown eyes lingered on me.

"See you at the office tomorrow." She sipped her drink, peering up from beneath dark lashes.

"I'll get the info to you tomorrow." Declan stood, reaching for my hand. "Thanks again for coming. I look forward to talking with you more in Vegas."

"For sure."

I was already dreading the trip, but I had to follow through. I didn't want to screw this up for my brother.

I made my way through the maze of people and found Olivia near the door, talking to some guy in a leather jacket. He had to be hot in that thing.

Olivia shook her head at the man and pointed at his chest. Maybe an ex?

I walked past the two of them, catching her eye on my way to the exit.

The crisp air slapped me in the face as I stepped through the door. I stuffed my hands in my pockets as the valet left to retrieve my car.

"I'm sorry."

My shoulders arched back as a thrill ran up my spine. I slowly turned to face her. "Sorry for what?"

She released a sigh. "Asking you to lie for me."

I shrugged and tried to think of something to say, but it was too hard to concentrate when she was standing so close to me, smelling so damn good. Fortunately, the valet pulled up in my Jeep. "I'll see you around, I guess."

"Connor?"

"Yeah?" I didn't turn around.

"Goodnight," she whispered.

I hopped into the car and clenched the steering wheel, forcing myself not to look.

6

OLIVIA

"ONE MORE TIME. COME ON. HIT IT HARD."

My gloved hand pounded the bag, and I had to reel it back and shake off the pain. "Ughhh . . ."

"That's what I'm talking about, girl." Bobby, the bartender from the club, came from behind the punching bag and slapped me lightly on the back. "You ready to spar?" He handed me a bottle of water.

I sucked the bottle dry. "The question is, are you?" A grin teased my lips.

"Always ready." He reached for the blue gloves he'd set on a folding chair by the boxing ring.

I pulled the white headgear over my ears. "Don't take it easy on me."

"Have I ever?" he asked once we were in the boxing ring, squaring off.

The gym was Declan's, and he'd insisted I take advantage of the place, especially now that I was working later in the day. Bobby, who reminded me of a young Will Smith, never hit me even remotely hard. It drove me nuts—I was used to sparring with guys who were willing to slam me to the floor. I wanted—no, needed—an intense match up. Especially after last night.

Bobby touched his gloved hands to his black hair—he never wore headgear—before raising them in front of his face.

My right hook caught him in the jaw, and I shifted my weight to my left side to come at him with a fast crescent kick.

"Feisty today, huh?" A lopsided grin formed as he threw a soft jab at my mid-section.

My white T-shirt was already clinging with sweat. Earlier, thoughts of Connor had me pounding the punching bag like I was fighting for my life.

I blocked Bobby's left punch and returned with a second blow to his jaw. Even if he decided not to take it easy on me, I knew I could take sweet Bobby down.

My focus shifted to find Declan entering the large private boxing area. "What's he doing here?" I lowered my gloves and took a step back.

"He does own the gym," Bobby said with a touch of sarcasm in his voice.

"No, shit," I responded and raised my hands back up. "But he should be at the office."

"I don't know. Maybe he needed something to hit as much as you do." He smirked.

I laughed. "What? Need me to go easy on ya?"

"Hardly." He swung, but I ducked out of reach.

"I told you to use the gym, but really—you box?" Declan climbed into the ring, stepping under one of the red ropes that surrounded the fighting area. "You're full of surprises."

"Do you need me for something?"

He folded his arms and directed his attention at Bobby. "You mind if we have a few moments alone?"

So, he'd come here for me.

"Sure." Bobby winked before climbing out of the ring.

I removed my headgear and started taking off my gloves. "What's up?" I asked, still a little breathy from the fight.

"Is my doing business with Connor Matthews going to be a problem for you?"

Without realizing it, I took a step back. My eyes widened. "What do you mean?"

He closed the short distance between us and placed his hand on my shoulder.

Take your hand off me, I wanted to yell, but I stayed still and silent under his touch.

"Connor mentioned he screwed you over. Just hoping you can move past whatever it is he did . . ."

My breath caught in my throat for a moment. What in the hell was I supposed to say? My short fingernails pressed into my palms. "I haven't seen Connor in nearly ten years. It's ancient history."

He angled his head and kept his eyes on mine. "You're sure?"

Hell, no. "Of course."

"Good. Then I want you to head over to his office for me."

"What?" This time, I couldn't help it. I stepped away and out of his reach.

Declan crossed his arms, taking a defensive stance. "I want you to drop off the Vegas info."

I propped my hands on my hips. "You don't think my showing up to his office will have the opposite effect?"

"Why would it if the past is behind you?" Giving me a pointed look, he said, "Make sure he's happy. Make sure he's at the club this weekend."

"He's that important for business?" *This can't be happening.*

Declan's expression softened a little. "Yes, he is."

"Then he'll be there." My chest tightened as I thought about whether or not I'd be able to follow through with my promise.

"And Olivia? Next time you plan on sparring, call me, instead."

Now that was something I could do. "What about now?" I hadn't meant to be so obvious, but my excitement at the thought of hitting the bastard echoed in my voice. I'd grown to hate the man in the last nine months working for him.

"I have a meeting. But I'll definitely take a rain check."

I watched him duck under the rope and exit the ring. He nodded at Bobby, then strode through the boxing area and back to the main gym. I huffed and tossed my gloves and headgear into my bag.

"You done for the day?" Bobby hovered as I zipped up my bag just outside the boxing ring. The room was empty, except for us. Declan only allowed his employees and friends the use of the boxing room, which was tucked away in the back of the gym.

"Unfortunately. I have an errand to run for the boss man." I picked up the bag and slung the strap over my shoulder. "See ya tonight." I patted him on the shoulder and started for the locker room.

Thirty minutes later, my fist tapped the door three times. I waited, my stomach a ball of nerves. I couldn't believe that it had come to this.

The door swung open. "You're late."

I stepped past Blake, removing my Mets baseball hat and sunglasses as I walked down the hall.

"What took so long?" he asked.

"Traffic." I sank into the leather chair and pressed my hands to my jeaned thighs. "Why were you at the club last night? You don't normally make an appearance on Wednesdays."

"Trying not to be too predictable." Blake's blue eyes studied mine for a moment before he sat across from me on the couch.

The apartment was our home away from home, for now. Last month it had been a penthouse in the Upper Eastside, and the time before a brownstone in Harlem.

"You were in an awfully pissy mood last night—wouldn't talk

to me even when I called your damn phone. That's a breach of protocol."

My eyelids snapped shut. I still didn't want to say a thing.

"Who was it that Declan was talking to last night? And you, too."

I wanted to tell him it was none of his damn business, but in all fairness, it was. "Connor Matthews. He inherited his father's company. Matthews Tech." I slowly opened my eyes and tried to push the image of Connor out of my mind.

Blake rubbed his clean-shaven jaw before smoothing a hand over his short, dark blonde hair. "The same Matthews Tech that designs and manufactures weapons?"

"Yeah," I whispered the word, still in shock myself. "Before you ask, let me tell you that I don't know anything. This is the first I've heard of any business between Declan and Matthews Tech." I stood up and crossed my arms. "But he had me sign an NDA, so I have a feeling it's only a matter of time."

Blake was nodding. "This is good. This might finally be the lead we're looking for."

"Declan invited Connor to Vegas this weekend." I didn't want to tell him more, but I knew he'd find out. "There's a problem."

"What?" He crossed his arms, and his biceps popped up like a tent.

I swallowed the lump in my throat, afraid to tell him about Connor. I didn't know what it would mean for the investigation. "Connor and I have a history."

His shock was immediate as he pressed his hands to the sides of his face, dragging them down as he contemplated a response. "Did he mention to Declan he knew you?"

It was obvious we knew each other . . . "Declan thinks Connor screwed me over. I told Connor that I'd lied on my resume to get the job, and not to say anything about me."

"And *did* Connor screw you over?" He cocked his head, and his expression hardened.

Yes. Cut out my heart and sliced it with a machete. "No. Well —just don't worry about it."

He blew out a breath. "You trust this Connor guy to keep his lips sealed?"

Despite our history, I said, "Yes." But I honestly had no idea.

"I want you to get close to Connor." His eyes lit up like there was a bulb behind them, like he could actually see a bright light before him.

"No. Absolutely not. I just—couldn't . . ." I turned away from Blake and walked to the window.

"This could be our lucky break." His fingers splayed against my back and regret poured through me. He whispered in my ear, "When this is over . . ."

Chills licked my spine and moved throughout my body as I spun to face him. "No, Blake." I pressed my hand to his chest. "You and I—that can't happen again. We tried it before, and it just didn't work. Besides, you're my boss now."

"We can make it work." The darkening of his blue eyes was familiar to me—I knew what he was thinking, wanting. Well, that wouldn't be happening again.

I shook my head. I was in no mood to deal with hurting his ego. And knowing Blake, rejection was more painful than the actual loss of being with me. "What did you have in mind with Connor?" I changed the subject.

He turned away from me. "How well do you know him?"

I chewed on my bottom lip for a moment. I didn't know how much to divulge. "We dated in college. Things just sort of ended." With him running away . . .

Insert metaphorical stab wound.

Choke on the pain for a moment.

Breathe.

Move on.

"Do you think you can get him to trust you? Open up to you?"

Connor Matthews—open up to me? It seemed unlikely,

especially since I got the distinct feeling that he had toughened up in the last decade. I knew he'd gone into the Marines and even heard he'd been a badass sniper. Now, he was a lone wolf. A bodyguard. He was nothing like his rich father. And I remembered he never wanted to be like the old man.

I was doing it again. Letting Connor hurt me. I couldn't walk down memory lane every time Connor's name was mentioned. There was too much hanging on the line to let Connor trip me up.

"Olivia?"

Blake's deep voice arrested my attention. "I don't know if I can do this," I admitted, rubbing my forehead with pained irritation.

He reached for my wrist and tugged my hand free from my face. "You have to do this. You've been in deep for nine months—you can't back out now."

He was right. This was only my third undercover assignment after completing training at Quantico. And the only reason I was given such a high profile assignment was because I'd forced Blake's hand, that and he still had a thing for me.

"I'll see if I can get Connor to open up to me, but he may be innocent. His father, on the other hand, was a world class jerk."

"Find out, because we're running out of time. If we don't produce some results soon, we might have to stop the investigation."

I swallowed. No. God, no. I was finally where I needed to be. We were too close.

"Do what it takes. Get me evidence."

As if he needed to encourage me . . .

"We'll need to push the envelope a little more. We came up empty while you were at the office, but now that you're at the club, there are few things we can try to get the evidence we need."

Knowing Blake, those "things" would probably be dangerous. "I've been working for Declan since late September. I spent almost eight long months working in his office, biding my time, gaining his trust. The office job was our way in, and the fact that I'm now at the club means it paid off. You have to give it some time." But would Declan ever really let me in? If he didn't, Connor might be my only way. But would Connor make a deal with him?

I needed Connor to.

And yet, I hoped to hell he didn't . . .

7

CONNOR

LAUREN LEANED BACK IN HER BLACK LEATHER DESK CHAIR AND brought her thumb to her lip, pulling her bottom lip down just slightly. Was she done talking?

"Thank you for explaining the Saudi deal to me." I started to get up.

Lauren had her hand in the air, gesturing for me to wait. "This deal is just the start. Our competitors are raking in sales in the tens of billions. This deal only got us on the map."

I sat back down in my seat and started for the tie at my neck, but realized it wasn't even there. I'd already tossed it. "Where are you from originally?" The question slipped from my lips before I realized I'd asked it.

She arched her shoulders back. "I'm American."

"You have an accent, don't you? I feel like I keep hearing it, and I was just curious." I don't know why I was asking this, but I was hoping to distract her from her big ideas.

"I'd prefer not to talk about it."

What? Well, that wasn't the response I was expecting, but I'd drop it.

"Connor, please think about—"

I held my hand out in front of me. "Lauren, I don't want to make any major decisions. I don't think the company should take on too much until Mason's here."

Her eyes widened a fraction. "I don't advise slowing down." She was now the one standing. Her hot pink heels flashed as she walked to my side.

"I'm not cut out for this." I was itching to get to the gun range in Vegas on Friday. An old Marine buddy of mine lived in Vegas, and my first order of business upon arrival was to meet up with him and shoot something. I'm not violent. Not crazy—well, not certifiable, at least. But I was tense. Wired.

Yes, firing a few rounds would make a world of difference.

"Connor," she folded her arms across her chest, her dark eyes steadying on mine, "I'm not sure you realize that our company is on the brink of something revolutionary."

What in the hell was she talking about? I stood up. I didn't appreciate a lecture from Mrs. Sales on my father's company. Shit, it was my company. No . . . Mason's. It would never really be mine.

I pushed my hands into the pockets of my gray slacks, clearing my throat. "What's up, Lauren?" I narrowed my eyes at her, my jaw tight. For some reason, I got the feeling there was a hell of a lot more going on.

"Have you talked to Wes yet?"

Wes. Who was he again? "R&D guy?"

"Yeah, the head of the department of research and development." Her hands fell to her sides, and she took a small step closer to me, wedged between us was the chair in which I'd previously sat.

This woman was a praying mantis. The way her sharp eyes bore through me, how she held her ground as if she owned the damn company. Normally a strong woman would turn me on like Olivia once had, but today, I wasn't in the mood.

"I'll meet him. Promise." I inhaled a breath and tilted my head.

"Anything else?" I allowed a bite to my voice, wanting her to know the irritation had begun to spread through my limbs like a disease.

Her hand was on my shoulder; her long pink nails a perfect match to her shoes. "I don't want the company to lose momentum. Just think about it, okay?"

With my eyes still on her hand, I responded, "Fine." I stepped back and started to leave.

"Connor?"

"Yeah?"

"See you in Vegas tomorrow."

I nodded without turning to face her and escaped through the door, working out the tension in my neck as I strode past cubicles and fluorescent lights. Maybe it wasn't Lauren I was mad at. Maybe I was still pissed at my father. I didn't want to be here. He was probably laughing at me from heaven—or hell.

My secretary, Elsa, stopped me just outside my door. "Connor," she said, smoothing a hand over her short, white bob, "there is a Miss Taylor in your office."

"Taylor?" Shit. That was Olivia's new last name. My stomach twisted like melted steel. I gripped the knob, surprised by the fact that the door was closed. "Thanks," I muttered to Elsa and pushed my way in.

Olivia jumped back from whatever she'd been peering at on my desk and bumped into my chair. Her cheeks brightened, and she forced an awkward smile to her face, exposing her "kill-me-now" dimples.

Why couldn't she have gotten ugly in the past ten years? She still had those high cheekbones in her heart-shaped face, the small, straight nose, the full lips I wanted to sink my teeth into . . .

I was still standing in the doorframe, just staring. As I moved into the room, she pushed her dark hair over her shoulder and stepped around the desk. "Looks like it might storm," she remarked, placing an envelope on my desk.

I sucked in a breath as she picked up the red tie I had tossed in the chair in front of my desk. She took a seat, still holding on to my tie, playing with it between her fingers . . .

I pressed a hand to my desk, trying to ground myself, and squeezed my eyes shut. The last Halloween we'd spent together, she had dressed in a mafia suit and had worn a red tie. Later that night we'd used the tie—

"Connor?"

My eyes flashed open. "Why are you here?" I rolled my sleeves to my elbows. It was getting too damn hot.

She dropped the tie on the edge of my desk, and I thanked God for that, but then she was touching her blouse, and it took all my willpower not to think about her full breasts beneath her silk shirt. "I'm sorry. Declan wanted me to drop off the hotel and club information, and . . ."

Her attention shifted from the tie to my eyes, and I had to take a step back. Her hazel eyes were full of mourning.

Did she feel guilty about the past?

Did it matter?

"I want to put the past behind us." Her chest rose and fell with subtle breaths.

My shoulders arched back as I looked away from her. "If I do business with Declan, we can be civil. We don't need to talk about the past," I forced myself to say with a clenched jaw. I sat down in my seat, worried the floor would swallow me if I stood much longer. She had far too much of an effect on me. It wasn't right.

"Thank you." She stood up. "I'm afraid Declan will fire me if he doesn't think you and I can work together."

I deliberated her words, not sure how I felt about lying for her. "I may not like working with you, but I won't ruin your life." *Not the way you ruined mine.*

But, I couldn't think like that. Everything happened for a reason, right? If she hadn't screwed me over, I would never have joined the Marines. I might have ended up a replica of my father, the thought of which made me physically ill.

"Friends?" There was a slight wobble to her bottom lip as she regarded me with a somber expression.

Her hand was in the air, outstretched over my desk. "Sure," I said as I tried to digest my strange emotions. I finally took her hand as I stood. The warmth of her skin, and the feel of her hand in mine created a strange sharp pain in the pit of my stomach—an all too familiar haunting pain.

Still holding her hand, my eyes snapped shut, and I swallowed, almost choking on the desert heat of the Middle East. Memories ripped through my mind: the IED tearing a chunk out of my platoons Hummer, my face buried in sand, my body broken and bruised . . . My friend's wail as he tried to pop his dislocated shoulder back into place.

"Connor?" Olivia's voice had me shooting back to the present, safe within the four walls of my office.

My eyes opened in dismay. "Shit. Sorry." I released my grip on her hand and watched as she rubbed her one hand with the other. And instead of offering some lame excuse, like normal, I said, "I was thinking of Iraq."

Her lips parted but then closed. I was pretty sure she had no idea what to say, so I helped her out. "You remind me of the blistering Iraq heat—easy to get burned."

She lowered her eyes to the floor as her hands slipped to the sides of her cream-colored pants. "See you in Vegas," she said with a flat, emotionless voice.

God, what was wrong with me? "You still afraid of flying? Of heights?" I found myself asking with no clue as to why.

"No," she said as her eyes landed on mine. Her head angled and her lips parted. "Well, maybe a little." A moment of tension rocked the room between us, and she turned away.

I burned a hole in her back as she left my office. How could I let her get to me after all our history? It was like the last ten years were a dream, and I was a twenty-two-year-old kid in love again.

But I had been naïve. And I had no intention of being duped again.

8

CONNOR

THE BULLET PIERCED THE TARGET, AND I PEERED THROUGH THE sight. I had nailed the paper figure in the head, from six hundred meters away.

"There's not much left to that paper." Ben removed his sunglasses and tipped his head in my direction. "You all right?"

Still kneeling, I aimed and took one last shot. "Everything's wrong." I stood up and squinted at him, the desert sun burning my eyes. I could feel it turning my tan skin darker.

"Here, man." Ben reached into the cooler for a bottle of Corona and popped the top off.

"Thanks." I set my rifle down and swallowed the chilled gold liquid. "This is a nice place you have." Ben was a couple years younger than me, but we'd been in the Marines at the same time. He had been in a different unit, but our paths had crossed during training and in Iraq. I tried to remain close to my fellow veterans since I'd been out of the military. We needed each other if only to be sure we all kept sane.

"Thank you." He scratched the black stubble on his jaw and his light green eyes focused on mine as he hopped up onto the back of his truck bed. "Twenty acres of absolute nothing. Told you my place was better than a gun range."

"You happy here? Working as private security?" I reached for my shades and leaned against the side of his truck, taking another sip.

"Yeah. It's okay. I'm not a huge fan of protecting big wigs with a lot of money, though." He smirked at me. "Although now it seems you're a big shot, too. How come you never told me your father was some rich businessman?" He raked a hand through his black hair.

I shook my head and kicked my boot at the dirt. "I'm not like him." I released a breath. "I was wild in college, partying and throwing his money around." Then I met Olivia. *You bring out the wild in me. You make me feel so alive. And I never want us to end,* she once told me.

But it did end.

"Connor?"

"Anyways," I choked out the word, my mind moaning and protesting the memories which assaulted and battered my brain, "the Marines changed me, and I realized having bricks of money isn't my thing."

He released a deep, throaty laugh. "Well, shit. Money isn't the problem. It's what you do with it that can be." He reached for his baseball hat and put it on. "But I know what you mean. When I was recruited to play for the Dodgers, I totally let the fame and money go to my head." He took another sip of his Corona. "I'm almost glad I blew my shoulder out."

"I always forget I'm friends with a famous athlete," I joked.

"Well, now I'm friends with a billionaire."

"Hell, the company might be worth a lot, but I'm not. And it's just temporary." Thank, God. I was almost ready to display a countdown clock in my office. The time when Mason came home couldn't come soon enough.

"When's Mason's tour over?"

"Just over five months." Too. Damn. Long.

"What will you do after he takes over?"

"Same as before." I pushed away from the truck and set my Corona on the ground before reaching for my rifle.

"You liked that life?"

I thought about Lydia, the girl I'd rescued almost a month ago. "Yeah."

"What about a love life? You ever going to settle down?" He jumped off the truck bed and stepped up behind me as I kneeled on the ground.

I once thought about it. Olivia's name tickled my throat. "I'll settle down the day you do," I answered instead.

"I'm living in Vegas. That's never going to happen." He laughed.

"Then I guess you have your answer." I fired off a round and waited until the bullet tore through the target, destroying it completely. "Wanna come to the grand opening of a club tonight?" I'd almost forgot why I was in Vegas.

"Sure. Need a wingman?"

God, just the opposite. I needed a shield.

* * *

Olivia

IT DIDN'T MATTER HOW CROWDED THE CASINO WAS—HE WAS impossible to miss. With his back to me, I took note of the silvery-gray suit he wore instead of his usual jeans and T-shirt.

The frantic beeping of the slot machines matched my heartbeat pound for pound as I crossed the room.

A woman with long, blonde hair pressed her hand to Connor's back, which had me stopping about ten feet shy of the table.

I didn't see Lauren anywhere, but she might have already met up with Declan.

Blowing out a nervous breath, I closed the distance between myself and Connor and cleared my throat.

The blonde turned, and her dark green eyes narrowed on me. She kept her hand on his back as she tilted her head up, letting me know he'd been claimed.

"Connor?" His shoulders flinched. The woman's hand dropped to her side as her red lips pursed together. "Hi." I smoothed a hand over my black dress.

His green eyes settled on my mouth once he faced me, and his chest swelled. "Olivia. How are you?" The deep timber of his voice made my core clench.

"Good. Declan sent me for you."

"Give me a minute." He turned back to the table as if unable to stand the sight of me and slid a stack of chips to the double zero. What was he thinking? That had to be twenty grand.

"Looks like you've figured out what to do with your father's money." Shit, I hadn't meant to say that out loud.

"It's my money," he was quick to respond.

"Same thing, right?" Damn. Damn. Damn. I needed to stop.

He was clearing his throat, his back still to me. "My money from before. My job paid well." He shook his head. "Not that I need to explain myself to you."

"Double zero!"

Some kind of luck.

The woman placed her hand on his arm. "Nice!"

Connor turned to me, ignoring the woman who swooned over him as large denomination chips were pushed his way. "I don't plan on keeping my father's money. Or the business. FYI." There was grit in his voice.

Maybe he wouldn't make a deal with Declan, after all. "Really?" I tried to sound disappointed. Angling my head down, I looked up at him from beneath my lashes. I had to play the part.

"Okay if my friend comes to the club?"

I blew out a breath and looked over at the woman. She stared back at me, and her eyes went round, her plump injected lips curving into a smile.

"My friend, Ben, lives in Vegas. I invited him. Hope that's okay?"

The temptation to smirk at the woman faded as Connor took a step closer to me, pushing all the oxygen from the room. "No problem."

Connor turned to the woman. "Have a good night."

I couldn't hide a smile as we left her behind. "How was your flight? Mine didn't have any turbulence." Thank God. I wasn't sure if I was capable of making small talk with him, but I'd give it a shot.

He glanced down at me from over his shoulder. He was tall— more than half a foot taller than my five foot seven, and his broad shoulders made me feel that much smaller. I combed my fingers through my hair, and realized that could be considered flirtatious . . . but I didn't mean it like that. Did I?

"The flight was fine." He was cold. Hard. Icy, even. The muscle in his square jaw tightened as we walked.

Why was he so angry with me? I had every right to hold a grudge for the way he'd abandoned me, but what in the hell was his excuse?

I needed to focus. He was a job now.

"Does your boss always do business like this?" he asked as we weaved our way to The Phoenix. He must've already scoped out the location—the hotel was a maze.

I shrugged. "I guess so." How much did Connor know about Declan? I couldn't believe that Connor would ever do business with a criminal. Of course, on paper, Declan appeared to be a legit businessman. I couldn't exactly enlighten Connor on the truth through.

What if Connor blew my cover?

Even after all these years, it was hard to turn off the switch on my feelings. We'd been together for a year. Still, that was the longest relationship of my life.

We stopped for a minute on our way to the club. "Let me text my friend," he said. I couldn't take my eyes off his hands as he tapped at his iPhone. Those hands had once touched every inch of my body . . .

I didn't know I was biting my lip until I saw Connor staring at my mouth. Something dark—dangerous, even—lurked behind his eyes. "You ready?" I checked the silver Movado on my wrist. It was half past eleven.

"Yeah."

We bypassed the line and headed through the lobby of the club, which was lit only by black lights. I nodded to the two men standing guard outside the two elevators. I halted just in front of them and turned to face Connor, but he must not have been paying attention—he plowed right into me. My back pushed up against the closed elevator doors, and he sucked in a breath as his hand braced against the door.

I shot him an apologetic look.

He stared down at me, and even in the dim light, his eyes flickered.

"You okay, Miss Taylor?" Seth, one of the bodyguards, asked.

Connor kept his eyes on mine as he took a step back, giving me room to breathe. I could vaguely hear a few of the women in line nearby: "Hot." "Sexy." "So fuckable." I couldn't disagree.

"Yeah. Thanks, Seth." I swallowed, looking back at Connor. "What's the name of your friend? So I can put him on the list." I rubbed my semi-sweaty palms against the sides of my dress and wondered whether my chest had grown overnight. Or perhaps the dress had shrunk. It was far too snug tonight.

"Ben Logan," Connor said, directing his attention to Seth.

Seth leaned forward. "Looking fine tonight, Liv. You put these girls to shame," he whispered, jerking a thumb at the line behind him.

Connor's jaw tightened as his eyes focused on Seth, like Seth was a predator I needed protection from. It was enough to make me laugh. Connor was far more dangerous to me than Seth could ever be.

Connor's hand touched my elbow, and he motioned when the elevator doors chimed and opened. "Ready?" he asked, a hint of irritation in his voice.

Blinking a few times, I followed him in. "There's plenty of room," I said to Seth.

Seth held up his hand and shook his head while groans slipped from the lips of women in line. "Just you two."

After the doors had closed and we began our fifty-one story trek up to the club, Connor said, "You should think twice before wearing a dress like that to work." His voice was rasping, hoarse.

My lips parted as my eyes grew wide. Who the hell did he think he was? Our gaze met in the mirrored elevator doors. "And I think you should keep comments like that to yourself," I hissed.

He took a step back and turned away from me, looking out the glass wall as the lights of the city shrank below. "Nice view." He tucked his hands in his slacks pockets.

I all but jumped out of the elevator once it opened. "Declan's waiting outside."

"Outside?"

"Yeah. There are two dance areas, but the best one is on the rooftop." I tried to ignore the uptick in my pulse and began down the dark, narrow hall, which was lit only by the flickers of phoenix-from-the-flames drawings. I welcomed the fresh air as we stepped out on the patio of the nightclub, which was nestled at the top of the hotel.

"Nice place."

I stole a look at Connor out of the corner of my eye. He was checking the place out, probably as enamored with the club like everyone else.

The DJ was spinning hip-hop and the stripper pole in the

middle of the dance floor was sans stripper . . . for now. "This way."

Connor's eyes remained on the crowd, a mesh of bodies smacking against each other to the music, some dancing well, others rhythmically-challenged.

To get into the club, people have to be invited. Even those waiting in line downstairs were on the list to get in. This wasn't just for the grand-opening, Declan planned to maintain the hyper-exclusivity of the place.

It took me a moment to find Declan, but as I scanned the room, I spotted him tucked away in one of the VIP booths off to the side of the bar, with Lauren standing at attendance. My stomach lurched at the sight of her, and I wasn't sure why. As we approached the booth, Connor trailing a few painful steps behind, I noticed that Lauren's barely-there red lace dress looked like it was pasted on her body. Was this her business casual attire?

"Declan. Lauren." I fixed a smile on my face as we stopped near the booth.

Declan scooted out and rose to his feet, dressed in a tailored, three-piece retro brown suit. He looked sharp. Lethal.

"What do you think?" Declan unbuttoned his suit jacket and motioned for us to have a seat.

"It's great." Connor gestured for me, and then Lauren, to slide in first.

Lauren's brown eyes, enhanced by jet-black eyeliner and false eyelashes, focused on Connor as he sat down. She scooted between Connor and me, her thigh unnaturally close to his. I had to tear my gaze away from her hand, which was draped over her lap, but only a few inches away from his leg.

Who was she into—Declan or Connor? Maybe she wanted both. Yeah, I could totally see that.

But Lauren wasn't Connor's type, was she? Of course, he may have changed in the last ten years—wait. What was I thinking?

"You okay?" Declan was snapping his fingers at me.

Shit, I was losing my edge. Blake thought having Connor involved might help me break the case, but he was wrong. Having Connor around might cause me to lose my damn job—or worse.

"I was saying that we should enjoy the club tonight and talk business tomorrow." Declan's eyes creased at the corners as he pushed a lopsided grin to his face. "What do you think, Liv?"

I really hated that Declan sometimes referred to me as Liv, but I needed to suck it up like I'd done the last nine months, and smile. I needed to play the smart but slightly naïve girl Declan had come to appreciate, and hopefully, would open up to.

"Why don't you two dance?" Declan gestured at Connor and me.

Connor glanced in my direction with his lips in a straight line.

I gulped and straightened my spine. "Um."

My orders were to get close to Connor. But how close would be too close? I studied Connor's strong profile out of the corner of my eye and waited for his answer.

A grin stretched across Declan's face. "Come on. Enjoy yourself." He stood up once again, allowing Connor to exit.

Hesitant, Connor started to slide out of the large booth.

"Save me a dance," Lauren said once he was standing.

He nodded at her but kept his eyes on me. I was still sitting, wasn't I?

"Maybe we shouldn't," I finally said, my bottom glued to the seat.

"I will, then!" Lauren rushed to her feet and reached for Connor's hand before he could respond.

Connor released a barely noticeable breath as he looked away and to the dance area. With slow steps, Connor and Lauren moved deeper into the whirl of activity. Once in the dedicated dance area, Lauren's hand swooped around to his back, and she pulled herself up against him.

Why was I watching them? I winced as a hand patted my knee. It was Declan's. When had he sat back down? And why in the hell was the bastard touching me? "They make a cute couple," I said, trying not to choke on my words.

"You have a thing for him, huh?" He removed his hand—thank God—and studied me.

"What? No!" Resting my hands on the table, I stared down at my short, red painted fingernails, forcing myself to keep from looking over at Lauren and Connor dance.

Almost ten years since he'd completely abandoned me, and for some Godforsaken reason I was still in heat over the damn man. "Want a drink?" I tried to side-step Declan's concerns.

"Liv." His icy fingers touched my chin, tilting my face in his direction. "Dance with him."

"Why?"

"Go after what's yours. I promise you won't regret it."

What was *mine*? Connor wasn't mine—not even close. Until the other day, I'd forgotten that we shared a planet. I'd written off his very existence a long time ago.

Okay, so maybe not entirely. Maybe when I got into the boxing ring to spar, I pictured him sometimes.

And his father, too.

I half-smiled at Declan as I scooted out of the booth, careful to keep my dress from riding up too high.

"Good girl."

The slap on my ass had my head spinning in his direction as I rose to my feet. I controlled the urge to ball my hands into fists, curtailing the desire to slug him in the face. But I'd been trained at Quantico, for Christ's sakes. I could handle Declan Reid.

9

CONNOR

GRABBY HANDS DIDN'T NORMALLY BOTHER ME, BUT KNOWING Olivia was at the club made Lauren's wandering paws feel wrong, somehow. I wasn't cheating, though. It was ridiculous to feel that way.

Olivia was standing at the bar, her back turned to me, just on the outskirts of the dance area. I'd tossed my suit jacket and rolled my dress sleeves up. The night air was still warm, and I was burning up. My hands slid down Lauren's exposed back as I pulled her closer, and another sensation of guilt crawled up my spine.

When I caught sight of Ben, relief slammed into me. Thank God, an excuse to stop dancing. "Lauren, I have a friend I'd like to talk to," I yelled into her ear.

She pouted before wetting her lips and leaned in close. Her hand touched my chest and started south, but I caught her wrist and stepped back. Was this girl trying to get me sued for sexual harassment?

Hell, wasn't she the one harassing me?

I released her wrist and shouted out Ben's name as I fought through the crowd.

Ben had just set his sights on Olivia, like every other man in the club, it seemed. She tilted her head back and laughed as they talked.

I cleared my throat, which had little effect given the loud music. "Ben."

"Hey, man." He slapped my shoulder and Olivia's lip tucked between her teeth as she focused on her drink. "This is—" Ben turned to Olivia and cocked his head, waiting for her to produce a name.

"Olivia."

Standing before them, I started to feel like a third wheel. "We know each other. She works for the man I'm meeting with; the owner of this club."

His mouth formed an O-shape, and he nodded and took a small step to the side, offering a little more room between him and Olivia. He studied me for a second, attempting telepathy, perhaps.

"So, you're Ben Logan?" She reached for her martini and took a sip, her eyes still wandering. "How do you know each other?"

Why'd she care? Was she just making small talk?

"We met in the military," Ben responded. He grabbed his beer from the bar and looked off into the swarm of good-looking people who danced fast and furious to the beat. Olivia and I used to dance to this kind of music every weekend back in the day.

"Want a drink?" She finally gave me the gift of her gaze.

"I'm good." Olivia's presence was already intoxicating enough, and I wasn't sure if I could trust myself around her, even with just a drink or two. I was so angry with her, but damned if I didn't still want to pull her against me. Even just for a second.

"Loosen up, man. Haven't seen you for a while." Ben pressed a hand to my shoulder and angled his head. "How about a shot of tequila for all of us?"

Tequila. Damn. A smile threatened my lips.

"Ah. You remember?" Ben's eyes lit up.

"How could I forget?"

Olivia's eyes darted back and forth between us. "What?"

Ben set his beer down, turned toward the bartender and motioned for his attention. "Three shots of tequila."

Olivia raised her hand in the air as she shook her head. "Oh no. I'm working."

Ben ran a hand through his dark hair and narrowed his eyes at her. "Oh come on, if you can have a martini you can have one shot."

Despite the shouting and loud music, Olivia's voice was alluring. "Only if you tell me about your tequila story." She set her martini glass down on the bar and folded her arms.

"We were both between tours. We took a trip to London, and—"

"She doesn't need to hear this," I interrupted, warning him not to continue with the clenching of my jaw.

"Oh come on," she begged.

"No."

"Let's just say the *Hangover* movie had nothing on us. He woke up naked near Buckingham Palace and had the nerve to taunt the soldiers and—"

"Stop, Ben."

"You weren't arrested?" Her mouth edged open in surprise.

"Um, yeah! I had to bail his ass out of jail—once I gained consciousness." Ben laughed.

"Ignore him. It wasn't that crazy," I lied.

"So, what do you say?" Ben grabbed two shots, handing them to Olivia and me.

"No salt?" Olivia teased.

"Nah," Ben answered.

What the hell . . . We clinked our glasses and a splash of liquid spilled on Olivia's hand. I wanted nothing more than to take her hand to my mouth—but I didn't. Instead, I gulped down the shot and focused on Olivia as her shoulders arched back and her face puckered.

"So, are you working tonight or having fun?" Ben asked as he set his glass down on the bar.

I looked at Olivia. "I guess I'm off tonight." This was all so strange. Had my father been in charge, would he be at the bar with Olivia right now? I scanned the dance area, searching for Lauren, and spotted her pressed up against some muscle-bound guy with tattoos. "Where's Declan?"

Olivia shrugged. "I assume he's mingling with the A-listers . . ."

"And what are you supposed to be doing?" I asked.

"I was ordered to dance with you, actually." She was staring down at the empty shot glass in her hand.

"Really?" Was she nervous? If she even apologized to me for what happened when we were together, could I forgive her? Probably not.

"You should dance." Ben's eyes were laser focused on a tall brunette standing off to the side of the dance area. "I'll see you in a bit." He started for the woman, and within in a minute he had the woman smiling. Ben, always the charmer.

"So?" The corners of her eyes crinkled as she smiled. A forced smile, maybe.

"I guess one dance won't hurt." Maybe I needed another shot, something to alleviate the tension circulating throughout my body. "Come on." I didn't reach for her hand like I wanted to, nor did I get a shot. I moved to the center of the crowd of dancers, and she followed.

A mixed Avicii song blasted through the speakers, as I touched her back and pulled her closer. Her breasts pressed against my chest, and I reached for her wrist, slinging her arm over my shoulder.

She inhaled sharply and peered into my eyes. The vibration from the bass poured through me as we moved like old times.

I couldn't hear the music after a few minutes. Everything was white noise. Nothing else existed except Olivia.

At some point, I realized we'd been dancing for a hell of a lot longer than one song. My shirt was practically sticking to my body, and I noticed her long neck glistening. "You tired?" I whispered into her ear, and her body shuddered at my breath.

"Looks like you're having a good time."

Olivia jerked away from me in one sudden movement with Declan at our side. Her cheeks were already red from dancing, but I could have sworn they deepened to crimson as she focused on Declan. "I should walk around. Check on how things are going." She brushed a loose strand of hair from her face.

"Relax. Everything's going great. You don't need to work," Declan responded.

"If that's the case, I might head to my room."

"I'll walk you." The words had slipped from my lips before I had the chance to stop them.

"Come back, man. The night has only just begun."

I checked my watch. It was quarter past one already, but yeah, in Vegas, that was like ten p.m. "Sure." I rested my hand on her elbow, and she nodded to Declan before we headed inside.

There was no one standing by the elevators, but why would there be? No one would leave the grand opening of a club this early, except Olivia. I was surprised Declan didn't object to her leaving. I figured he'd want her there until the sun rose.

"Do you regret what happened between you and me?" I couldn't help myself. The past was hanging in the air between us, heavy and thick.

She pressed the elevator call button. "Regret?" she snapped and squinted at me. "I'd hardly—" The elevator doors opened, and a few people strode out of it, pushing past us, cutting her off.

Olivia entered the empty elevator and faced the glass window. Apparently, she didn't intend to finish her thought. Following her inside, I hit the first-floor button and rubbed the back of my neck as the doors closed. "Liv . . ."

Her shoulders slouched forward at the sound of my voice, and she slowly faced me.

I blew out a breath, exhausted from the emotions pulling at me, and closed the gap between us.

"I don't want to talk about the baby." Her voice was low and grave but coated with a tender sadness.

"Neither do I," I rasped before I banded my hand around her hip. I pulled her against me, my lips on fire as they touched hers.

* * *

Olivia

THIS WASN'T A PART OF THE PLAN. KISSING MY EX-BOYFRIEND wasn't how I wanted to get the information I needed. But, holy shit. He tasted so damn good.

His tongue mingled with mine, stealing my breath. His hand fisted my hair, and my head tilted back. "I want you," he growled after breaking the kiss.

The elevator doors chimed, and I shifted away from Connor's hold. I couldn't look him in the eyes. I was both embarrassed and angry with myself for giving in. How could I still feel something for this man?

I stared down at the red carpet as I brushed past him and exited the elevator.

"Liv." He reached for my arm and spun me toward him, not giving a damn about the people who were still standing in line outside the elevator. "Are you okay?" he asked breathlessly.

"Sure." I nodded like an idiot, moving my head up and down like some lifeless being. "Tired." I pulled my arm free from his grasp. I couldn't handle the way his fingers burned my skin, sending shivers of desire through my body.

He motioned for me to walk, and I was grateful he didn't say anything. What was there to say? We'd kissed. It's not like we hadn't done it before.

Men were supposed to get better with age. Was that possible? Connor had been incredible even when we were young. I swallowed back the memories of his sweat-slicked body riding me atop the rooftop of his apartment when we were young.

"Where's your room?"

Goosebumps crawled across my skin as we walked through the casino and toward the main lobby. The swarms of people at the machines and the green felt tables, pissing their money away were tiny blips on my radar. "Eighth floor."

Fluorescent lights bathed the lobby, mimicking sunshine to keep gamblers awake and spending. We entered a hallway filled with depictions of Greco-Roman art along the walls. The silver-doored elevators gleamed before us.

"You have your key?" he asked once we stepped inside the elevator.

I bit my lip for a moment. "In my bra."

His eyes averted immediately to my cleavage. "You're kidding?"

I turned away from the camera, which was perched in the top right corner of the elevator, and slipped my hand inside my bra. "See?" I revealed the small white card.

His light green eyes steadied on mine, and I wondered if he was going to kiss me again.

Instead, he blew out a breath and waited for the doors to open. "Left or right?"

Why was he even walking me to my room? It wasn't like there was a safety issue at the hotel. What were his intentions? His almost bruising kiss popped into my head. Did he want to take it further?

It sure didn't seem like it, the way he was acting.

Blake's orders came to mind. Did Connor know anything? If I tried to pump him for information, what could he possibly tell me?

Of course, if he didn't know anything now, he might know something later. If I gained his trust . . .

I wanted to scream. I hated this. And I hated how I felt like a teenager again, unsure and aching inside.

"What's up?" Connor was smiling—one of the first times he'd smiled at me like that since we'd bumped into each other. It wasn't a forced, tight-lipped smile, but a real knock-your-panties-off kind of smile.

Once outside my room, I swiped my card, unlocked the door, and opened it. "Want to come in?"

"Not sure if that's a good idea." His palm went to the wall just outside the door, and he leaned in closer to me. I tilted my head to look up at him, noticing his strong forearm and the way the material of his shirt constricted against the swell of his muscular chest.

"We should talk," I suggested in a low voice, worried if I spoke above a whisper it would crack.

"About what?" The muscle in his jaw tightened, and his eyes creased as he narrowed them at me. He was Mr. Serious, now—a man I'd never met when I was younger. Connor had always been the live-free-or-die guy. The bungee jumping, skydiving, dancing in a restaurant even though it was, well, a restaurant, kind of guy.

"I don't know. There's all this tension between us, and we have to work together now. I meant what I said at your office. Put the past behind us and be friends." God, that was total bullshit. I wish it could be true, but how could I ever trust him enough to be friends? Besides, my job was in the way.

"Olivia," he leaned closer until his face was inches from mine, "you and I were never meant to be friends."

I wet my lips, drawn into his pull. "What were we meant to be?" My eyes closed, and I waited for his lips to touch mine again.

But when my eyes fluttered open, he was standing a foot back with his hands tucked in his pockets. "I should go."

What?

His eyes were cast down and focused on the carpet. "Please, can we try?" I had to do this—I had to win him over. It was my job, right? I didn't want to make amends with him for any other reason than that.

"Try what?" he asked with a terseness to his voice that set me on my heels. His eyes were now on me, and something dark was there—something I'd never seen when we were younger. I know the military can change a person, but this was pure and utter hatred.

"Connor," I said softly, "come in."

Sure, let the tiger—no, the lion—into my room. He was going to eat me alive.

He rubbed his neck with his large hand and came inside. Shaking my head and fighting my guilt, I shut the door and turned to face him. He moved straight to the terrace, opened the door, and stepped outside.

The terrace overlooked the Vegas strip. Sitting down in one of the chairs, I mentally scolded myself for admiring his backside as he pressed his hands to the railing.

"How have you been?" I crossed my legs and leaned back in my seat, attempting to be casual.

"Great," he said sarcastically. Okay, maybe I deserved that. His father had just passed away a few weeks ago. "Listen . . ." He had turned to face me, but his voice stopped as his eyes settled on my legs.

"What?"

His mouth twitched as he dragged his gaze up to my face. His pupils dilated, taking over the soft green of his eyes. "I can't be here with you," he said in a deep voice, shaking his head.

I stood up, my legs trembling a little as I moved toward him. He touched my face with the back of his hand, and I leaned into his touch. "Connor, what happened to you?" I snapped my eyes shut as painful memories hurdled to my mind.

A few moments of silence, and then, "*You* happened to me."

My cheek tingled from the loss of him as my eyes opened.

He'd already gone.

10

CONNOR

I LEANED BACK IN THE LOUNGE CHAIR, MY LEGS STRETCHED OUT, wearing only my black swim trunks. The sun was hot on my skin as the poolside DJ spun an engaging mix of electronic music. Vegas was wild. If I were in a better mood, I'd have enjoyed it.

Lauren was walking my way in a tiny black bikini, her boobs practically spilling out of her top. She shifted her sunglasses to the edge of her nose and flashed me a smile as she sat down in the empty lounge chair next to me. She plopped her large bag down between our seats and slapped my knee. "Hey, cowboy."

Really? Did I give off a horse-riding, rodeo vibe? I brought my bare feet to the ground and removed my aviator sunglasses. The sparkling, cool water of the pool beckoned me.

"What happened to you last night? You never came back." She reached into her massive bag and dug through it for a moment. Then she pulled out a bottle of tanning oil and handed it to me. "You mind?"

The woman would fry, but who was I to judge?

She lay on her stomach and swept her brown hair over her shoulder, offering me access to her back as I stood. My breath hitched when she unclasped her bra strap. What the hell? This had to violate some code of business ethics. I shook my head and poured the oil onto my palms. "I was tired and went to bed. Sorry. How was it?"

"It was amazing. You missed out."

I rubbed the oil over Lauren's back, and her shoulder blades pinched back a little. I wasn't the least bit turned on.

What was happening to me? It had been almost a month since I'd gotten laid—since before my father died. I still couldn't believe I'd kissed Olivia. And the things I had thought about doing to her tight body last night . . . shit, *now* I was getting hard. I hoped to hell the bulge in my shorts wasn't apparent—*that* was a lawsuit waiting to happen.

My phone began to ring, vibrating noisily against the side table, and I did my best to wipe the oil from my hands with my towel. "Sorry," I muttered as I grabbed my cell.

"Tell me that you didn't come back last night because you went back to that girl's room—Olivia, right?"

Ben, Jesus. "No. I was tired."

"What? Really?"

"Sorry to disappoint," I said and mouthed to Lauren, "Be right back."

"When do you go back to New York?" Ben asked as I weaved my way through the rows of sunbathers to the outskirts of the pool area. "Monday's the plan, but I don't know. Part of me wants to high-tail it out of here tonight."

"Why?"

Olivia, mostly, but I wasn't about to give him the satisfaction. "Could you do me a favor? Could you ask around about Declan Reid?" I shoved a hand through my hair. "Discreetly."

"Sure. The guy who owns the club, right?"

"Yeah."

"What for?"

"I don't want to raise any flags, but maybe you could gain some insight about him without anything pointing to me . . . I might do a business deal with him, and I just want to make sure he's legit."

"You getting the vibe he's not?"

"I don't know. This whole businessman thing is new to me. Maybe everyone does it this way." I thought longingly of the three job offers I'd turned down this week: bodyguard, rescue attempt, and a missing person case. It was hard puttering around in Vegas when I knew I could be out there helping people.

"I'll see what I can find out. No worries."

"Thanks, man. Ring me later." As I started back for my seat, I spotted Olivia standing at the edge of the pool, by the deep end. My mouth clamped shut in frustration as my eyes raked over her insanely hot pink bikini.

It looked like she was about to jump in the water, but two men were flanking her sides. And she didn't look happy. Before I realized what I was doing, my feet carried me through the maze of chairs.

Olivia was waving her hand between the two men, and one of them had placed his hand on her hip. Gritting my teeth, I shoved my phone in my pocket, prepared to use my fists to remove the men if necessary.

But I didn't get the chance. I stilled about ten feet away when Olivia twisted the man's hand back, and he dropped to his knees before her.

Wow. When had Olivia become such a badass?

"Back off," I growled on approach just as the man was rising to his feet.

Once the men walked away, Olivia angled her head at me. "I had them. They were just drunk and stupid." She folded her arms, and her eyes bore into me. Her skin was glowing from the sun, and her chest heaved.

"Where'd you learn to do that?"

"I took defense classes, and I box."

The woman got sexier every minute.

This was bad.

"Anyway, I was trying to swim, so if you don't mind . . ."

Before I had a chance to respond, she slipped into the pool and disappeared beneath the water, her hair fanning out behind her.

I rubbed my jaw, not sure what the hell to think. I still needed to cool off. The pool would be big enough for the both of us.

I hurried back to return my phone. Lauren's eyes were shut with wires trailing from her ears. Good, I didn't want to dive into small talk. I tucked my phone under my towel and went back to the pool.

The water felt like a warm bath, but it was still better than roasting beneath the sun.

"Are you following me?"

Olivia was just a foot away. Her hair was slicked back, revealing her flawless face.

Beautiful. I couldn't think of a better word to describe her.

I was going stiff again. Shit.

She shook her head, huffing, and started toward the crowd of people gathered at the other end of the pool, flailing their arms to a David Guetta remix.

Without thinking, I started after her. My hand shot through the water and touched her back.

Turning toward me with wide eyes, she swallowed. "What?"

This wasn't right. How could I do a deal with Declan if it meant being around Olivia? I couldn't control myself around her.

"Tell Declan I can't do business with him." My hand fell to my side, splashing into the water. Her mouth formed a sexy O and dirty thoughts pushed into my mind. What in the hell was wrong with me? "Sorry," I added.

"Declan will be upset." Her plump bottom lip slipped between her teeth.

"Goodbye, Liv—Olivia," I said, my voice breaking a little as I turned away. I moved toward the closest set of steps, preparing myself to book the next flight back to New York, but Olivia's fingers on my back arrested me.

"You're doing the right thing," she said, loud enough for me to hear over the music but low enough not to draw too much attention.

What was she talking about? But I didn't ask. I didn't even look back.

I grabbed my stuff carefully, glad that Lauren's eyes stayed shut. She could stay and party in Vegas for all I cared. I'd shoot her a text from the airport to let her know there would be no deal.

I wanted the best for the company, for my brother, but I couldn't be around Olivia for another minute.

* * *

Olivia

"THIS WAS OUR BEST SHOT. WHAT HAPPENED?" BLAKE BARKED. I was thankful the phone was set to speakerphone and safely resting on the dresser next to me.

"Maybe he figured out that Declan's shady." I zipped up the side of my sequin dress and studied myself in the full-length mirror in the hotel room. "Connor wouldn't have been able to help us if he's not crooked, anyway." Thank God.

"I'm not buying that. Last night you told me that Declan still hadn't talked to Connor about business. Why would Connor all of the sudden jet out of there?" A crackling sounded through the phone as Blake blew out his breath. "What'd you do, Liv?"

"I didn't do anything. I don't know what happened. He said he couldn't do business with Declan." I sat in the desk chair and spun to face the window, which overlooked the strip's infamous Eiffel Tower.

"Get him back." Blake's sharp voice grated on my ears. What had I ever seen in him?

"I can't."

"He's one of our best leads so far."

"Not if he's innocent. If he's a straight-up guy, there's no point in getting close to him," I protested.

"There's only one way to find out, isn't there?" Blake insisted. "Besides, Declan's going to flip when he learns Connor took off. What if he fires you? The last nine months will be for nothing."

Unfortunately, Blake was right. Declan would be more than pissed, and he'd probably blame me since he knew about our history.

Before I could speak, there was a knock on my door. "I gotta call you back." I slipped the phone into the dresser drawer and hurried to the door.

I peeked through the peephole. Declan's pinched face sent me a step back. *He must know.*

When I opened the door, Declan walked right in. "Lauren just got a text from Connor."

"Oh yeah?"

"Don't play dumb, Livvy."

So it was Livvy, now?

"What?" Folding my arms, I leaned against the wall, trying to bottle my hate for the man.

"You're screwing with a very important business deal." Dressed in black slacks, a black dress shirt, jacket—and even black tie, Declan looked dangerous. He stalked toward me with predatory steps and placed his palm on the wall near my shoulder. I could almost feel his warm breath on my face.

"Declan," I warned, wondering if I'd need to drop his ass to the floor.

He cupped the back of my head with his free hand and pulled me close to him until his mouth was at my ear. "Get out of Vegas and go back to New York. Make this right," he hissed.

Both of his hands dropped to his sides as he stepped back. I thanked God.

"I want a meeting scheduled with him when I'm back on Tuesday." His eyes darkened to black as he focused on me.

I wanted to lash out at him, but I bit my tongue and forced a nod.

"Leave now." He walked through the door, glancing over his shoulder at me before disappearing.

11

CONNOR

I STUDIED THE TEXT ON MY PHONE. BEN HAD NOTHING TO TELL ME about Declan yet. Maybe that was a good thing.

"Sorry, what were you saying again?" I shoved my phone back into my jeans pocket—I'd given up on the suit—and looked at the man before me.

Wes didn't look like the brilliant guy I'd pictured. The head of research and development looked more like the leader of a biker gang, given the tank top, his large tree trunk arms covered in tattoos, and his shaven head.

"You ready to see what we've been working on?" Wes patted me on the shoulder and motioned to the massive double doors in front of me. We were in the basement of the building where, according to Wes, "all of the cool shit takes place."

"It has to be better than pushing papers upstairs."

Wes grinned and approached a glass screen mounted on the wall next to the doors. He pressed his palm to the screen and said his name.

"Identity confirmed. You will have five seconds to now enter your passcode," a female voice stated.

Wow. What were they working on that needed a handprint, voice recognition, and a passcode?

The doors slid open to reveal what could only be a gun lover's paradise. Weapons lined the sterile, white walls: everything from old-fashioned revolvers to hard-core assault rifles. I followed Wes down to another door, which also required verification.

Wes rubbed his hands together, a smile on his lips, as we entered a room. There were several people standing in front of the far wall, which was completely covered in a screen lit up with images. "Here's where all of the magic happens." Wes introduced me to all ten employees, although by the end of the introductions, I'd already forgotten the first nine names.

"We have a project that is going to change everything for Matthews Tech. We'll become the premier defense company in the country."

That was a bit hard to believe.

"Have you seen or heard of the electromagnetic field railgun?"

"Sure. The military is wrapping up tests, but there are some issues with it. Such as its massive size."

Wes smirked. "Well, we have some of the best minds here. Your father hired engineers from NASA, scientists from MIT, and myself, of course. Not only have we created the EMF railgun, we improved it." Wes tapped on a keyboard, and the image of a hand-held gun appeared on the wall.

The crowd of employees surrounded us, eager for my reaction. "That can't be an EMF gun." The gun with its silver handle, which led to two thin rails, or strips of metal, looked like something out of some science fiction film.

"Applying Faraday and Lenz's laws of electromagnetic energy, we're able to generate magnetic fields to produce voltage . . ." Wes lost me as he pointed to several mathematical equations that came on the screen. He rambled on about the science behind the weapon and didn't gain my full attention until he motioned for someone to hand over the prototype of the weapon. "Basically, it's light years ahead of its time. The military is building the big gun for a naval vessel—this one here is for up, close, and personal."

My jaw went slack as I weighed the gun, which sat heavy but balanced in my palm. It was game changing . . . and a dangerous device. If it got into the wrong hands . . . "Does the government know we have this?"

Wes took the gun back. "Not yet. Unfortunately, your dad never got to see the final results. We finished it just last week." Wes pressed a small silver object on the butt of the gun, and a microchip popped out. "The weapon is useless without the chip," he added while handing the gun and chip off to another team member.

I folded my arms and leaned against the counter behind me. "When do we present this to the Department of Defense?"

Wes laughed. "No clue, that's not my department. I just design the stuff. The people in suits handle the rest."

"Okay," I drawled, not sure what I was supposed to do now. I glanced at my watch. "I have another meeting, but it was nice to meet you." I was pretty sure he wanted a slap on the back and approval from me, but I wasn't sure how I felt about this. And what was more terrifying: The fact that my father's team of civilians had managed to do something that the military hadn't? Or the fact that no one seemed to know what to do with it?

* * *

Olivia

"No one is in the club. You're good to go," Blake's reassurance was a whisper in my earpiece.

I'd done this kind of thing numerous times before, with a team member hacked into the security cameras, but it always made me nervous. I hurried down the hall of The Phoenix and to Declan's office.

"Hey Olivia, it's me now." Sean was our tech guy. He could hack into anything and everything, including FBI computers. He'd once done just that, to prove we needed to beef up our security.

"Hi, Sean."

"Make sure you place the device I gave you flat against the screen of the keypad," he instructed.

"I remember." I reached into my pocket for the thin black strip. I pressed it to the keypad screen and held my breath as I waited.

"Got the code," Sean announced.

That was fast.

"You can remove the strip. Type six, five, six, nine, one, one, zero."

I tapped the numbers and released the breath I'd been holding as the door popped open. "I'm in." The lights automatically turned on as I entered the room. Shoving the device into one pocket, I retrieved another small object from my other pocket.

"Great. You know what to do now."

I peeled off the back of what appeared to be a quarter, revealing a thin, adhesive disc. I stuck it to the modem. "You getting anything?" I asked as I walked around behind Declan's desk.

"It's uploading. Only one percent so far," Sean answered.

It would take forever. But Declan wasn't supposed to be back from Vegas until tomorrow, and the club was closed on Mondays, with no deliveries in the afternoon.

"You think we'll find anything on there about his relationship with Konstantin?" Sean's voice popped into my ear.

Konstantin. A man I hated more than Declan. A lot more.

"How many times have we caught Declan and Konstantin meeting on tape? Five times now? We need more than a little video footage of them just being seen together, though," Blake came on the line, and his announcement had me rolling my eyes.

I didn't need a reminder as to why I'd been playing the good little secretary for Declan for so long. "I sure hope we find something soon. Otherwise, this whole charade will have been a colossal waste of time." I rubbed my sweaty palms against my jeans and waited. There was no point in attempting any of the desk drawers or filing cabinets in the room. Not only did they require a key, but I also doubted Declan would leave a paper trail of his criminal activities. Hell, even the computer was a longshot, but we had to try.

"Sean, you're wiping away the proof of my entry from the video feeds, right?" Not that Declan would have any reason to check the security footage, but just in case . . .

"I'm looping the feeds now . . . shit!" There was a muffled sound in my earpiece.

"Sean? What?" Panicked, I pressed my hand to my ear. "Sean?"

"Get out of there, Liv. Declan is on his way," Sean shouted.

Adrenaline zipped through my body, and I started for the door. "What about the computer?"

"Just get out of there," Sean cried out.

"But if he catches me . . ." I rushed out of the office, pulled the door shut behind me, and spun away toward my office.

"Olivia?" The hairs on my arms stood at Declan's soft voice. "What are you doing here?"

I slowly turned to face him. "Hey. I thought you didn't get back from Vegas until tomorrow." I closed the gap between us until we both stood outside his office door.

His long fingers tapped at the keypad, and his office door opened. "Come in."

Declan allowed me entrance first. My heart was ready to burst through my chest as I glanced over at the modem.

"I had an important business meeting arise, and so I needed to get back early. Why are you here?"

Oh yeah, I still hadn't answered that. I made my way toward one of the cages in the room and feigned interest in it, hoping to divert his attention. I pressed my hands on the metal, tracing the frame of the cage with my fingers. "Thought I'd get some work done without any distractions."

His hand on my back turned me toward him until our chests were just inches apart. He stared down at me, and his hand went to my chin. He tilted my face up to meet his eyes. "You finally ready to ask me about those?" His eyes darkened; I could feel the bulge in his pants press against my stomach.

Disgust slammed my system, but I had to maintain my composure. "Maybe sometime I'll ask you about them," I answered in a whisper.

His hand slipped up to my cheek before he took a step back, making no attempt to hide his desire. "I have people coming soon."

I nodded. "While I'm here, do you need anything?" I moved around to the front of his desk as he took a seat. "Damn laces," I muttered as I bent forward.

With my heart in my throat, I reached for the adhesive disc, but it was stuck.

"You okay down there?" Declan chuckled, and I worried he'd duck his head under the desk to see.

"Yeah," I answered as I tried once again for the device.

I popped upright with the device pressed against my palm. Pushing my hands into my pockets, I forced a smile to my face. "I'm not really dressed for a meeting, though." I kept my hands in my pockets, not wanting to raise any questions, and glanced down at my white T-shirt.

"No. I guess you're not. Besides, I don't think you're ready for this meeting."

"What do you mean?" Although I was only there to bring him and his associates down, part of me rankled at the thought that I might be unprepared for anything Declan might throw at me.

"Olivia, what are you willing to do for this job?"

Here it was—finally. Would he offer me the chance to learn more? Oh God, please . . .

He rolled his dress sleeves to his elbows, exposing his tattoos, and laced his fingers together before him. "If I were to tell you that you could be richer than you ever imagined—what would you do?" His eyes creased as they focused on me, his lips a tight straight line. The muscle in his jaw clenched.

For the first time, I found myself intimidated. Was it because we were alone? No, Blake and Sean could help me if things turned for the worst.

"So?" He angled his head and his mouth parted.

Removing my hands from my pockets, I pressed my palms to his desk. "I would do anything," I answered, keeping my eyes on his.

"Then get Connor on board," he said slowly. "Because otherwise, you're out of a job." He leaned back in his chair and his hands slipped to his lap.

I shuddered at his words and straightened. "Consider it done."

"Good." Declan cleared his throat. "And Olivia—"

"Yes?"

I wanted to knock the smug bastard in the face.

"The next time I find you in the building alone, I'll forget about my decision to keep things professional between us . . . and I'll provide you a full tutorial on the cages."

12

CONNOR

"I wanted to offer my condolences."

I switched the call to speakerphone. "Thanks." I drummed my fingers on the desk, uneasiness crawling up my spine. "I wasn't aware he did any business with your bank."

"He only recently opened an account and a safe deposit box with us," the banker responded.

My fingers stilled; I straightened in my chair. "Okay. What's your location? I'll swing by and close out his account. No offense, but I see no need in using your bank when all of the other funds are tied up elsewhere."

"I understand, sir. You'll want to be sure to bring the key and the passcode."

"I'm sorry?"

The banker made a gurgling sound before speaking. "He opened a premier box—even in the event of death, the box may not be opened without the key and passcode. And he only gave authority to himself, you, and your brother, to open it."

"So if he didn't leave me the key, what happens to the box?" This was ridiculous.

"You could request a court order, sir. Beyond that, the box will remain available to you or your brother for ten years—then it will be disposed of by the bank. So if you find the key and code among your father's things . . ."

Elsa came to the door as I was shaking my head. I motioned for her to enter the room. "If I can't find the information, I'll go the legal route."

"Of course."

"How long has my father been a client?"

"Recently. He opened the box just about a month ago."

A month ago? "Can you tell me the exact day?"

"Just one second," he answered, and I could hear him tapping at a few keys. "May sixteenth."

My mouth dropped open in surprise. "You must be mistaken. That's the day he died."

Silence greeted me.

"Hello?"

"Sorry, sir. I'm surprised to hear that. But it's correct. The sixteenth."

Could it be a coincidence? I doubted it. "I'll be in touch." I looked up at Elsa as I hung up the phone. "Do you know anything about my father opening a safe deposit box at Capital James Bank?" I asked as I walked around in front of my desk.

She placed a file on the desk next to me and shook her head. "No. Sorry. But here's the passcode for the research area, as you requested."

I took the scrap of paper from her and plugged the number into my phone.

"Connor?" She removed her glasses and shut her eyes for a brief moment before opening them. "Tyson's sister called."

"Oh good." She hopefully knew the whereabouts of my father's driver. "What'd she say?" I folded my arms and leaned against the desk.

"She doesn't know where he is. In fact, she said she's been trying to reach him for a while. She's worried."

"Oh. What did you say to her?"

"The truth. And she had no idea Edward passed. She hasn't talked to Tyson since before . . ."

"Something isn't right. I'm going to make a few calls and see what I can come up with. Don't worry." I rubbed the back of my neck as tension knotted at the base of my skull.

"Lauren will be back tomorrow, right?"

"Yeah." What a waste that trip had been. I needed to blow off some steam. "Elsa, I think I need to cut out of here early. Call me on my cell if you need anything." I grabbed my keys and started for the door, but paused.

I had planned on finding a local pistol range but realized we probably had one in the building. "Elsa?" I called out.

"Yeah?"

"Do we have a gun range here?"

"Yes," she answered before her lips curved into a smile. "In the basement. The key code to the lab will give you entrance."

"Thanks." I slipped my keys and phone into my pocket and made my way to the elevator. Once inside, I pressed my palms to the mirrored wall and stared at my reflection.

Without a moment of warning, my mind flashed to the kiss in the elevator with Olivia. It felt like a punch to my gut.

I groaned and opened my eyes as the elevator chimed.

I entered the restricted area, passed the wall of weapons, and stepped inside the lab. "I'd like to shoot something," I announced to Wes once I spotted him.

He grinned. "Follow me." We made our way down a hall and stopped just outside a dark blue door. "There are earmuffs and a wide selection of weapons inside. Have fun." He slapped my back with his big arms, and I thanked him before pushing open the door and stepping inside.

There were three zones set up for individual target practice. I moved through the empty room to the wall of weapons and grabbed a 9mm, some ammo, and the earmuffs.

Before I could load my weapon, my head snapped up. I didn't even need to see her to know she was there. It was her scent —vanilla.

"Elsa, why'd you bring her down here? This is a secure area." I set the gun down and faced them.

"I'm sorry, sir. She said she's a family friend. She insisted it was an emergency, and your phone was going straight to voicemail. I—I . . ."

Family? Hell, no. I held up my hand, not bothering to fight the anger splayed in the lines of my face. "It's fine, Elsa. You can leave us alone." I waited for my assistant to slip away. "What's going on, Olivia?"

She moved toward me with slow steps, wearing jeans and a T-shirt that strained in just the right way over her breasts. "I know I shouldn't be here, but you wouldn't return my messages, and I really need to talk to you." She pressed a hand to her chest and released a breath.

I reached for the gun and began to load the ammo in the clip. Her eyes lingered over my weapon, and I wondered if it frightened her.

"I need you to meet with Declan tomorrow," she said in a low voice.

"I told you no."

"He's going to fire me if you don't show." Her voice was laced with desperation.

"He can't fire you because of that." Earmuffs on and safety off, I raised my gun and aimed at the target of bin Laden. I should've offered her earmuffs, but I was too angry to give a damn.

The bullet pierced the target in the chest, and I lowered the gun and glanced over my shoulder at her.

She stepped up to me with her hands on her hips.

"What?" I let the earmuffs drop to my neck as I trained my eyes on hers.

"Tell me what to shoot. If I get it, then you'll come tomorrow."

90

Was she out of her mind?

"Come on. I know you love to gamble."

All the times we'd been to Atlantic City . . . I tried not to smile.

"Sorry. No deal." I turned back, but her hand on my shoulder held me fast.

"I can't lose this job, Connor. Please." She leaned closer, her perfume suffocating me.

"Just make something up." She'd always been good at lying. Why stop?

I raised my arm to shoot.

The slug tore at the paper, off to the side of the target's head.

Shit. I never missed.

"I'll escort you out. You shouldn't be here."

"Connor."

"What?" I shouted, immediately regretting the vile tone of my voice. But damn, I hated her—well, I was trying to. But my restraint was weakening . . . and I couldn't stand feeling weak.

"Just show up tomorrow. You don't have to do the deal, but he thinks I'm the reason you left Vegas. If he blames me, I'm done."

"You *are* the reason I left." I set the gun down and pressed my palms against the table, leaning forward a little, trying to maintain self-control.

"Could you stop being so stubborn?"

"Could you stop being so beautiful?" I snapped back without checking the filter on my mouth first.

Her eyes widened, but I rubbed a hand over my face in one quick movement and shook off the irritation that was at its peak. "Fine. Shoot the target between the eyes, and I'll go tomorrow. Miss, and I never have to see you again."

It was the easiest solution to my problem—she'd never make it.

She grabbed the 9mm and studied me over her right shoulder. "A little space, please."

I held up my hands and took a few steps back. Now all I could focus on was her trim waist, which led to her hips and her perfect, heart-shaped ass.

When the bullet whistled free from the gun, my gaze drifted to the target and my mouth dropped open. Not just a little open—jaw to the floor.

It couldn't just be luck. No one picks up a 9mm one day and makes such a flawless shot. Hell, she hadn't even flinched. "What in the hell is going on?"

She set the gun down and shrugged. "I told you I took self-defense lessons, didn't I?"

To say I was turned on was an understatement, and I sure as hell hoped she didn't glance down at my jeans.

"What time is the meeting?" I asked with defeat.

"Just come to the club tomorrow night. The later, the better."

"Fine."

"Thank you." She lifted her fingers to her collarbone. "Have dinner with me? You can call it a business dinner if you want."

My gaze dipped to her long fingers. For a brief moment, I wished it was my hand so close to her heart.

"Why?"

"I—"

"Is that sushi bar we used to go to on Wall Street still open?" No. What was I thinking?

A long pause, and rasp to her voice, "I don't know."

"Well, let's find out." I had no idea what had possessed me to agree. I motioned for her to exit and I walked behind her, trying my best not to check her out as she moved.

"Thank you again for tomorrow," she said before moving through the doors of the elevator. Her cheeks reddened. Perhaps she remembered our elevator kiss, just as I had.

"I can't make any promises that I'll do business with him, but I'll show. A bet is a bet." We walked to the parking garage, and she stopped in front of a red Audi.

"A company car," she said after she noticed me eyeing the car. It was a high-priced ride for a personal assistant.

"I'm pretty sure we only offer Fords at our office."

Olivia smirked. "You think you'll keep referring to the company as yours? Is it growing on you?" She opened her car door.

"No. I'm much better at dodging bullets," I said.

* * *

Olivia

I HAD A JOB TO DO, BUT I HAD TO KEEP REMINDING MYSELF THAT my past with Connor couldn't interfere with the end goal.

But Connor was innocent. He had to be. His father, on the other hand, was a bastard. Would he have been in business with Declan, though? Edward Matthews may have been a world class jerk, but was he a criminal?

Snagging a spot in front of the restaurant was pure luck, especially at this time of day. The place was still open after all these years, and part of me was disappointed. I didn't want to get close to Connor for the sake of my job. That wasn't who I wanted to be.

I tapped my fingers on my steering wheel, waiting for Connor to appear. My heart skipped into my throat at the sight of him. Nothing was sexier to me than a man in well-worn jeans, and God did Connor know how to wear them.

He caught sight of me and rubbed a large hand over his face, probably contemplating what in the hell he was doing with me.

I gulped, opened my door, and closed the distance between us. "Hi."

"Guess it's still here." He swung the door open and took a step back, allowing me entrance.

"Thanks." I tucked my hair behind my ear and walked past him, trying to ignore the heat that radiated from his body.

"Two," I told the host. "A booth, if you have one."

"Sure," the host responded, and we followed him to our table.

It was a small place—nothing fancy at all. But the best food in town, in my opinion, was usually from some cheap hole-in-the-wall place. Connor and I had once made it our mission to eat at every sushi restaurant in New York. But eventually, we gave up, because none was better than this one.

"I can't believe you never ate sushi before me."

"I ate sushi." I slid into the seat across from him.

"California rolls don't count. I'm talking about the kind that—"

I rushed a hand in front of my face. "Don't tell me. You know the rule. I'll try anything as long as I don't know what's in it."

"When was the last time you ate sushi?"

With you. But I didn't want to tell him that. It would seem—strange, at the least. "I don't know. Anyway, order for me. Okay?"

Once the waiter appeared and Connor ordered, he leaned back in the booth and propped his elbow up on the top of the seat, stretching his arm out. It shouldn't feel this normal, this right, to be here with him.

My eyes closed at the familiar lyrics playing in the trendy restaurant. It was a song about being locked away, a harsh reminder that I might have to arrest Connor if he wound up making a deal with Declan.

My stomach tightened at the thought of Connor in handcuffs.

"Olivia? You okay?" His hand was on my shoulder. I opened my eyes, and he pulled back and slipped both hands to his lap.

I pushed a smile to my face. "Sure," I lied. Lying was part of my playbook now.

But what lies did he know about me? Had his father told him the truth? Perhaps that was why I never saw him again after—no, I couldn't think about that.

"What's going on, Liv?"

Looking up from the table, I focused on his green eyes. God, he called me Liv, didn't he? "I'm just stressed. Work has been challenging."

"Tell me about Declan. Should I trust him?"

He shouldn't. But I kept my mouth shut and did my job. I wouldn't entrap him, though. "Declan is a bit of an asshole, to be honest."

He smirked at my response, and I realized how much I missed his smile. The dark stubble on his jaw was so damn sexy, too. He really rocked the five o'clock shadow. And the full beard. Okay, so basically he looked hot all the time.

"He's a narcissist and womanizer. But also a savvy businessman. Remember that club we used to hang out in? The one where we met?" Pain seared my insides at the memory.

"How could I forget?" His voice was like velvet, soft over my skin.

I hoped to hell he couldn't see through me right now—to see behind the mask I'd been wearing to hide the pain. "He owns the club now. Well, sort of. He co-owns it." I had to be careful not to say too much. I was giving away information I hadn't learned from Declan but from my undercover op.

"Really?"

"His influence runs deep." Like with the Russians. "Most people who work with him make a ton of money, including your father, I assume." Did he know anything about his father's dealings with Declan yet? "Declan must be a good business partner if your father was working with him." My lies made me sick.

Connor waved his hand in front of him. "I don't exactly trust my father's judgment."

"Yeah, you and me both." Shit, I hadn't meant to say that out loud. His facial expression didn't change, so perhaps I was off the hook for that one. "Has Declan told you anything—"

"Nothing important."

"It sounds like you aren't really interested in continuing business with him, regardless of me."

"Doubtful." He shrugged his shoulders but kept his eyes steadied on mine. He took a shallow breath and reached for his water again. Was I making him nervous?

"Olivia, I—" His cell rang, cutting him off. "Sorry. I have to answer this."

"Sure."

"Jake. Hey, I was just going to call you tonight. You a mind reader?" Connor's voice was lighter now, and less gritty. He must reserve his deep, throaty voice for me—it was all wrapped up in anger with a dash of sexual tension . . . okay, maybe more than a dash. I had it bad for him, too. But wanting him was wrong on so many levels.

"What? Okay. Sure. Call you back in twenty." He ended the call and reached for his wallet. "I'm sorry, I have to leave. Something important has come up." He placed forty dollars on the table and stood up. "This has been . . . well, it's been—"

Yeah, I had no words either. "No problem. But I'll see you at the club tomorrow, right?"

He took a moment to consider my words and nodded at last. "See ya."

I pressed my elbows to the table and covered my face with my hands, trying to fight off the heartache.

I hadn't cried in almost ten years, and I wouldn't start now.

13

CONNOR

"WHAT'S UP?" I SAT ON THE EDGE OF MY DESK AND HELD THE phone tight in my hands, worry gripping my body. The last time I'd seen Jake was at our friends, Kate and Michael's, wedding.

"What's going on?" his Texas accent rang clear through the phone. "I just had someone in my office asking me about you." Jake was a high-level FBI agent. Unlike me, he used a badge to help others.

"What do you mean?"

"I got a call from some agent in the New York office. He started asking me questions about you. He said he wanted to give me a heads up as a courtesy, because he knew we served in the Marines together."

I scratched the back of my head and stared out the window. The sun was starting to dip out of sight behind the skyscrapers. "And?"

"I asked him his name, and he said he couldn't tell me anything. So, of course, I told him to go to hell."

What was going on?

"I checked the system for any open investigations, but came up empty."

My mind scrambled and landed on the first thing that made sense. "Shit."

"What?"

"I was going to call you earlier. There has been some weird stuff going on since I took over my father's company."

"God, I'm sorry. I meant to tell you I'm sorry about your father when I first called . . ."

"No, it's fine." I pushed my fingers to my forehead. "Anyway, I was going to ask you to look into something for me."

"What is it?"

"The day my father died, he went and got a safe deposit box at a bank he'd never used before. It's shady, too. Like, I can't open it without a key and passcode, or a court order. Why would my dad open it the day he died? And his personal driver, who'd been with my dad for just about forever, went missing right after my father passed."

"Really?"

"It gets crazier." I shook my head in disbelief. "My father's company just developed a hand-held electromagnetic field gun."

Jakes gasped. "What? You can't be serious. That's not possible."

"If I hadn't held the thing in my hand this morning, then I'd tell you it was bullshit."

"Wow. That's nuts."

"But here's the part I'm curious about. I met with this guy, Declan Reid. He runs Reid Enterprises, as well as several nightclubs. Declan said he had some sort of business arrangement with my father, but . . . I don't know, I get a bad feeling about the whole thing."

"Hang on a sec. Let me see if I can pull something up."

I listened as Jake tapped at keys. "There has to be a connection between the call you got and this—right?"

"I don't know. There's nothing in the system on Declan Reid, either. Of course, some investigations are sealed to avoid leaks."

I was on my feet, unable to shed my nervous energy. "I don't know what's going on."

"I take it your father didn't leave you the key and code to the safe deposit box?"

"No, but—" I remembered the envelope my father's lawyer had given to Mason and I. "Can you do me a favor? Can you take a look at the video footage on May sixteenth for the Capital James Bank in New York?"

"Sure. What should I look for?"

"Just verify my dad was there, and if you see anything out of the ordinary . . ."

"And what was the driver's name? I'll try and locate him."

"Tyson Beckham."

"Want me to call Michael?"

I thought about it for a second, but answered, "No."

"Oh come on. He lives for this shit."

"Hopefully it's nothing. Besides, he just got back from his honeymoon. I don't want to drag him into this."

"Alright. I'll see what I can find out."

"Thanks, man. I owe you. Ring me when you know something." I hung up and started for the parking garage. I rushed to my Jeep and hopped inside the passenger seat. After unlocking the glove compartment, I searched for my father's letter.

"What the hell!" I grabbed the user's manual and tossed it to the floor, along with a few receipts I'd stashed in there.

Where was it?

How could the letter be gone?

14

CONNOR

I WAS WOUND TIGHT, AND THE MASSIVE AMOUNT OF CAFFEINE I'D been consuming all day was doing nothing to help my nerves. Sitting inside my Jeep a block from The Phoenix, I read my brother's message for the fifth time today. He had been unable to call me, so he emailed me. I had asked him what our father's letter had said to him.

Mason's response was that it had basically been a one-page apology about his failure as a father, but how proud he was of him. Mason said the letter gave off the vibe that he knew his time was coming.

He died of a heart attack, though. Nothing suspect given his prior heart problems. I scratched my jaw where the stubble was becoming itchy.

Was I overreacting?

No. A Fed was asking questions about me, and the letter my father gave me was now missing.

Normally I wouldn't be fazed by this kind of stuff. I was usually laid back when it came to high-tension situations.

But now that it was my life, my leg was shaking and my brain sizzled.

I still hadn't heard back from Jake. With any luck, he'd turn up something and soon.

I pulled my car up to the curb in front of the valet, adjusting my thin, gray tie before stepping out of my Jeep. I had decided to wear a suit tonight. Well, minus the blazer. For some reason, once I got out of the shower I went straight for the least damn comfortable thing in the closet.

I tried to tell myself it had nothing to do with seeing Olivia.

As I handed my keys to the valet, I paused and studied the young kid in front of me. The only time my keys had been out of sight were when they'd been with the valet at the club last time. Did one of these kids steal the letter?

I couldn't exactly round them up and ask them, but I'd have to look into it.

I cursed under my breath as I made my way into the club, wishing I had opened the letter when I had the chance.

The ideas and theories rattling around in my brain came to a screeching halt when I spotted Olivia sitting at the bar. Her body was partially turned, her profile showing.

I stopped walking and tried to tear my gaze away from the red sleeveless dress that hugged her body. Her toned legs were crossed, and she was sporting red heels to match her dress.

She'd worn a similar dress the night we'd celebrated New Years' Eve in Toronto. We had been standing out in line waiting to get into an event at a club. The snow pounded us. As we hugged each other in line, trying to fight the biting wind, we promised ourselves that we'd spend our next New Years together somewhere warmer. Much warmer.

Of course, we never got the chance.

I kicked the memory from my mind, fighting back the strange emotions that bit at me.

I swallowed the lump in my throat and reached for my tie, loosening it so I could breathe. The music in the room faded to background noise as I started toward her.

"Hi," was the only word that escaped my mouth.

Her red lips parted as she slipped off her stool and flashed me a smile. "Thank you so much for coming."

I expected to see a wave of relief on her face, but her body looked rigid. Tense. What had her stressed?

"Mm. Hm." A woman to Olivia's right was staring at Olivia out of the corner of her eye. She twisted her black hair between her fingers and held her hand out in front of me. "I'm Claire. And who might you be?"

"Connor," I answered, but kept my eyes on Olivia's hazel ones, which glowed green beneath smoke-gray shadow.

"Claire and I used to work together," Olivia announced, and I saw her elbow dig into the woman's side.

I half-smiled as I tucked my hands into the pockets of my slacks.

"You want to dance?" Claire asked.

Guess Claire didn't take kindly to hints. I would've laughed at Olivia's death-stare if it weren't for the fact that worry had crushed me flat.

"Claire, Connor's here to meet with Declan."

Claire's mouth opened wide as she nodded. "Oh. Catch me later, if you're around." She winked and walked past me, but I didn't turn to see where she was heading. Frankly, I didn't care.

"Sorry about her. She can be a bit much." Olivia smoothed a hand over her dress, and my eyes traced its path.

"Is he ready?" I cleared my throat, hoping to flush away my desire for her once and for all.

Her eyes pinned to my face. "You sure you want to see him?" she asked, her voice breaking.

"What?" I gasped. "You begged me to come."

Her mouth opened, but no sound came out. She blinked her eyes once and motioned for me to follow her without another word.

What was up with that?

"Declan? He's here," Olivia said once we reached his door.

"Lauren?" I hadn't seen her at the office today, and I didn't tell her I was coming. What was she doing in his office?

"Hi, Connor." Lauren stood up and smiled at me, pushing her hair off her shoulder so that it wisped against her back. "Glad you changed your mind. I think you'll see that doing business with Declan will be highly lucrative for our company."

Our company? "We'll see."

"Olivia, why don't you stay?" Declan suggested

A line appeared between Olivia's brows; surprise, if I had to guess. But her face assumed a blank mask as she closed the door.

My eyes met hers as she started my direction, and she motioned for me to have a seat next to Lauren. She remained standing, off to the side of Declan's desk.

How could she work for him? It didn't make any damn sense.

"Connor, I'm just going to cut the bullshit and be honest with you." Declan slid a piece of paper across the desk, and I grabbed it. "Your father offered my company the first right of sales to that weapon if I guaranteed he'd get the Saudi deal last October."

Staring down at a graphic image of the electromagnetic field gun, the one I'd just held yesterday, my mouth opened. Seriously? "How exactly did you help him secure the deal?"

His eyes glinted at me. "As I mentioned, I have influences over there."

"Isn't that corporate bribery?" I accused.

Declan waved his hand, dismissing the notion. "That's just jargon. What matters is that the deal we made helped him garner the money he needed to turn his vision into a reality."

"My father always wanted to create an EMF gun?" My voice dripped with sarcasm, but Declan didn't seem to notice, or care.

"Not just any EMF gun. He wanted to be the first to create one that could be used in hand-to-hand combat." Declan rose to his feet and folded his arms. "Unfortunately, he passed away before he ever got to see his vision fully realized. But, thankfully, he has a son who can carry on his legacy."

"The weapon will go to the DoD," I said without hesitation.

Declan cocked his head, and his eyes darted to Lauren.

"Connor, your father made a promise," she coaxed. "Our company will still sell to the U.S. government, but Declan has connections through his international business relationships. We can become the leading player in weapons defense. It was what your father wanted." Her voice was smooth, but pleading.

"And you benefit from this how?" I stole a glimpse of Olivia. Her lips were in a straight line as her eyes remained locked on Declan. Was this the first time she'd heard about this?

"Well, we get the purchasing rights to sell the gun in selected areas of the world. The weapon has the potential to bring in tens of billions of dollars. Plus, we get a small commission on all weapons deals we help negotiate and establish," Declan explained.

"And that's not illegal?" I straightened in my chair.

"No," Declan was quick to reply.

"Who are you hoping we sell the weapons to?" This was total bullshit. I wasn't a businessman, but I was pretty sure this violated some sort of law.

"It can be anyone. The Saudi's again. Turkey, maybe. Russia. Our allies, of course."

Sure. Let's sell an advanced weapon to Putin. Just great. Maybe the North Koreans, too, while we're at it. The guy was out of his mind if he thought I'd ever agree to this. Had my straight-edge father lost his mind, as well?

"Olivia, what do you think?" Declan shifted to face her.

She laced her fingers together and rested her hands against her abdomen. "Sounds like everyone will make a lot of money." Her lips curved into a forced smile. I was probably the only one in the room who knew Olivia's real smile. That wasn't it.

"I only just learned about this weapon." There wasn't a chance in hell I'd do business with him, but I needed to string him along, to find out what had been going on before my father died. "How'd you even know the gun was complete?"

Lauren held up her hand and gave a slight, twitchy shrug. "I told him the good news as soon as Wes let me know it was finished. I knew your father planned to go through with the deal. I should have run it by you first, though. I'm sorry."

Was Lauren a part of this? I wouldn't be too surprised. I remembered that she asked me for a ride last week to our first meeting with Declan, and she had gone back for something. I had given her the valet ticket. She had access to my Jeep. To the letter.

I stole another look at Olivia, who was staring at the paper in my hand. She swayed, slightly. Was she in on this, too?

"Listen, I'm not expecting you to say yes this second. I can have some papers drawn up so you can look over the fine print and details. I'll show you the papers your father signed, as well, if that will make you feel better."

I folded the paper as I stood and shoved it into my pocket. "I need to process all of this. Let me know when you have documents for my lawyer to look at."

Declan pushed to his feet, holding his hand out in front of him. "This needs to remain between us. No lawyers. The information is too sensitive to be shared with anyone."

I didn't say anything. I was never good at acting, so I just nodded.

"I would hold off on letting anyone know the weapon is complete. Once my people verify the weapon and we sign a contract, you're free to—"

"Last time I checked, the weapon belongs to Matthews Tech, which means I can do whatever the hell I please," I blurted, unable to hide my irritation. "Did my father let you dictate his business to him?"

Declan smoothed on a grin and gripped his chin, his eyes pinned on mine. "I like you. I value honesty."

Yeah, sure.

"Think about what we've talked about, and I hope we can make a deal. I'm sure when you see the numbers, you'll be as excited about this as I am." He faced Olivia. "Why don't you get Connor a drink?"

"I'm good. Thanks." I angled my head at Lauren. "A word, please." I left Declan's office without looking at Olivia and waited in the hall for Lauren to join me.

"Sorry," Lauren said once she pulled the door closed behind her. "I should've—"

"Damn right you should have talked to me first. Don't ever go behind my back again."

She pouted and leaned a little closer to me as Declan's office door opened.

Olivia's eyes rounded with surprise, and I moved away until the wall pressed hard against my back. Lauren's hand fell to her side, and she shot Olivia a tight-lipped smile.

Olivia tucked her hair behind her ear and moved past us. She had the wrong idea about Lauren and I. "I'll see you at work tomorrow." I was in no mood to have any type of conversation with her. My ability to trust Lauren was growing thinner by the moment.

I didn't give her a chance to say anything; I hurried down the hall in search of Olivia. "Wait up," I called after her as she reached the bar.

She turned to face me. "You and Lauren, huh?"

I tugged at the knot of my tie, loosening it. "Not even close." Not that I needed to explain. "Can we get out of here?" I needed to see how much she knew about Declan, to try and chip away at the façade of the so-called deal my father had made with Declan before he died.

She cupped her neck with her hand, tilting her head back as she shut her eyes.

"You okay, Olivia?" I looked over at the bartender, who was now pressing his palms to the counter and focusing on me.

"I'm good, Bobby. Thanks," Olivia responded as her eyes flashed open.

The bartender kept his eyes on me for a moment longer as he slowly wiped down the counter. "Let me know if you change your mind," he added in a deep voice.

I tipped my head before focusing back on Olivia. Without thinking, I found my hand on her forearm. My damn hands kept wandering to places where they didn't belong.

She lowered her eyes. "We can go back to my place."

15

OLIVIA

"Did Sean decrypt any of the files from Declan's computer?"

"He thinks we should have something by morning. I don't know if it'll be useful, but we'll see," Blake answered. "How'd it go tonight?"

I shoved both hands into my hair and leaned my forehead against the steering wheel while I thought about what to say. "I have a lot to tell you, but I'd rather do it in person. Connor's on his way to my apartment."

"Why?"

"He wants to talk." Was Connor going to make a deal with Declan? The thought made me ill. If Connor knew who Declan was—really was—would he consider it? Despite our past, I wanted to protect Connor, but I knew I wasn't allowed.

Lies. Lies to get to the truth. That's how it was supposed to work.

As I turned off my car I remembered what else I had wanted to tell Blake. "Can you look up Lauren Tate? She was at the meeting, and my gut's telling me that she's more than just an employee at

Matthews Tech. She's pretty damn friendly with Declan, and pushing the deal hard."

"I'll look into her."

"Thanks. See you in the morning."

"Stay safe."

I ended the call, shoved my burner phone in my purse, and hurried to the elevator so I could get to my place before Connor arrived.

I halted when I stepped out of the elevator, not expecting to see him standing outside my apartment door. His back was pressed against the wall with his head lowered and eyes shut.

"How'd you beat me here?"

He pushed off the wall as his eyes flashed open. "I know the best roads to take—even after all these years." He stood off to the side of the door, his eyes on me, and I tried not to inhale the piney scent of his cologne as I shoved my key in the lock.

"Want something to drink? Wine? Beer?" I shut the door after he entered. "Tequila?" I teased.

The heated look he shot me had my stomach doing somersaults. "Only if we use salt this time." He popped open the top button of his silvery gray dress shirt. His tie was missing; he must've gotten rid of it in his car.

"How about wine?"

"Sure." He followed me down the hall and into my living area. It wasn't a big apartment—less than eight-hundred square feet. A tiny living room connected to a small galley kitchen. But what the apartment lacked in entertaining space, it more than made up for in bathroom. The master bath had a giant claw foot tub, and sleek gray tiled shower, which had a window overlooking the city. I was such a girl when it came to bathrooms.

"Sorry my place is so small," I said as I retrieved a bottle of wine from the rack. "Pinot okay?" I grabbed the wine opener from the drawer in front of me.

"Sure," he answered while coming up behind me. "Let me," he

offered, his breath whistling through the hairs on the back of my neck.

A flash of heat tore through me. "Thanks," I said, gulping. I bumped into him as I tried to move out of his way. The kitchen was too small for the both of us. "Sorry." As I tried to get free, my hands found his chest.

I could feel his heart pounding beneath my palms, and his gaze dipped to my mouth. "You're in my way," I sputtered before pulling my lip between my teeth. I needed to get it together. We'd been in my apartment less than five minutes, and I was already growing warm from the memory of his mouth.

My body was betraying my mind.

"Sorry," he muttered and stepped to the side.

My hands slipped from his hard chest, and I clenched them at my sides for a moment, pressing my nails into my palms, hoping to slow my heart and gather some control over my libido.

He turned away from me, and I reached for the glasses. I heard the familiar pop of the wine uncorking. "Here." I held out the glasses and watched as he filled the red liquid almost to the brim.

"Rain."

"What?" I shook my head.

"It's raining." He set the bottle down on the counter and tipped his head to the kitchen window. Water drops flicked against the glass, the soft noise becoming hard splatters as the rain grew more intense.

"Guess we got inside just in time." I left the kitchen. It was too small—I couldn't breathe. I sank on the brown leather couch and stared at the table.

He leaned his shoulder against the cut out framed entrance to the kitchen and took a sip of his wine. "I don't want to lie to you, Olivia."

My head jerked up in surprise.

"I came here for one purpose."

My heart thundered in my chest, and my body ached with the need to be touched by him.

"Being around you is hard for me. But this is how serious I am about this deal with Declan."

Oh. I forced my shoulders back and tried not to shrink with disappointment. There was no need to be upset about the fact that he didn't come here for . . . "What are you trying to say?"

He moved away from the wall and slipped into the lone, tan chair by the sofa. He set his wine on the glass coffee table and rested his hands on his lap. He looked casual—even his lips were relaxed—this was new.

"I want the truth from you. Should I make a deal with Declan? I want to turn this company over to my brother in a better condition than it was left to me, but I'm not sure if I can trust Declan."

You can't, I screamed on the inside. "I can't tell you what to do." But God, did I want to. He may have burned me in the past, but I didn't want to see him mixed up in this. Of course, Blake would kill me if he knew I'd steered Connor away from the deal. Hell, Declan would, as well.

"Connor—" I cut myself off. I had no idea what to say. I wished he'd never walked into the nightclub that night. "You run a billion-dollar company now. You need to make that decision for yourself," I forced myself to say.

He pressed his hands to his knees. "You're right."

"But . . . I'd say to go with your gut." What was I saying?

Connor reached for his wine, and I brought my glass to my lips.

"Why'd you lie to me?"

I spit out my wine, and it sprayed onto my dress. "Shit." I jumped to my feet. "What are you talking about?" Did he know? I racked my brain, trying to consider how he'd figured out I was FBI.

"You should wash that out before it stains," he said in a monochromatic voice.

"Um. Yeah." Relieved to have a minute to gather my thoughts, I rushed to my bedroom and shut the door behind me. I peeled off my dress, tossing it to the floor, and rummaged through my dresser until I found a yellow T-shirt and black yoga pants.

"What's wrong with you?" I lashed out at myself in a hushed voice as I stared at my reflection in the dresser mirror. I needed to get a grip. I wasn't some nineteen-year-old, lovesick girl. I was a trained agent.

"You okay?" A fist tapped at my door.

"Yeah." I swung open the door, and Connor's muscular body filled the frame. His eyes shifted over my shoulder and to the bed.

He propped a hand to the wall just outside my bedroom and tilted his head. "Why'd you lie, Liv? Why'd things go down the way they did?"

The past . . . He was talking about our past, not the present. I released an inner sigh, and I ducked under his arm, exiting my room and re-entering the living area. "Your father told you, huh?"

He nodded.

"Well, if you had stayed around instead of running away to join the military, I could've explained." He shot me an 'are-you-kidding' look. "Fine." I shook my head. "Do you remember the first time you asked me out on a date?" My hands tightened into fists at my side. Not because I wanted to hit him, but because it helped me think—helped me contain my emotions.

"Of course I remember. I asked you out how many times before you said yes?" The skin around his eyes crinkled as his lips pulled together into a semi-smile.

I moved to the window and stared outside as the sky opened up before us. The rain slammed the city streets. "You and your friends were sitting near me at the bar. I heard you guys talking. I could tell you all had money. Your friends, Tim and Freddie, were comparing their expensive sports cars, and you—well, you were just looking at me. You weren't saying anything. But I listened to them talk. I couldn't help it—they were loud." My eyes searched for his reflection—he was back in the tan chair.

"And?" he pressed.

I relaxed my shoulders but kept my eyes on his through the reflection. "I heard your friend Tim tell you to hit on the bartender —that was my sister, and you said she was too young for you. You only dated older women." My voice faltered as I spoke, and I hoped he didn't notice. "Well, if my sister was too young for you, then you'd never be interested in me. I was younger than her. And so when you asked me out, I said no. Not only was I too young for you, but we ran in completely different circles."

"That still doesn't explain why you lied." His voice was thick, cutting.

I turned to face him, and his eyes focused on mine. His face was all hard lines and his jaw ticked, noticeable even beneath the stubble.

"You wouldn't give up. I figured you'd go off to grad school or something, not hang out in the city. Anyways, I told you I took time off high school, which was why I was only going into my sophomore year. I just didn't want to let myself even hope there could ever be a world where someone like you dated someone like me. I never thought we'd last more than a few dates."

"Someone like you?"

I swallowed. "Yeah. I was barely nineteen, poor, and had a shitty life. You were twenty-two and rich." God, it sounded so pathetic, saying it out loud. But I'd been young and foolish. I was different now. Wasn't I?

"I kept coming to that club every weekend because of you. Hoping that you'd finally say yes."

"And I did."

"But why lie?" He scrutinized me, probably wondering if I'd lie to him again, right now.

I lowered my head and stared down at the hardwood beneath

my feet. "I thought that once you discovered I was so young, that I was only allowed at the club because my sister had got me a fake ID . . ." I couldn't continue. I didn't want to think about her. It hurt too much.

I leaned forward and pressed my hands to my thighs. At the moment, I wasn't a tough FBI agent. I was a young kid again, someone broken and afraid.

"Olivia?" Connor was at my side, his hand on my back. "What's wrong?"

"I thought you would've at least come to her funeral." I stood upright and stepped away from his reach, trying not to cry.

His eyes grew wide. "What are you talking about?" He was shaking his head.

"You don't know?" How could he not have known what happened? No, he ran off to the Marines as my life spiraled out of control.

A stabbing, burning pain bubbled in my chest, and I pressed my hand to my throat, struggling to breathe. "I've worked too hard to let you do this to me."

"What are you talking about?" he demanded as he moved in front of me and cupped my chin, forcing me to look him in the eyes.

"Jessie died," I gasped as tears pooled in my eyes. "She was shot while bartending at the club."

"Oh God. I'm so sorry." His hand dropped heavy to his side, and he took a step back and turned away from me, running a hand through his hair, mussing it up.

"She was caught in the crossfires of a turf war between the Russians and Irish. I didn't know the place was owned by the Irish mob; that's how she got me the fake ID. I never would've taken it had I known . . ." My mind flashed to the night, and my body trembled. "I saw it happen. I was at the club that night. Drinking my sorrows away. And I couldn't save her." My voice cracked. "The club cleared out during the gunfire. She motioned for me to run before she ducked down behind the bar." My beautiful sister. My only real family. Our bucket list had been extensive, and it included doing so many things together.

"I'm so sorry. If I'd known—" He pulled me to him. His arms were warm around me. "I'm so sorry," he said once again, his voice breaking.

"A bullet ricocheted and hit her." My body was shaking. The emotions pulling at me were too strong to fight. After years of bottling everything inside, turning to my work to hide the pain . . . I sobbed.

He didn't try hushing me. He just held me, rubbing my back.

After I calmed myself and wiped the tears and black streaks of mascara from my face, Connor scooped me into his arms and carried me to my bedroom. He shouldered open my bathroom door and gently released me.

I leaned against the counter, rubbing my arms, and watched him move to the bathtub and start the water. "What are you doing?"

He glanced at me over his shoulder as he tested the temperature of the water and adjusted the knob. "How about a bath? I'll be right back."

He came back with a full glass of wine and set it next to the tub. "I'll be just outside in the living room—I don't want you falling asleep in there. Take your time." The back of his hand touched my cheek, and I sucked in a breath.

"I'm sorry for—"

His finger touched my lip, silencing me. "Try and relax," he said in a low voice as his light green eyes held mine for a few long beats.

He blinked, shook his head a little, and left.

Once the door was closed, I retrieved candles and matches from beneath the sink. I peeled off my clothes in a haste after lighting the candles, turned off the lights, and rushed into the tub. I shut my eyes once the water swallowed my body, and I tried to ignore my brain's protestations. How damn odd it was to be in a bath while my ex was just outside. And not just any ex, but a man I needed to spy on—and possibly arrest.

The pain eased up a little as my body relaxed. My thoughts drifted as I heard the rain pound hard on the streets, which were a couple stories below my apartment. I really hoped the case would end soon. I wasn't sure how much more I could bear.

A twinge of guilt poked my core. And then the guilt expanded to a gaping hole in my stomach.

"Connor?" I called out, not sure what the hell I was doing.

"Yeah?" he answered, his voice muffled by the door.

"You can come in."

The door opened slowly, and I was grateful for the bubbles and dim lighting.

Connor leaned his back to the counter, folded his arms, and faced me. He didn't look the least bit skittish. In fact, he appeared comfortable standing in my bathroom while I was naked a few feet away. And his confidence turned me on.

My skin flushed and warmth spread through my limbs. I wanted him. And God did it hurt. I stared at his magnificent body. He'd popped open a few more buttons, exposing his tanned chest and throat. His sleeves were rolled up, his shoes were off, and his jaw was tight. Resolute.

I wondered what God was thinking when he'd designed such an amazing specimen of a man. Did he draw up some architectural plans first—carved, sculpted, chiseled . . . a little of this, a dash of that . . .

I must've been more than tipsy, I realized.

"Are you okay, Olivia?" His voice was low and gravely. I wondered why, but then I caught sight of his massive hard-on.

Oh wow, did that make me forget everything. My knees popped up above the water, and I sat up a little more without thinking, my nipples lifting above the surface of the water.

Connor pushed away from the counter and stood above me, his eyes darkening with lust.

I wanted him, even just for tonight. I shut my eyes, trying to ignore my brain, which was shouting, "I can't. I'm undercover. It'd be wrong!" But when my eyes opened and focused on his mouth, that voice grew silent.

"Connor," I said his name like a cry.

The water raised as Connor, fully clothed, stepped inside the bath. I stared at him, part in shock, part in awe, as he braced the sides of the tub. *Oh my God.* I found his legs and my hands slid up his slacks. I shifted forward onto his lap.

His dress shirt clung to the hard muscles of his chest. His large hands held my face as he guided me closer to him, crushing my lips with his.

My naked body pressed against his clothed one, and I moaned into his mouth, wishing I could feel his skin. I needed him, more than I'd ever needed him before.

Just for tonight.

Only for tonight.

My lips parted from his as I steadied my eyes on him. "I need to touch you." It had been so long, and yet it felt like we'd first made love only yesterday.

Connor slipped me off of him, and I groaned at the loss of his touch. He stood and unbuttoned his wet shirt. No, he didn't rip it off—he wasn't some overplayed Fabio—but as I watched him tug off his shirt, I almost thought he was. The shadows from the flickering candle flames played off his muscled chest and perfect abs as he reached for the button of his pants.

I couldn't wait any longer. I stood up, offering him full view of my body.

His eyes dropped down to my breasts and continued until he pulled his gaze back up. "You're so beautiful," he rasped.

I stepped up to him, trying to ignore the fact that I was now freezing. Goosebumps scattered over my body and my nipples were fully erect from the cold.

Although his pants were still on, he reached for me and pulled me into his arms, leaning over to sweep my legs from under me. I reveled in how warm his chest felt against mine.

He carried me into the bedroom and yanked at my bedspread with one hand. "Thank you," I said as he lowered me onto the bed. I covered my body with the comforter and studied him.

A smile teased the corners of his lips as he dropped his pants and removed his socks. He pulled back the covers and joined me in bed. "Are you sure you want this? After what you told me tonight —" He reached for my hand and laced his fingers with mine.

The time would never be right, but I wasn't sure if I could tell him now. A dim sense of responsibility battered my brain, and I squeezed my eyes shut.

My eyes opened as he released my hand. He was getting out of the bed. He must have known I was having second thoughts. "I let myself get carried away."

I didn't know what to say. "Let me throw your clothes in the dryer." I pulled the sheet from the bed and wrapped it around my body.

He looked down at his boxers, which were wet, and crooked a smile my way. "You don't happen to have anything big enough to fit me while they dry, do you?"

I came around to his side of the bed, the white bedsheet clinging to my body. His smooth muscled chest, his trim waist, the oh-so-sexy shadows below . . . I captured the memory of him in my mind.

* * *

Connor

I COULDN'T BELIEVE WHAT HAD ALMOST HAPPENED. WE HAD BEEN

so close. But, no. It didn't feel right, not after the revelation about her sister. We'd both lost control in the bathroom—our bodies had taken over—but thankfully, we came to our senses.

We were wrong for each other. It hadn't worked before, and I had the scars to prove it. But the woman was making it hard for me to hate her. I couldn't even pretend to, anymore. Not after what she went through with her sister. I couldn't imagine losing Mason, my brother. It would kill me.

And Olivia and Jessie had been close. Her sister practically raised her after their father remarried . . . and her mother—well, she'd been out of the picture for a while. That was why Olivia and I made the decision to keep the baby. To raise the baby together. To give the baby a family.

Or at least, that's what I had thought we had decided.

It had gutted me when she changed the plan without telling me.

"Connor, your clothes are dry."

I pushed my thoughts to the side and forced my attention on Olivia. "That was fast." I rose from the couch, clutching the blanket around me, and grabbed my clothes from her. "Thank you."

"You can use my bedroom." She forced a smile to her face— one of the fake smiles I'd learned to know.

I nodded and moved into her bedroom, shutting the door behind me. I dropped the blanket to the floor, holding only the clothes in my hands.

We had spent the last twenty minutes in silence in her living room, both feeling the pangs of discomfort. Thankfully, she'd changed out of the sheet. I didn't think I'd be able to handle seeing her wear the sheet any longer without sporting a painful hard on.

"Sorry about tonight," she softly said when I came out.

I finished buttoning my shirt and looked up to meet her eyes. The pain and sadness were still there. "I'm so sorry about Jessie. Did they catch whoever was responsible?"

Her face blanched as white as the sheet she'd worn earlier.

119

"No." But then her expression changed and a mask veiled her face. But the mask was thin, and I could see through it—I could see her. She couldn't hide from me, not even after all the years between us.

"Will you be okay?" I worried about leaving her alone.

She inhaled a breath through her nose, her mind obviously working. "Yes," she whispered and rubbed her arms.

I wanted to comfort her again, but I knew if I touched her, I wouldn't want to stop. "I should go," I rushed the words from my mouth before I could change my mind. I grabbed my keys off the end table by her sofa and shoved them into my pocket. "Are you sure you're going to be okay?" I asked again, unable to shake my concern.

"I'm fine," she drew out the words with obvious emphasis. "Really."

I wanted to protest her answer, but I turned away and started for the door.

"What are you going to do about Declan?"

I placed my hand on the doorknob. "You think we can work together?"

"Do you?"

I turned to face her, and she was standing only a few inches away. I touched her shoulder, and she flinched, but I kept my hand there anyway. "I think I can."

Her lips became glossy after she wet them. "We can make it work," she answered in a somewhat strained voice.

"Then I'll call Declan tomorrow. I'll make the deal."

16

OLIVIA

"HE WAS AT YOUR PLACE PRETTY LATE. WHAT HAPPENED?"

I gasped and took a step back from Blake, crossing my arms. "Were you spying on me?" I wondered if my eyes were bulging with the rage I felt.

Blake glanced over at Sean, who was standing a few feet away with a laptop in his hand. "Can you give us one sec?"

Sean nodded at us and retreated to the bedroom. We were at our meetinghouse in Brooklyn, not too far from the Metro Detention Center. That was the federal prison I hoped Declan would wind up in. He deserved to be thrown in the hole for twenty-three hours a day. And Konstantin and the Russians he was partnered with? Well, they were worse; they merited a special place in hell.

"Were you watching me?" I asked Blake again, with grit in my voice.

He touched my shoulder, but I jerked back free of him. "Olivia, I was just keeping an eye on you. Connor could be dangerous. We don't know."

"Nothing happened, Blake. He spilled something on his

clothes, and I had to dry them." Not quite a lie to my apparently jealous superior.

He rubbed his jaw and eyed me.

"Did you find anything on Lauren Tate?" I maneuvered to a different topic.

"She's clean."

I turned my back to him. "I find that hard to believe. There's something off about her."

"Trust me. I would've found something."

"Alright." Maybe she was an opportunist and saw dollar signs when she looked at both Declan and Connor. Hell, maybe I just didn't like the way she looked at Connor. But that was insane. Connor wasn't mine—not anymore.

Still, the ripcord had been pulled, and there was no stopping now—the memories began parachuting in my mind the second I had laid eyes on Connor at the club.

I'll never stop loving you, Liv. There's nothing in the world that could make me run away. Connor's words from the past planted root in my mind.

Everyone runs, Connor. I had responded to him, remembering my mother, my father.

I'll never leave. We'll grow old together. I'll die first because I wouldn't survive a day without you, he had told me. I'd actually believed him.

But I shouldn't have. He took off like everyone else in my life had.

"What did you learn last night?" Blake's voice slipped into my ear, interrupting my thoughts.

Turning around, I took a deep, grounding breath, and answered, "He's going to make a deal with Declan."

"And what's the deal?"

I pressed my back to the window, irritation pushing through my body, making my legs feel shaky. "His company invented an EMF railgun. A hand-held one."

"What?" That was Sean from the other room—apparently eavesdropping. "You're shitting me?" He re-entered the room, taking quick steps toward me. His eyes darted to Blake and back to me.

"Declan obviously wants the weapon." I described everything I'd remembered from the meeting, hating myself for keeping the truth from Connor. He wouldn't do the deal if he knew how deep this whole thing ran, would he?

"Wow. That weapon is like Sci-Fi shit. I'd love to see it," Sean remarked.

I reached into my pocket and handed Sean a folded piece of paper. When I'd gone to dry Connor's pants last night, I found the printed image of the weapon folded in the pocket. Thankfully, it hadn't been too badly damaged by the bath.

Sean eagerly unfolded the paper and studied it. "This is sick." He handed the paper to Blake and pushed dark strands of hair out of his eyes.

"And what did you find?" I asked Sean and slouched onto the couch.

Sean grabbed his laptop and powered it on. "We stumbled upon the holy grail."

"Don't get too excited." Blake held his hand in front of him.

I rubbed my hands up and down my thighs, nervous apprehension spiking inside me. Sean sat next to me, but Blake remained standing before us. "What am I looking at?"

"This is an aerial photo of a location just outside Baghdad." Sean pointed to the screen. "This guy here is the Russian general Josef Zhuravlev. And he's meeting with what looks like a group of insurgents. They're trading crates for briefcases. The assumption being money is in those briefcases." He zoomed in on a cargo box off to the side of Zhuravlev. "Recognize that?"

My hand went to my mouth. "Oh my God. That's the Matthews Tech logo on that box."

"There're more of these images. Another one in Islamabad,

BRITTNEY SAHIN

Pakistan. Two more in Syria," Sean said. "I almost missed these. The pictures were filed under vacation photos 2016."

"I know you feel guilty about encouraging the deal with Connor and Declan, but I hope these images help you see the light," Blake's voice cut through me.

"When were they taken?" I asked.

Sean answered, "All in April."

"Connor's father was still alive and in charge. You can't pin that on Connor." I felt some strange need to defend him.

"And Connor is continuing business as usual," he shot back. "He told you he's making the deal." He gaped at me, his blue eyes piercing mine as his lips twisted into a scowl.

"Whether Edward knew his weapons were going to terrorists is questionable. But I do know Connor would never turn weapons over to terrorists. He's only agreeing to Declan's proposition because he thinks it's good for the company. Connor spent years in the Middle East fighting terrorists—there's no way he'd supply them with weapons to turn a profit." I had my own issues with Connor, but they were mine to have. I wasn't about to ruin his life just because he broke my heart.

"I know what you're thinking. The answer is still no." Blake's biceps flexed as his arms crossed over his chest.

I was gathering my thoughts when Sean cleared his throat at an obnoxious level. "I'm surprised Declan has incriminating photos of the exchange on his computer." Sean looked at me, his forehead pinching together with concern. He was trying to redirect the conversation and avoid what was about to be a shouting match. "If Konstantin found out he had these pictures, he'd blow a fuse." Sean slid his laptop on the coffee table in front of us.

I looked back at Sean, ignoring Blake. "You think he's keeping the pictures in his back pocket in case the Russians ever tried to screw him over?"

"All I know is that if these images ever got leaked to the government, there'd be major issues between the U.S. and Russia.

124

The photos could also be used to make sure Edward never backed out of the arrangement," Sean said.

"This is bigger than we thought." I knew we'd uncover something eventually, but I honestly never thought our investigation would relate to terrorists. We couldn't let Connor get any deeper. I pushed to my feet and folded my arms. "So our local Russian mob boss, Konstantin, is working with General Zhuravlev. And Declan is the middleman between Matthews Tech and Konstantin."

"Destabilizing the Middle East means continued war, an increase in defense spending, an increase in rebuilding efforts . . ." Sean rattled off the domino effect.

I nodded. "Makes sense. Reid Enterprises has been turning a huge profit by winning projects in Iraq to rebuild the infrastructure. And the Russians want a reason to push into the territory. It's been looking like a new Cold War these last two years, with the Middle East as the age-old playground between Russia and the U.S." I touched my neck and tilted my head back, thinking.

"Konstantin helped Declan rescue the crumbling Reid Enterprises," I added. "In exchange for the help of the Russian mob, Declan had to do something for him. Apparently, that something was to get his hands on weapons."

"Which is where Matthews Tech fits in," Sean finished. "I did some research. Matthews Tech was almost in the same situation that Reid Enterprises was in a few years back. As of last summer, their financials were frightening. Edward Matthews was on the brink of closing down."

"And the Saudi deal saved the company and made him a fortune." Wow. Edward Matthews had made a deal with the devil —well, with two of Lucifer's imps. "We have Konstantin on camera meeting with Declan several times. We have an obvious connection between Declan and Konstantin in relation to their partnering on some clubs and restaurants, and now we have these photos. This is good."

There was hope, right? I had something to cling to, didn't I?

"Illegally obtained, they mean nothing." Blake finally joined the conversation. He had remained a bystander in the conversation between Sean and me until now, which suited me just fine. It annoyed me how much Blake wanted to peg Connor as an enemy. "The photos aren't enough. We need to catch the deal in action."

I inhaled a sharp breath and released it through my nose. "Shouldn't we bring Homeland or the CIA in on this? Now that we know we're dealing with arms sales to terrorists on foreign soil?" I shook my head. This couldn't be happening.

"I'll get in touch with a contact of mine in D.C. We need to follow the weapons to the end point and bring down anyone connected to the pipeline," Blake answered.

Yeah, including Connor?

"I really don't think Connor's a bad guy."

Both Blake and I turned to face Sean.

Sean shrugged his shoulders. "I made a few calls, and—"

"You did what?" Blake barked out.

"Sorry, when we discovered Connor's involvement I asked around." Sean took a step back from Blake.

It was nice to know I had Sean on my side, but Blake was right to be upset. If Sean's calls tipped anyone off . . .

Blake turned away from Sean, but I had a feeling he wasn't quite finished with him. "Olivia, you know what you have to do," Blake's shrill voice gave me the chills.

Great. His anger was back on me.

"I don't want to discuss this issue further." Blake pointed to the picture of the EMF gun in his hand. "Make sure the exchange happens, and we can finally end this and bring them all down." Blake moved directly in front of me, his eyes focused on mine, drilling into me. "Do it, Olivia. Prove to me I didn't make a mistake by bringing you on this case."

* * *

Connor

A CALL FROM DECLAN INTERRUPTED THE TEXT I WAS SENDING OUT to my friend Ben, in Vegas. "Hey, Declan."

"Are you into MMA, by any chance?"

Why the hell was he calling me about mixed martial arts? "Um. It's okay. I guess."

"Well, I'm friends with John Jackson, and he's swinging by around lunch time to square off with me in the ring. Feel like stopping by? I own a gym a few blocks from The Phoenix."

I had no interest in spending time with Declan, nor did I care to meet some famous fighter. What was his angle? As much as I wanted to tell him to go to hell, I knew I needed to keep up with the act if I wanted to find out the truth about whatever shit storm my father had fallen into before he died.

"Connor?"

I glanced down at my Omega. Half past eleven. "Be there in an hour. Just text me the location."

"Sounds good. Maybe we can talk a little business while you're here, too."

Of course. Why else would he want me there? "Sure. See ya." I hung up the phone, finished my text to Ben, and stared at the stack of paperwork on my desk. God, I just wanted to shift it over about two feet, and let it fall into the waste basket.

The vibration of my phone alerted me to a text. And then another. The address from Declan and a message from Jake.

Thank God. Jake had asked me to call him on a secure line.

"Good or bad news first?" Jake. Always to the point.

I stood up and clutched the phone to my ear. "Good news."

"The good news is I got my hands on the bank video cameras, and I was able to see your father, along with his driver, at the bank on the sixteenth. Nothing looked out of the ordinary, though, so I'm not really sure what else, or who else, to be looking for."

I grumbled. "Okay. Well, I have news, myself. My father's

lawyer gave me a letter at the reading of the will. I never opened it and shoved it in the glove compartment of my Jeep. After you and I talked last, I went to grab it, wondering if my father revealed anything to me. I vaguely remembered the envelope having some weight to it. Maybe he left the key and code to the safe deposit box in there? But the letter's missing. I have to assume it was stolen."

"Someone's been watching you since your father's death?" Jake exhaled. "Did you check with Mason? Did he get a letter, too?"

"Mason said his was a basic apology letter."

"Then why do you think your letter had anything more in it?"

"Because Mason's my younger brother, and he's in the middle of a tour of duty. My dad wouldn't lay anything heavy on his favorite son, not with him already in harm's way in the Middle East."

"Okay . . . Well, did anyone have access to your car?"

"There's one person who had the keys to my Jeep, and I think there's something going on between her and Declan. Can you look up a Lauren Tate? She's the director of sales here at the company. I checked her file. She's only been with the company since September—a month before the arrangement started between Declan and my father. And before that, she was getting her MBA. Kind of interesting that she'd go straight from college to a job as the director of sales, right?" I rubbed a hand over my jaw. "I'm new to this and all, but she needs experience for a position like that. Hell, all the other directors at the office are at least forty and have well over ten years of business experience."

"Well, shit," he drawled. "I don't know why your father hired her, but I think it's safe to assume she's part of this in some way or another." Jake was silent for a moment. "When did she have access to your Jeep, though?"

"Last week." The night I bumped into Olivia.

"That doesn't make sense."

"What? Why not?"

"If someone saw you put the letter in the Jeep after the reading of your father's will, you really think they'd wait several weeks to snatch it? That'd be too risky. How would they know you didn't open it before you put it in there? Or that you wouldn't open it later . . ."

I lowered my head. He had a point, but what'd that mean? My chest tightened as I thought about various possibilities. "You think someone had eyes on me inside the lawyer's office?" I tried to remember the building. The people inside. But my father had just passed away, and I wasn't exactly paying attention to every man and woman I encountered that day.

"Where'd you go after you left the lawyer's?"

My fingers twitched on my desk, and my mouth edged open. "Gambling in Atlantic City."

"Your father passed away, and you went gambling?"

"I sound like a horrible person, but I don't deal with things that well, and I was pissed at my father for dying—leaving before we ever had a chance to make amends. We'd barely spoken to each other in the decade since I'd left New York." Jake didn't know the full scope of my relationship with my dad. No one really knew, not even Mason.

I could hear him breathing on the other end; he was probably not sure what to say. Jake was never good at dealing with feelings. His or anyones. "I have to assume it wasn't Lauren. Someone probably took the letter while you were at the casino. But I'll still look into her and let you know what I find. I'll be in town tomorrow."

"You're coming here?" I walked to the window, holding the phone tight to my ear. Dark, threatening clouds were gathering in the sky.

"Yeah, there's more that I meant to tell you before we started talking about the letter. And it's the reason why I want to come."

I forgot all about the bad news Jake had previously mentioned having. "What is it?" I asked with a flicker of worry coloring my voice.

"Well, the thing is, your father's driver booked a flight the day after your father died—to El Salvador. I looked at the flight manifest. He never made it on board."

My skin prickled with worry, and my heart rate kicked up a notch.

"I made some calls. There are a couple unidentified bodies that match the description of Tyson, but most of them didn't check out when the detectives got a look at his photo. One said his John Doe was in pretty bad shape—too hard to guarantee it's Tyson based on the picture. But he went out on a limb to say it's a possible match."

"Damn." I sat back down, needing to comprehend what Jake was telling me. "You think it's him? You think Tyson was murdered?"

"I don't know, but if it is him, I'm betting both your father and Tyson were killed."

I shook my head. "But he died of a heart attack."

"You and I both know that it could have been a drug-induced heart attack. They didn't do an autopsy, right?"

"No." Why would they? My father had a heart condition. "No one had any reason to think foul play."

"True." There was a long pause. "Have you packed up your father's personal belongings?"

I hadn't even set foot in my father's penthouse on Park Avenue. Mason and I had agreed to put in on the market once I got around to packing it up. Neither of us wanted to live there. "I haven't gone yet," I said, feeling almost embarrassed to admit it.

A foreign pain poked my core, and the sensation grew until it transformed into a loud noise in my head. Like a banshee howling, followed by the words, "He's dead." I squeezed my eyes shut, trying to ignore the eruption of sadness.

Where had that come from? I still hadn't shed a tear since his death, but I was on the brink of losing it. I could feel it. And if my father was murdered . . .?

"We should swing by there tomorrow. Was your father on any medicine?"

I shook off the layers of emotion that weighed me down. "I assume. He had a minor heart attack two years ago and had a stent put in."

"We can check for pill bottles. Someone may have swapped his pills. I doubt they'd put something in a drink because they wouldn't be able to guarantee he'd consume it. But if your dad took pills on a regular basis, that's definitely a start."

"It could also be a waste of time. If someone swapped his pills, they wouldn't leave evidence behind."

"How'd your father get to the hospital? Who made the call? Who found him?" Jake rattled off questions, and I had to take a second to wrap my head around all of it.

"I don't know." I never thought to ask. "I'll find out when we go to his place tomorrow."

"I'll also take another look at the bank cameras. It sounds more like there's a connection between the bank and your father's death. We can work on getting a court order for the box when I come. The only drawback with that is it will alert anyone who has been keeping tabs on you. They might take some sort of action if they think you're going to get that box open."

There had to be something damn near awful in that safe deposit box if my father and Tyson were killed for it. If I tried to open it, would they come after me? I could handle it if they did, but I also didn't want to blow my chance of uncovering whatever craziness was going on. "Let's hold off on doing that for now. We'll save opening the box for when we know more about what's really going on."

"We can monitor the bank cameras from here on out, in case someone shows up trying to get access to the box," Jake suggested.

"No one should be able to get the box open, even with the key and code. Only Mason and I are capable of opening it." I tilted my head back. When I took over my father's company, I expected paperwork and boring meetings, not to be caught up in the middle of shady deals and a murder investigation.

"You okay?"

No. Nothing about this was okay. My father was dead. My ex-girlfriend—I hadn't mentioned that part to Jake yet—was either in league with the enemy or was about to get caught in the crossfires. I opened my eyes and glanced at the text that popped up on my cell. Ben was still coming up empty, so it seemed. "Thanks for your help, man."

"Connor, this is what we do. We have each other's backs. Always."

17

OLIVIA

WIPING THE SWEAT FROM MY BROW, I INCREASED THE SPEED ON the treadmill and ran harder. Faster. I couldn't make it early enough to meet Bobby to spar in the morning, but I still needed to get in a workout. What a mess I was in.

My mind drifted to my conversation with Blake, and I jabbed again at the arrow button, increasing the speed once more. My feet slammed hard against the black rotating fabric as possible outcomes danced around in my head.

I couldn't keep the truth from Connor. I couldn't spin more lies.

If Blake found out I told Connor the truth, I could lose my job, which didn't scare me. What terrified me was the idea of not putting Declan and Konstantin behind bars. If Connor didn't sell the weapons to Declan, then Declan would just go to someone else.

There'd never be justice. Only more death.

I almost tripped and fell off my treadmill as my mind dipped into dangerous waters.

The thought of Connor behind bars flipped my stomach. Something had changed between us last night. Whatever anger he had with me, and I for him, had weakened.

We'd come so close to sharing my bed. Strange pangs of regret pulled at me. Of course I knew it was absurd to feel that way. It should've been the other way around.

My chest was near exploding from the intense run. Just as I tapped the buttons on the treadmill to slow down, I caught sight of Declan. It was lunchtime—his workout time. I was in no mood to talk with him. He'd probably press me about Connor if he saw me, and I was already getting that from Blake. I didn't need two bossy men in my life pushing me where I didn't want to go.

I hopped off my treadmill and started for the locker room, hoping Declan wouldn't spot me, but he turned my direction just outside the doors that led to the private arena.

Ugh—eye contact made. There was no escaping him now. He beckoned me from across the room, and I rolled my eyes as I made my way to him. "Hey, Declan."

"I didn't expect to see you here." His voice was smooth as silk, and it creeped me the hell out.

"Oh, well I was just heading to the showers." I folded my arms across my chest, but realized I probably looked angry or bitchy, so I dropped my hands back to my sides.

"How about you watch me fight, instead?"

If that meant watching him get his ass handed to him, then I was all for that. But I could care less about whatever poor sap Declan had arranged to fight because I was pretty sure whomever it was would throw the fight, to ensure the master of the universe kept his head remaining in Mt. Olympus. "Who are you fighting?" I faked an interest.

"John Jackson. The pro-fighter."

Of course. Declan had invested in the club John Jackson owned, not too long ago.

Memories jabbed at me as I thought about the club.

"Sure. I'd love to watch," I finally responded.

"Declan!"

No. I turned around to see Connor approaching us.

"By the way, I invited Connor to come," Declan whispered in my ear. His breath set my body trembling, and not in a good way.

Connor focused on me as he stopped in front of Declan and I. His facial expression gave no indication of his feelings as he stared at me.

I noticed his clean-shaven face and had to force myself to look at the floor for a brief moment.

Sexy with stubble, hot with a beard. And no beard with smooth skin? *Groan.*

I cleared the damn lump that had formed in my throat and swallowed the images—the memories—of Connor's ripped body.

"Hi," I think I said at some point. I cursed myself for allowing my mind and body to succumb to the strange, primordial urge to have sex with him. We had a horrible past. Not to mention I was supposed to screw him over and probably arrest him. What was wrong with me?

Declan tipped his head. "Ever seen this woman fight?" Declan nudged me in the arm.

I forced a small laugh. I was growing impressed with my ability to act around Declan, but why couldn't I use those same skills when it came to Connor? "I'm not that good."

"I'm pretty sure I don't believe that. I saw you handle that guy by the pool in Vegas. Remember?" Connor's eyes remained laser focused on mine.

"Come on. Jackson should be here any minute, and I need to warm up before we fight." Declan held the door open, and Connor gestured for me to enter first.

"Thanks," I said as I walked into the empty boxing area. "Too bad Bobby isn't around. He would love to meet a famous fighter. Is he a boxing champ?" I played dumb.

"UFC. Mixed martial arts champion," Declan said brusquely.

Hopefully, at the very least, I could watch Declan get knocked out by the pro. I tightened the knot in my ponytail, realizing what a mess I must look like.

"You feel like getting your hands dirty?" Declan asked Connor as he removed his T-shirt. For the first time, I saw that his back was a canvas. Angel wings sprouted from each side of his shoulder blades; they appeared to move, to flap, as he cracked his neck and rolled his shoulders, loosening up.

Declan, the fallen angel.

"I'll help you warm up if you'd like. We can throw a few punches." Connor stole a glance at me before removing his shirt. The man didn't have any tattoos, but he didn't need the paint. His back, his chest, his pecs were already works of art.

And my mind was drifting to dangerous territory again. If the sight of Connor's body could reduce me to a puddle of girly hormones, what business did I have in being an FBI agent?

Then again, I'd helped the FBI take down a hitman in Boston last year. I needed to remind myself that I was also *that* woman— the woman who'd stared death in the face and come out on top. My first and only kill. And, I hoped, my last. Although the guy was a world-class felon and murderer, it was never easy to have blood on your hands.

The sound of a fist pounding into flesh brought my attention front and center. Connor's gloved hand connected with Declan's stomach.

Both men had abs of steel, but Declan was slightly leaner. Connor was a former Marine. He could handle Declan. I was sure of it. And I couldn't help but stand just outside the ring, inwardly cheering him on.

"You ready to make the deal?" Declan asked Connor as he ducked away from one of Connor's shots.

"I'm still thinking about it." Connor's answer surprised me— he had told me yes last night. Did he change his mind? Hope seized my heart, but how would I take down the entire evil empire without the help of intimate knowledge of the weapons exchange?

We'd just have to come up with a new plan.

"What's holding you back?" Declan snuck an uppercut, but Connor jerked his head, saving himself a blow to the chin. They were both taking it rather easy.

"I'm not sure how I feel about making a deal when I don't really know who else I'm doing business with." Connor threw a right hook, followed by a left.

Declan dodged both and answered, "I'll ask my contacts if they're willing to meet with you if you sign the contract."

I sucked in a breath at Declan's words. A face-to-face!

"That'd be ideal." Connor lowered his guard, and Declan took the chance to send a hard jab.

The sound of the punch smacking into Connor's cheek had me cringing.

Surprisingly, Connor didn't let it affect him too much. He sprang back at Declan with his own shot. "I don't think we need these." Connor's eyes focused intently on Declan as he slipped off his gloves and held his fists up in front of his face.

Declan nodded and followed suit, but before either could take another swing, the doors to the room pushed open.

"Declan. My man!"

It must have been John Jackson, and he had two other men at his sides. I took a step back, gasping, but tripped. My butt smacked hard against the concrete floor.

I grimaced and looked up at Connor's hand reaching for mine, helping me up.

"Are you okay?" Connor stared at me like I was the sun and moon all rolled into one.

I focused on his sweaty chest for a moment, before pulling my eyes back up to meet his. "Yeah. Clumsy."

He smiled and released my arm. "Guess the big shot's here," he joked in a low voice.

I tried to return his smile, but I was too nervous. I lowered my head and stared at my sneakers, hoping to avoid notice.

"Connor Matthews, meet John Jackson, lightweight champion of the world," Declan said as he ducked between the ropes.

John Jackson was about six feet. His body was pretty fit but not too bulky, and his arms were banded in flashy tattoos. His head was shaved, his nose a little crooked, and his ears massively swollen from one too many punches. "Hey, man." He slapped Declan on the back and nodded at Connor.

The two men who had entered the room with John Jackson both greeted Declan as well.

"You up for a few rounds?" Declan tapped John on the arm.

John's eyes were on me, and I did my best to keep my balance, still terrified of being identified by the men who had come in with John. I'd known they were back in the city; I'd been expecting to see them at some point. I had just hoped they wouldn't see me, too.

"And you are?" John angled his head and held out his hand.

"Just leaving." I gripped his hand fast and hard before dropping my arm back to my side.

"You don't want to stay for the fight?" John glanced at Declan.

"I'd hate to see my boss get beat up." I couldn't exactly go with "fighting isn't my thing," could I? That'd never fly. But damn, I needed to get out of that gym and fast.

"You should stay," Declan said in a voice that was more a command than a suggestion.

Connor looked over at John. "Where are you from? Your accent . . ."

"My mother's Russian. I grew up outside Moscow and moved to the States when I was fifteen," John responded.

Connor reached for the T-shirt he had discarded and pulled it over his head. "Congrats on being champion."

"Thank you."

He rooted around in his bag and pulled out his cell, then tapped at the screen. "I have a meeting in Jersey, so I should probably head out." He toyed with his phone another second before looking up at me. "Walk with me?"

Oh God. He was saving me. "Is that okay?" I asked Declan, knowing he'd say yes. He needed to make Connor happy to get him to agree to the deal.

A deal that apparently involved selling an advanced weapon to terrorists.

"Sure." Declan nodded at me and focused his attention on John. "Get changed. I don't have all day to kick your ass. I have meetings, too." He laughed.

"You've never beaten me. And you never will." John cracked his knuckles but kept his eyes on mine.

Chills dashed up my spine, and I averted my eyes to the floor again, worried that John's friends would call me out. All would be lost. But I was equally anxious that I'd lose control and lunge at the men—claws out, ready to kill.

"You ready?" Connor slung his bag over his shoulder.

"Yeah," I said, trying to steady my breath, to hide my heaving chest.

"Enjoy your night off." Declan reached for a water bottle before switching his attention to Connor. "Can you make a decision by tomorrow?"

"I'll let you know," Connor was quick to reply, his voice steady.

I shuffled past John and his men, avoiding eye contact, and released a breath once outside the boxing area. "Thanks for saving me. I didn't feel like hanging out in a room full of egos and testosterone." Or having my cover blown.

"Of course." We started past the free weights, passed a row of treadmills, and stopped outside the ladies' locker room.

I was hanging on by a thread, my sanity at the threshold. "How come you haven't told Declan that you'll make the deal?" I moved out of the way for a woman to enter the locker room and stepped back closer to him once she was gone.

I needed to tell him the truth.

"Having second thoughts. Not a fan of getting into bed with strangers."

Because he was a good guy. Well, except for when he screwed me over. "I'd better shower." The words rolled off my tongue by some small miracle.

"You're off tonight." He slung the weight of his bag behind him and pushed his hands into his pockets. "Maybe we can get together?"

My heart started flapping like it had grown wings. "Another business dinner? We got interrupted at our last meal."

"I have a friend coming in from out of town tomorrow, and I'll be tied up for the next few days. I might swing by the club at some point and let Declan know my decision, but I'd like to see you tonight if that's okay."

"Why?" I didn't mean for the little three-letter word to slip from my lips, but it came out before I could clamp my mouth shut.

He took a step back from me and removed his hands from his pockets. "I have no idea why to be honest."

What was I supposed to say? "I was going to grab dinner with a friend tonight." A big fat lie. "But maybe I can change my schedule around. Can you call me later? I'll let you know."

He frowned as he programmed my number into his phone. "We shouldn't see each other, right?" His doubts mirrored my own. But my reasons for holding back were so much bigger, and he had no idea.

"I don't know." I sighed and touched my neck. It was impossible to think clearly, knowing those men were still so close.

"You okay?" Connor's hand was now on my arm.

"I'm just thinking about my sister," I said, and it felt good to be honest for once.

My skin grew cold at the loss of his touch. "Sorry," he mumbled.

"It's okay." Lie. Lie. Lie. "I'd better shower."

I needed to cool off, to strip away the pain, anger, and fear that crawled beneath my skin.

Before he could say anything else, I shoved open the locker room door and disappeared inside.

* * *

Connor

"Just sent you some photos. They aren't the best. I had to snap them fast and without notice." I leaned against my kitchen counter and stared out the window, which offered a view of Central Park. A light mist of rain had started.

"Who are they?" Jake asked.

"The one in the middle is John Jackson, a pro-fighter. All three had Russian accents. Can you see what you can find out about them?" I moved to my fridge and grabbed a beer. I'd spent ninety minutes in traffic and had decided to head home instead of back to the office.

"I'll do my best. The picture quality isn't great, but maybe this Jackson guy has prints on file, and I can cross reference his name to any known associates."

"Great. Thanks."

"I looked into Lauren Tate's background."

"And?"

"She's clean. Born and raised in New York. Her father is a construction worker, and her mother never worked. She graduated from Rutgers with an undergrad in business law and finished her MBA August 2015, right before she started working at Matthews Tech. She has no record. Not even a parking ticket."

I took a sip of my dark wheat beer and processed what he'd said. I was having a hard time believing Lauren was legit. "She always lived in New York?" I probed.

"Born and raised. Her parents are native New Yorkers, as well."

"Then her background is bullshit." I set my beer down and pressed my palms to the counter. "She has an accent. It slips out every once in a while."

"She's trying to hide an accent?"

"I asked her about it, and I think she lied to me."

"Do you think you're just paranoid?" he tested.

I stood up straight, pinching my shoulder blades together. "No. If she wasn't so damn up, close, and personal with Declan, then maybe I would let it slide."

"What type of accent?"

"Russian, maybe."

"Shit. That can't be a coincidence."

I reached for my drink again, needing to cool my brain before it overheated. "Why would Declan even want me to meet those guys?"

"I don't know."

This was giving me a headache. "When's your flight? We can talk more about this in person."

"My flight leaves Dallas at nine. I should be at LaGuardia around noon."

"I'll pick you up. Text me when you land."

"Sounds good."

"Thanks for coming. See you tomorrow." I tossed the burner phone I'd bought in Jersey on the couch and brought the beer to my lips. How much did Olivia know about Declan? Although my judgment was clouded by both anger and by lust, I wanted to protect her, even if she was on the wrong side.

I dug into my pocket for my regular cell and scrolled through my contacts.

Olivia Taylor. I still didn't understand why she wasn't going by Olivia Scott. She mentioned fudging her resume, but why her name? There had to be more to the story, and I planned to find out.

A half hour later, I parked my car in the garage around the corner from her apartment building. The clouds opened up, and I was hammered with rain as I made my way down the street to her building.

I pushed my wet hair off my face with both hands, shaking my head like a damn dog.

I impatiently waited in the empty lobby outside the set of elevators. I shook my T-shirt and was thankful it wasn't drenched. The rain had only started to pound onto the street just as I closed in on her building. I didn't want to make it a habit of needing to strip and have my clothes dried every time I was around Olivia.

Once inside the elevator, I pressed my hands to the wall and shut my eyes.

Part of me hoped Olivia wouldn't be home. I needed to talk to her, and yet I knew it was such a bad idea to be going back to her place. My mind spun with all I wanted to say. A knot formed in my stomach, the kind I used to get when I was positioned on a rooftop in Iraq or a mountain in Afghanistan, my brow sweating as I peered through the scope—waiting. Watching.

What was it about Olivia that had me feeling like I was in the middle of a war?

I opened my eyes at the sound of the elevator doors popping open, and I attempted to ease the tension from my neck as I walked to her room.

At her door, I hesitated for a moment, my fist hanging in the air. I could hear music playing inside her apartment. Was she alone?

I never got the chance to knock. The door opened, and I dropped my hand to my side.

Olivia leaned against the door frame and crossed her arms. "I thought you were going to call." She fought the smile that threatened her lips. "Were you so confident I'd rearrange my dinner plans for you?" There was the feisty personality I remembered from our youth—and God did I love it.

"Of course," I responded and tipped my head down a little, but kept my eyes on hers.

Her cheeks bloomed to echo the red of her T-shirt, and she stepped back, allowing me entrance.

I pulled the door closed and followed her into the living room. "Was there ever a dinner?" I challenged.

She approached her iPad on the coffee table and lowered the music. "Maybe," she said as she flashed her dimples. "Why are you here?" Her mood shifted pretty damn fast, and an underlying edge cut through her voice. "I thought you said seeing each other was a bad idea. You're confusing me."

I was confusing myself. "We should talk."

"About?" She remained standing a few feet in front of me, just inside the living room by the coffee table, with her arms folded in defiance across her chest.

"I want to talk to you about your job."

Her forehead creased, and her lips parted a fraction. No sound.

"This deal with Declan may not be legal, and I'd hate to see you get caught up in the middle of it all," I confessed, although I couldn't outright tell her all my concerns. She'd betrayed me in the past, and I wasn't certain she wouldn't do it again, even though my gut was telling me she was innocent.

"So, you decided not to do the deal?"

Was that relief? Her face changed to a blank slate before I could be sure. "I *am* doing the deal, but I don't think you should be involved. It seems risky, and I'm getting the vibe that Declan's business partners may not be on the up and up. But my father's company might fail without a partnership with Declan . . ."

I hated lying to her, but I couldn't open up. Not yet, at least.

"Which would be worse—handing over an unsuccessful company or a jail sentence?" she spat, but then covered her face with her hands for a brief moment. "Sorry. I'm supposed to be on Declan's side."

Supposed to be on Declan's side? What did that mean?

She shook her head and steepled her hands together, her fingertips brushing against her lips. "Connor. I'm an adult. I'm capable of making my own decisions. Is that the only reason you came here?"

No. My damn body ached to simply be near her. "Olivia, you shouldn't be working for Declan. You're better than that." I didn't mean to say being a personal assistant wasn't a good job, but—with Declan? "You were preparing to rule the world when we were young. You were going to be a lawyer. Hell, a senator. Or more." I took a step closer to her, and she attempted a step back, but bumped into the table. Her palms rubbed against her jeans as her eyes focused on the floor.

"Things change."

Of course—her sister. This wasn't what her sister would have wanted for her, but who was I to say? And who was I to remind her of that pain?

"What about you, Connor? Are you the man you always wanted to be?" She looked down at my hand, which was now on her arm, and I tugged her close to me. I tipped her chin up and pulled her gaze to mine. "I don't know who I am anymore. I've been adrift for a long time," I remarked, a painful honesty slicing through my words.

"Why'd you join the Marines? What happened to you?"

I released my hold on her and exhaled sharply before moving past her and into her kitchen. "Got anything to drink?"

"Connor," she followed after me, "you haven't changed, have you? Always sidestepping the big issues."

I spun around, practically pinning her to the counter in the galley kitchen. My hands braced the granite top on each side of her, and her chest rose and fell enough to give her away.

"Connor."

My eyes narrowed on her as I angled my head, listening. "Do you hear the song playing?"

She nodded as she rolled her tongue over her teeth. We were so close I could almost feel her body quiver.

"Do you remember?"

"How could I forget?" She touched my arm and moved it, scooting free from me. "This song played the first night I finally agreed to dance with you." She grabbed a beer from the fridge and tossed it at me. "I didn't have a clue how to dance to house music. But you insisted, and God, did I look like an idiot the first time."

"You were adorable. I wasn't sure what you were doing at first. The jive, or something? But once you got into your groove, I knew I was done for. The way your body moves should be a sin." I cleared my throat, remembering her body against mine on dance floors all over Manhattan.

She swallowed and moved away from me again.

I removed the top of the beer and found her standing in the living room, her back to me.

The rain had stopped. It must've been a quick shower. My hair was still a little wet, but my clothes weren't bad. I'd forgotten all about them the second Olivia had opened her door.

I brought the bottle to my lips and sat in the chair, my fingers tapping the side to the thumping beat of the music.

"You going to answer my question? Why'd you turn into your father?"

"I'm not my father," I snapped, my body growing rigid at the very idea. "And are you going to tell me why you changed your last name and work for some creep like Declan?"

She faltered a little as she turned around. "I wanted a fresh start after Jessie died." She stared at her bare feet. "A new name. A new life."

I knew she was lying as soon as she looked up at me. Her mouth was tight, her brows slanted. She was panting, just slightly. What was she hiding?

I took another swig of my beer. Of course, I wasn't being totally honest with her, either.

"I answered. Your turn." She took a seat on the couch and pulled a pillow to her chest as if to guard herself.

"After the baby," I started, but had to look away from her. It hurt too much to look her in the eyes and talk about *this*, "my father and I got into a big fight about you. I was angry at everyone and everything. I decided to get the hell out of New York. I took off, and the next thing I knew I was in boot camp." I scratched my chin and released a breath. "I didn't talk to my father for a long time after that."

Her mouth opened as her eyes darkened, but she didn't say anything.

"I don't want to talk about our past anymore, though." I stood up and rubbed the back of my neck. I almost forgot why I had come.

"I think we need to talk about it." She folded her arms and rose to her feet. "You shouldn't have left me." Her voice was raw. Gritty. "You don't get to be pissed at me."

Was she out of her mind? Did she forget that she had wrecked my damn life? I couldn't do this. I thought we could both move on if we just avoided the elephant in the room, but who was I kidding? The tension between us was too thick to elude. "I'm out of here." I set the bottle down in front of me and moved to the door.

"Connor, wait."

My hand froze on the knob, but I couldn't turn around. My hands slid up and I pressed both palms to the door, lowering my head, not sure what to do. This woman had me skipping down memory lane one minute and ready to run the next. The flip-flopping was making me sick.

I knew it would be better if I never saw her again, but as long as she worked for Declan, and as long as there were unanswered questions about my father and the company, I would have to face her.

"If you don't want to talk about it, I won't press." Her hand rested on my back, and my shoulder blades flexed back at her touch.

"Damn it, Liv." My voice was deep and gravelly as I squeezed my eyes shut. "I hate myself for still wanting you."

"I'm in the same boat," she said in a soft voice.

I turned to face her, and I couldn't fight it anymore. I pulled her against me and snaked my hand through her hair, cupping the back of her head, as my mouth found hers.

18

OLIVIA

CONNOR WAS KISSING ME. AND I WAS LETTING HIM. NO, NOT JUST letting him. I was kissing him back.

I told myself to stop. I told myself to back away. But I couldn't.

Instead, my hands slipped beneath his slightly damp T-shirt. My fingertips brushed against his warm skin; he raised his arms, and I peeled the shirt off.

He lifted me up, and my legs wrapped around his hips as his tongue pushed into my mouth. As he carried me down the hall and to my room, I wondered how the hell something so wrong could feel so unbelievably right. *You're mine, Liv. Forever mine.* The memory of Connor's promises pushed into my mind. He didn't use his words lightly—they came in the moments that really mattered. For a nineteen-year-old-girl, those words had been everything.

Connor released me in front of my bed, and my feet found the ground. I started for my own shirt, desperate to have his hands on my body. His breath hitched, and his eyes darted to my chest once my lacy bra dropped to the floor.

I pulled air into my lungs as he lunged for me, his hands in my hair again, his mouth on mine. His fingers grazed my neck, traced the line of my collarbone, and dipped down to cup one of my breasts. My nipples tightened as he crushed his lips to mine, taking my mouth like he couldn't get enough.

"Fuck," he whispered after breaking our kiss. His eyes pinned me as frenzied need gripped hold. My hands shot to his chest, dying to touch his hard, rippled flesh.

He used his knee and nudged my legs apart. I gasped as he brought both his hands to my ass and lifted me up into the air.

I wrapped my arms around his neck and tilted my head back as he planted kisses on my throat. A moan escaped my lips, and he laid me on the bed.

His eyes darted to mine as he kneeled on the floor, and I propped myself up on my elbows. I stared at his hardened features as he started with my zipper and tugged at my jeans. He worked them off, leaving me only in pink panties. I luxuriated under his gaze.

He lifted my leg and kissed my ankle before his hands slipped up my legs, massaging and kneading my flesh as he kissed my skin, making my body sizzle.

I wanted to touch him, too—his arousal was obvious—but he was teasing and taunting me with his hands and lips. And then his face came close to my inner thigh and my hips bucked. I shifted back, my head hitting the bed as he tore the thin fabric of my underwear and replaced it with his mouth.

I gripped the sheets. I'd completely forgotten what it felt like to have a man there.

And oh God, was Connor an expert—the memories of our past times together played through my mind, the music from the other room serving as my own personal soundtrack.

Just when I was on the brink of coming, Connor was off me and removing his jeans and boxers. My body was shaking with need as he mounted me. I reached for him, wanting to feel him the way he'd touched me. His body arched when my hand closed around him. He lowered his head to my ear, and his breath flowed over me, driving me crazy. I bit into his shoulder, trying to keep myself from yelping as he removed my hand from him, sheathed himself with a condom, and worked himself into me. Filling me.

The void had been there for over ten years—waiting for him, ever since he left. I writhed beneath him, savoring the sensation of him inside me. *We're going to do this forever. Every day. And every night.* That's what Connor said to me after our first time together, after claiming my virginity.

I shut my eyes, hating myself for remembering.

My body jerked up as he moved out and back into me again; it gripped me back to reality, to the pleasure of the moment.

My nipples grazed his chest, and my body lined in goosebumps as he moved faster and faster; my hands clawed at the sheets as he throbbed inside me.

But then he stopped. My eyes widened, panicked. I was so close . . . no . . .

He shifted off me and to his back before pulling me up and on top of him.

Oh. He remembered. I positioned over him and pressed my hands to his chest. I sunk down, sheathing his length and began to rock, swaying my hips back and forth. His eyes glinted, his jaw tightened, and I could tell he was trying hard to hang on as I grinded and moved against him, the friction pushing me to the edge.

I tried to swallow back my emotions, but they fed into my desire.

His hands moved up and down my outer thighs, blazing trails of fire on my skin with each movement.

"Oh . . ." My core tightened, my sex clenched, and I sank on top of him as my body exploded with orgasm. His eyes squeezed shut as he held my hips. His body tensed and he shuddered beneath me.

I nuzzled my face against his chest, inhaling his piney cologne, and then slipped off of him. But he pulled me against him. His arm banded around my hip, holding me tight. *You're mine, Liv. Forever mine.* The memory of what we once had rushed back into my mind with a painful blow.

Despite the confusion, the lies, and the fear—I felt safe.

But when I woke up an hour later, he was gone.

* * *

Connor

I RESTED MY HEAD AGAINST MY STEERING WHEEL AND TRIED TO make sense of what in the hell had happened. What should never have happened.

I remembered the first time we were together. I hadn't known she was a virgin. She'd held that from me until I was buried deep inside her, and the realization of what I'd done, what I'd taken from her, hit me.

She didn't want me to know, she had said. She hadn't wanted me to take it easy on her. She told me she had wanted me: *Sexy. Hungry. And wild.* She was amazing then, and God, was she still incredible now.

My body stirred again at the thought.

I needed to go. She and I would never work. Our past was too messed up, and our present was just as complicated.

Perhaps we had satiated our need for each other. Perhaps now we could move on. But part of me wasn't sure if that'd be possible.

I gripped my steering wheel harder, hoping to control myself, but before I knew it, I was back inside the elevator of her building.

A woman clad in black leather pants and a tight gold top shot me an "I want you" look as we rode in the elevator together. Did I give off some vibe, or was I still hard from thoughts of Olivia? I ignored the woman and hurried away the second the doors peeled open.

I balled my hands into fists at my sides and stood outside Olivia's door. I had turned the lock on my way out, worried about

her safety, and she was probably asleep inside. She may not have even realized I'd left.

I needed to leave. To go home.

But I couldn't.

Instead, I rang the bell, knowing she wouldn't hear a knock if she were asleep. Plus, I could still hear the faint sound of music from inside.

After a painfully long minute, the door opened. Olivia stood before me in a full-length, creamy silk robe. Her hair was draped over one shoulder, and her mascara was smudged beneath her eyes, which made her look even sexier.

"What are you—"

I moved into her apartment, shoved the door shut behind me and cupped her cheeks with both my hands as I cut her off with my mouth.

She broke the kiss and stepped back. "You left." She steadied her eyes on mine. There was pain there. "Again."

"I'm sorry. I thought I should leave. I've been sitting in my car for twenty minutes and couldn't even turn on the engine."

"I don't want to sleep alone tonight," she said softly. And my control was shattered as her hands slipped to the knot of her robe. My hand seized her waist, and I pulled her tight body against mine.

"What do you want?" I rasped, still beholding her eyes.

"You." She pulled her bottom lip into her mouth as her robe fell to the floor.

My hand shot to her stomach and trailed down to her center, which was still soaking wet. "I'm going to lose my damn mind," I whispered into her ear as I stroked her soft flesh.

She bucked against my hand, and I pinned her back to the wall in the hallway. She tilted her head back, a moan escaping from her mouth. "I love you like this. Wet. Ready for me."

I felt her shudder against me as her fingertips gripped my shoulders. "Not yet. I don't want to come yet. Please."

I nipped her bottom lip before kissing her again, but kept my hand between her thighs, wanting nothing more than to feel her lose control.

My hand pinched her nipple as I continued to torment her. Soon, she was panting. Begging for release.

"Connor, please. Oh, yes . . ."

She clung to my body as she came, and I pressed my lips to her ear.

"I want you back in the bathroom where we started the other night." My voice was rough, because I could barely contain my need to be back inside her again. I don't know if I'd ever satisfy my need for her, but I knew how the story would end.

One of us would get hurt.

Shit, I couldn't think about it. All I wanted to think about was how I was going to make her scream my name.

I followed her into her bedroom, watching her body move with grace. She had no shame in her nakedness, her narrow waist, her perfect hips, her ass, which I wanted to sink my teeth into . . .

She entered the bathroom, dimmed the lights, and turned on the shower. I hastily stripped out of my clothes and joined her beneath the spray. She tilted her head back, allowing the water to pour over her. "My turn," she said before lowering herself in front of me.

I braced myself against the walls and looked down at her as she took me into her mouth. My muscles went taut, and my stomach tightened as she pumped me with her fist while she sucked.

I wanted this, but I wanted to be inside of her more. "Stop." I touched her shoulder, and she looked up at me. "Stand up," I said, and my voice sounded like a command.

"I'm not done," she said while continuing to caress me, making it hard for me to think.

"I need to feel you again." I groaned. "Be inside you."

Her lips parted, and she gifted me with her dimples before pushing up to her feet.

I lifted her up and buried myself deep inside her. With her legs wrapped tight around my hips, I braced one wall, holding on to her with the other. She shimmied up and down until the sensation had me reeling.

Shower sex is delicious, but also—realistically—a challenge. She slipped off me and released a deep, sobering laugh. "Are we getting older, or was it always this difficult?"

I was pretty sure at that moment, watching Olivia laugh and smile, I was about the happiest I'd been in a long time. I angled my head and just stared at her for a moment, fascinated that someone could be so beautiful.

The lies and the pain were gone in that moment. I refused to allow them to suffocate me, at least for tonight.

"Tonight, Liv . . . tonight, you're mine."

19

OLIVIA

BLAKE HAD ALREADY CALLED MY PHONE THREE TIMES THAT morning. I was grateful it was in the drawer in my nightstand on vibrate, but every time I heard the buzzing sound coming from my purse, it served as a quiet reminder that I was in trouble.

I was lying in bed with Connor, a man who planned on making a deal with Declan despite the fact that he worried it was illegal. And I had no idea what to do. How had it come to this?

I stared at Connor snoozing next to me, and I studied his masculine features. The sexy hard planes of his body, and the tough exterior . . . which only covered a sensitive, funny, and amazing man beneath the surface.

What really happened ten years ago? My hand slipped to my stomach, and I shut my eyes.

Connor and I hadn't meant to get pregnant. It was a mistake, but once we learned about it, we made the commitment to each other to raise the child together. We loved each other. It made sense. But I also knew that he'd eventually find out that I lied about my age and background. I was scared he'd hate me, that he'd run from me—leave me—like my mom had, so I kept putting it off. I promised myself I'd tell him the truth, though.

But I never got the chance. His father beat me to it.

A flash of anger shot through me at the memory of Edward, but the feel of Connor's fingers brushing my arm pulled me back to the present.

"How are you?" he asked with his sexy morning voice.

"Sore," I said before groaning.

"You're pretty damn flexible. Still doing yoga?" There was a hint of playfulness in his voice.

"No. Just born gifted," I teased back, and God, did it feel good to be carefree, even just for a blissful hour.

"That's for damn sure." He reached for my face and tucked the hair that had fallen in front of my eyes behind my ear.

"Do you ever work?"

He laughed. "I do my best to act like I'm working, but I haven't exactly been in the office all that much. But what will they do, fire me?"

"Good point."

"I probably should make an appearance at some point since I plan on calling it a day around noon." He grinned. God, his schoolboy, sheepish grin—I missed it. Missed him.

"Wait." I touched his chest, and he placed his large hand over mine. "Don't leave yet."

He brought my hand to his lips and kissed my knuckles. "As much as I want to stay in this bed forever and make up for lost time, you and I both know we can't live in a bubble. The real world will catch up with us eventually." He smirked. "Well, maybe we can steal one more hour." He leaned forward and kissed me, but I pulled back after a moment. "I'm not that sore, and I don't think it's fair to you that you're the only one suffering. I figure one more hour. One long and good hour—we can be evenly matched. Both barely able to walk."

I slapped his chest with my free hand and fought back the laughter. My groin ached at the thought of feeling him inside me again. "Connor?" I heard the buzzing of my cell phone again, and it was like Blake was in my ear, pulling me back to reality.

And I hated it.

"Yeah?" He touched my shoulder and kissed it. "What's up, Liv?" He tilted his head and studied me.

I leaned into him. "I've missed you." I hadn't meant to say that. The words just came out and dangled in the air between us.

His green eyes remained on mine, but he wasn't talking. I had no idea what he was thinking, but the silence between us was making it hard to breathe.

"I've missed you, too," he said while narrowing his eyes at me, his voice drowning in seriousness now.

I looked down at my hand, which was now tucked inside Connor's large one. "You wanna play hooky a little longer and grab breakfast with me?" What was I saying? I couldn't afford to play pretend.

"I'll cut out of work under one condition."

"Oh yeah. What's that?"

"You come to the airport with me to pick up my friend."

I thought about it for a moment, wondering why Connor really wanted me to go with him, but I answered, "Okay."

He tightened his hold on my hand and for some reason I asked, "What was it like being in the military?" I was still having a hard time picturing my laid-back ex-boyfriend being a Marine.

His attention darted to the wall, his eyes honing in near the ceiling where the pale blue paint was beginning to fade and flake. "It was interesting."

"Interesting?" I smirked. "Only you would describe it like that." I pressed my head back into the pillow, but my hand remained in his.

He glanced at me out of the corner of his eye, and his lips pushed into a smile. "I met a lot of good people there. I feel like I have a lot of brothers now, not just Mason."

"Oh yeah? Tell me about them." I don't know why I was

probing, but for some reason, it made me feel at ease learning about the man Connor had become.

"Well, my friend Michael Maddox is the glue. He keeps us in check." He laughed a little. "But he's intense. Better now that he's found someone—well, unless anything or anyone bothers his wife, and then he's like the Hulk."

I giggled. Like a real, girly-girl-giggle. I pressed my free hand to my mouth in surprise at the sound of the strange noise I'd made. Where had that come from?

"You met Ben in Vegas. And Aiden, well, he's this crazy Irish guy that we keep around because he's cool shit."

"Who's coming today? Is he military?" How could Connor be ex-military and friends with all these Marines—and still make a deal with Declan? There had to be more to the story. I wasn't buying it. The more I thought about it, the more I realized something had to be up Connor's sleeve. Of course that had to be the case, there was always more to Connor than meets the eye.

"You'll be meeting Jake. Women love Jake. He's got this whole Southern gentleman thing that they go nuts over. He's like a thirty-four-year-old Clint Eastwood—or maybe Eastwood's son."

I fanned my face with my free hand. "Oh. Can't wait to meet him."

I gasped as Connor playfully yanked me on top of him in one quick movement. God, he was strong. "I'm not sharing you." He sucked in a breath at the realization of his words, and I think we both wanted to pretend neither of us heard his comment because we both knew we were reliving the past—and there could never be a future for us.

Our current bubble was a breakable one. If I blinked, it'd shatter.

My palms were on each side of him on the bed, supporting my weight above his body. He pushed the hair off my face and held my face in his hands. "Did I ever tell you what made me realize you were the one the night we met?"

I gulped and shook my head no.

"Well, I spotted you at the club earlier in the night, before our eyes locked at the bar. You were lounging in a VIP booth by yourself, and you were reading a book. I was in shock. A, I couldn't believe you were reading a book at a club, and b, you were reading a book in pretty shitty lighting. I had this whole pick-up line ready. I was going to talk about offering you a light or something terribly lame." I smiled down at him, wishing for a minute I could be nineteen again. To be innocent. To have my sister back.

"Just when I was about to approach you some other guy beat me to it. I stopped a few feet away and listened. I was prepared to rescue you from his horrible attempt at picking you up—I'm pretty sure his line was far worse than mine—but the way you handled yourself impressed the hell out of me. You were so quick and witty. I'm sure the guy forgot to speak by the time you were done with him. And after he walked away, I knew I was done for. I had to be with you."

I couldn't believe he never told me that before. "How come you didn't approach me then? Why didn't you try out your line?"

He guffawed as his hands slipped to my shoulders. "You think I wanted to suffer the same humiliation as that poor guy? No, I waited. I plotted. But when I caught you looking at me at the bar while I was with my friends, I scrapped the plan and—"

"Failed."

A smile broke to his lips. "And failed. And failed . . ."

"Until I was so sick of you asking me out I gave in." I rolled off him and to his side. "Do you wish you gave up?"

He was quiet for a moment. "Everything happens for a reason, Liv."

"I guess." I rose from the bed and stood up. He propped his hands behind his head and just stared at me. His hard naked body only covered by a small scrap of sheet draped just over his groin— his corded tanned thighs, hard abs—he was a delicious sight.

"What are you looking at?" I glanced down at my naked body and back up at him.

"Just admiring God's work."

Jeez, and that's how I felt about him. "Wanna skip breakfast?" My heart was pounding, and my rationale thought didn't just fly out the window, it was launched. I was living in the moment. Something I hadn't done since, well, since Connor . . .

"You totally want to use me for my body again, don't you?" His white teeth flashed as he slipped the sheet from his body, exposing his erection.

I nodded. "Hell, yes." I laughed and crawled back into bed.

* * *

Connor

I NEEDED TO TELL OLIVIA THE TRUTH. SHE KNEW DECLAN WAS shady, but once she discovered who she was really working for she would quit. She had to, right? I decided to shelve my anger over the past. I had to keep her safe, to prevent anything bad happening to her.

I would introduce her to Jake and tell her the truth—that he was FBI, and he was helping me. Maybe she knew something that could help us.

I parked my Jeep in the short-term parking lot at LaGuardia and looked over at Olivia in the passenger seat. It was like old times, having her next to me.

She looked up at me beneath her dark lashes as she unbuckled her seatbelt. "What?"

I removed the key from the ignition. "Just remembering that time we got yelled at for making out in the bathroom on our plane trip to Italy." Wow. I had even glanced at her passport before we'd traveled, but I never paid attention to her birth year. I guess when you trust someone, you aren't looking for a lie.

Of course, that was the least of her offenses.

My nostrils flared a little as my memory became tainted, but when Olivia shut her eyes and tilted her head back, smiling, I let the pain fade away.

"That was a great trip. I never wanted to leave. How many times did we drink Limoncello when we were there? Or grappa? I miss that—how it instantly warms your insides." She opened her eyes, her tongue teasing me as it slipped over her lips. "Remember Pompeii? One of the only buildings that remained intact from the eruption of Mt. Vesuvius was the prostitution house. And you," she said while tapping my chest, "embarrassed the hell out of me on that tour by discussing all of the so-called items on the 'menu' there. Saying we should try the first three, but you didn't think you could bend far enough to try the fifth."

God, it felt like yesterday. "Well, I remember the fifth, and let's just say I'm game to try it now if you are."

Her dimples popped as she chuckled. "Maybe if you tell me the rest of the Buckingham Palace story, we'd have a deal."

My mouth opened, but I didn't speak. I just stared at her. The sun poked through the window, bouncing off her shiny, chocolate brown hair. She wet her already glossy lips.

She was poised. Elegant and beautiful. Yet this woman could drop a man to the ground with a flick of her wrist.

My body ached again with want. And my anger over her betrayal was slowly vanishing. Was I letting the good memories and my damn lust for her cloud my judgment?

I wasn't even sure if I cared anymore. It was a decade ago. She had been young, and so had I. People make mistakes. I was no saint. I should've at least confronted her when I learned the truth, but instead I tucked my damn tail between my legs, fought with my father, and took off to join the Marines . . . just to spite him, to say to hell with everyone.

"What about when we rented the boat, and you almost hit that guy?"

I shook my head. "In my defense, you took your top off, which was distracting!" A flood of heat torched my body at the memory and my eyes dipped to her chest.

"When you cursed at that guy in Italian, I about died."

"It's a requirement. You're bound by international travel laws to learn the swear words in the countries you travel." She slapped my chest, and I laughed. "But come on, he deserved it. He was checking you out."

"Because you almost collided with his boat!" She smirked at me, and I became speechless for a few long moments.

"You seem different," I finally said as she reached for the door handle.

Her shoulders flinched. "Good sex can do that, I guess."

I knew that wasn't what she wanted to say. There was more there, but she kept her back to me so I couldn't read her face. Smart. "Only good, huh?" I played right back. "I better up my game, then. Number five it is." I rubbed my hands together and beamed at her when she glanced over her shoulder at me.

She released a nervous laugh. "We'll see," she said in a low and sexy voice.

I attempted to curtail my desire. "We better go. His flight should've landed."

"So, who am I looking out for again?" she asked as we plodded through the busy crowd of people and to the baggage claim. "A super-hot guy?" She cracked a smile, and I slapped her butt, forgetting I was in an airport surrounded by people.

She whipped around to face me, and I could tell she was ready to kill me, but then her face fell. Her mouth edged open, and I turned around to see what she was looking at. "What?"

"Shit. I completely forgot. I have a meeting." The words rushed fast from her mouth.

I touched her back. "Oh. I'll take you after—"

"No. I'll get a cab. I gotta go. Sorry." Before I could speak, she turned away, disappearing into the crowd.

What the hell had just happened? I raked a hand through my hair and shoved it out of my face. It was getting a little out of control. Guess I needed a cut.

"Connor!"

I turned to see my friend on approach.

Jake and I shared a gruff, one-armed hug. "Hey, man. You check any luggage?"

"Nah. Just have a carry-on." He slapped my back. "Good to see you." His brown eyes shot to mine. "Well, not for these reasons, of course."

"Shit. I've been losing my damn mind," I said as we exited. The sunlight had me reaching for my shades, which hung at the neck of my gray T-shirt.

"Oh yeah? I'm betting you weren't expecting this when you took over the company."

"Hell, that's only the half of it. My ex-girlfriend, Olivia, is involved in all this, and it's screwing with my head." There. I'd said it. I told him about Olivia.

Jake stopped walking for a second. "*The* girl—the reason you took off from New York to begin with? The reason you joined the Marines?" he asked in a low voice, his brows slanting with concern.

I moved to the edge of the sidewalk and rubbed my forehead. "Yeah." Jake didn't know too much. I'd never really opened up and told anyone the full story. We'd been together on leave once, Michael, Jake, and a few other buddies of mine . . . I had one too many beers, and we were talking about why we had all joined, and I had stammered out Olivia's name.

"How is she involved in this?" He placed a hand on my shoulder and looked at me with concern etched on his face.

"She works for Declan."

He took an immediate step back. "Why didn't you tell me this sooner?"

I shook my head and started walking again. "I was trying to

make sense of it all. I told her last night that she should quit her job, that it's dangerous."

He kept up pace with me. "And?"

"She said not to worry about her, that she was fine. I was going to introduce you today. I wanted to explain to her that she's in over her head. At first I wasn't sure if I could trust her."

"But now you do?"

We reached my Jeep, and I unlocked it. "Yeah. I do."

"Even though she screwed you over in the past?" He tossed his bag into the back of my Jeep.

I thought about it for a moment. The Olivia I knew then was the same woman I knew now, but she'd hardened at the loss of her sister. But how things ended with Olivia and I was so out of character with the Olivia I had thought I knew—what if I had her all wrong?

Maybe we should talk like she had wanted to. But this was all too much right now. We needed to have the conversation about our past, but first, I had to deal with Declan.

"I'm afraid she's going to get hurt, Jake."

He nodded at me as he sat down. "Then we'll just have to make sure she doesn't."

20

OLIVIA

SHIT. DAMN. SHIT. BACK AT MY APARTMENT, I GRABBED MY burner phone and studied it in my hands. What was I supposed to tell Blake? I still hadn't even told him about who I'd bumped into at the gym yesterday. He was going to lose his mind when he found out.

And now this?

Five missed calls. Looks like Blake would be pissed at me for a couple reasons.

"What the hell, Olivia!" his voice roared through the phone the second he answered.

I crunched my face as I sat down atop the crumpled sheets at the bottom of the bed.

I could still smell him. His scent was all over. I grew warm at the simple memory of the morning. It had felt so—right.

"Olivia!"

I flinched. "Here. Sorry."

"Where have you been?" There was a long pause. "Were you with *him*? Connor?" Another long pause since I wasn't talking. "Did you sleep with him?"

"No, but that's none of your damn business, Blake," I snapped.

"He's a part of the op, Olivia. Everything's my business when it comes to the op." I could hear him blow out a loud breath.

If he was only my boss, I would say his anger had to do with his concerns about me crossing the line with someone we were investigating. But Blake and I had slept together, on and off, up until the investigation started. His voice rang more of jealousy than anything else.

"I get that he's your ex, but he's making a deal with Declan, which means he's on the wrong side of the law."

I wasn't sure about that . . . "I need to tell him who I am. This is non-negotiable for me," I said, trying to dodge his concerns about my sex life.

"You cannot tell him! You hear me? That's a direct order," his voice screeched in my ear, and I had to pull the phone away for a second. I pushed to my feet and walked around the barren bedroom. I didn't even have a single picture on the wall.

"He might find out anyway." My mouth tightened, nervous for Blake to hear the news. I didn't want him yanking me from the case. Although it was a case I shouldn't have really been on to begin with, given my history.

"What do you mean?" he asked slowly, his Boston accent thick in my ears.

"Jake Summers is in town. He's a friend of Connor's, apparently."

"Jake Summers? Whose—" The silence meant he'd probably just figured it out. "Jake Summers? As in the FBI director based in the Dallas office? *That* Jake Summers?"

Jake was well-known in the agency. He'd moved up in the ranks fast, which had him on everyone's radar.

"Shit—when Sean made his so-called phone calls asking around about Connor, he must have talked to the wrong damn person."

Jake. "Jake's being here is not the problem." I gulped. "He'll know who I am."

"I highly doubt that, Olivia." There was a trace of sarcasm in his voice. "You haven't been with the agency that long."

I exhaled a breath and walked to my window. "He was one of my instructors at Quantico."

"What?"

Jake didn't normally teach at Quantico, but he was brought in special to teach a class on counterterrorism in the United States. Identifying, investigating, and diffusing terrorist cells.

"Why did Connor bring an FBI agent to town? Is he here for a visit, or is Connor . . .?"

"I have no idea," I said, but part of me had a gut feeling that Connor had called in a favor from an old Marine buddy. He wasn't planning on making a deal with Declan. He was probably trying to take Declan down, like me. I just didn't know why.

And because I'd pulled him into the deal, I'd put Connor directly in harm's way.

I was sure Connor could handle himself, and the fact that he had a high-level FBI agent on his side, meant I shouldn't worry. But something nagged at my core, making me feel a little sick.

Maybe it was the lying.

Terrorists would be using weapons that Connor's company made—and Connor had no idea.

"I have to tell him who I am. We're on the same team." I sank back onto my bed.

"No. We don't know that for sure. I don't know what Connor's endgame is, but we have our own priorities. Just keep away from Connor while Jake is in town."

"But we can work together," I protested.

"No!"

"Blake. You're being ridiculous."

"Olivia, don't make me remind you that you take your orders from me. You work for me. We cannot tell anyone. Period."

"You're making a mistake." I wanted to say more. To yell and scream, but I bit my tongue. I needed to come up with an alternative to present to Blake, because I knew arguing with him would get me nowhere.

"I don't care what Connor's intentions are—when he makes a deal with Declan, he's going down, too. We've already discussed this. I'm really not sure why we're rehashing this again."

My nostrils flared.

"Can you come here so we can talk in person? We need to strategize." His voice was calmer now, at least.

I glanced at my watch. "I have a few things I need to take care of first. Swing by in a few hours."

"Stay out of trouble."

He hung up before I could say anything, which was probably for the better.

I went into my bathroom and swept my hair up into a loose bun, then placed my palms on the counter and stared into my eyes. It was lonely doing what I did. I didn't have any real friends. The only friends I made were for my cover.

Like Claire. And Bobby. I hated that they'd be blindsided by the truth when it all came out, but that was the name of the game. I couldn't risk them knowing.

I wondered how long I'd be able to keep this life up. Living lies, even if for a good cause. Would I ever be able to marry? Have a family?

My thoughts drifted to Connor. For the first time in a long time, when I thought about him, I smiled.

Connor

"Tyson went to the Middle East three times in April before your father died," Jake said as I parked my Jeep outside the police station.

"With my dad?"

Jake shook his head. "By himself, but the charges were billed to your father's credit card."

"Where'd he go?"

He reached into his pocket for his phone, studied it for a moment, then looked up at me. "Pakistan, Iraq, and Syria."

"That can't be a coincidence." I gripped the steering wheel tighter, my knuckles whitening. "What else did you find?"

"He was in Syria for two days. And Iraq and Pakistan once each. All trips were within a week apart."

"I'll have to look into a connection between my father's prior deals with Declan in relation to when Tyson flew abroad. Maybe my father had concerns about something and sent Tyson to follow up. And the evidence is in the safe deposit box."

"It makes sense." We stopped just outside the police station entrance, standing at the top of the stairs.

"Declan helped Matthews Tech secure the Saudi contract, but maybe my father regretted it later, or found out Declan was doing something illegal. Worse than simple corporate bribery."

"So, Edward tried to back out. Declan said no. And he collected evidence to bring Declan down—"

"Or my dad was blackmailing Declan. Had something in his pocket on him just in case." I wouldn't put it past my father. If he was willing to work with Declan in the first place, it was possible he was attempting to manipulate the situation for a better deal for himself and the company. But it was still a bit farfetched. My father had always been an honest man, so I had thought. "Hell, I don't know. We need more proof." I slipped my sunglasses off.

"We'll get it."

I nodded, and we made our way through the precinct and down the stairs to the medical examiner's office. "Is he expecting us?"

Jake had flashed his badge and worked his magic to get us in the police station and to the ME's office. "Yeah. We're right on time."

Two glass doors automatically slid open, allowing us entrance to the OCME, the Office of the Chief Medical Examiner.

"You must be Jake Summers." A tall and fit African American man approached us. After he'd shaken Jake's hand, his brown eyes shifted to me. "I'm Danny Bennett. I run the department. Jake told me on the phone that you have reason to believe my John Doe might be someone you know?" He folded his arms across his white coat.

I glanced at Jake before focusing back on Danny. The three of us were alone in the room. There was a body on a table a few feet away, and my stomach turned at the sight of it. An autopsy in progress.

Jake nudged me in the side. I still hadn't spoken, unable to tear my eyes away from the body, even though the sight of it made me ill. "Yes." I reached into my pocket for the photo I'd found of Tyson at my father's office; a different one than the image Jake had emailed the ME's office. "I'm looking for this man, and I'm hoping he's alive and not here."

Danny took the picture and studied it. "He might be a match for my John Doe, but the body is in pretty bad shape. You up for a look?" He handed the picture back, and I nodded.

We followed him through another pair of doors, and the cool air slammed us as we entered the room. Danny walked over to a silver wall with several black handles; it was basically a refrigerator for bodies. Great.

Danny pulled open drawer five from the middle of the wall, and he unzipped the body bag. My hand shot to my face, covering my mouth as I stared at the corpse. "Where'd they find the body?"

"The Hudson," he answered. "He died several weeks ago, but his body was only recently discovered."

"Doesn't look like he drowned," Jake remarked while eyeing the body.

The ME donned a pair of purple latex gloves and lifted one of the corpse's hands. "His fingertips have been severed. Missing." He opened the man's mouth. "Each tooth was pulled."

Bile rose in my throat, and I turned away from the body. It was hard to tell if it was Tyson. The body was discolored, and the flesh partially stripped. "Does he have a tattoo?" I remembered Tyson had a tattoo of the Marine Corps flag on his chest. We'd been at a family function at Martha's Vineyard once when I was fifteen, and Tyson had been there. My father had brought him everywhere like Tyson was his own personal secret service.

On the beach I'd noticed Tyson's tattoo, which prompted me to ask him about his time in the Marines. Our conversation had always stuck with me, and the night my father and I had the big blowout, I remembered Tyson, and I thought, *Why not?*

"He has a tattoo," Danny responded.

"Marine Corps flag on his chest?" I balled my hands at my sides, my chest flaring with rage. Tyson had been a good man. A better man than my father. He was someone I went to for advice when I was a teen. He'd worked for my father since I was twelve. I respected the man. And now—

"Yes."

"How'd he die?" I still couldn't turn around. Jake's hand was on my shoulder, and I leaned forward, pressing my hands to my knees.

"He had multiple wounds, but the final blow was most likely the stab wound to the left groin that hit the femoral artery. He was either tortured, or someone really didn't want his identity discovered. Probably both."

I sucked in a breath, held it a moment, and released it. I needed to get out of there.

"You gonna be okay?" Jake asked as my spine straightened.

"With Tyson dead, I have to assume that my father was also murdered." I turned to face Danny, who was zipping up Tyson's body bag.

"Is it possible that someone could fake a heart attack?" I knew the answer, but I was curious to hear a medical opinion.

"Of course. A lot of drugs can induce a heart attack. Even some common medicines, if abused, can result in heart failure, especially if someone has a pre-existing heart condition." He pushed Tyson's body back into the refrigerator. The thought of his body packed away like meat made me sick again.

"We need to get to my father's place and check it out."

"Thank you." Jake shook Danny's hand again, and I followed suit.

I handed Danny a small scrap of paper I'd brought with me, just in case. "Here's the name and phone number for this man's sister. You might want to have her come and ID the body."

"Thank you. Sorry for your loss," Danny said, averting his eyes to the floor. I couldn't imagine his job—having to meet with families and give them the worst news of their lives.

"Thanks." Jake and I left the police station and made our way back to the Jeep.

"You ready to go to your father's?"

I sighed. I had to do it eventually. "I guess."

Jake turned on the radio. Country music, of course.

I glared at him. "Hell, no."

"Oh, come on. This is *real* music." He drummed his fingers on his knees and looked out the window.

"I don't want to hear about someone's broken truck and dog running away."

"At least my music has lyrics. Unlike that techno stuff you listen to."

"I don't listen to techno. It's called house music." I pulled out onto the road, joining the pack of cars on the busy street. "They sing, F.Y.I."

"Uh huh. Sure." He grinned at me.

"Man, I don't know how I put up with you in the past."

"Oh shit," Jake said a few minutes later.

173

"What?" I stopped at a red light and looked over at Jake, who was holding his phone.

"I just got hits on the photos of those guys you sent me." With a low voice he announced the names: "Andrei Belyakov and Oleg Konstantin."

I quickly reached for the music, turning it off. *"Konstantin?* As in Alexander Konstantin?"

"Oleg is Alexander's nephew—his brother's son. And Andrei is one of Alexander's hitmen." He tapped at his phone. "Tyson's murder has Russian mafia written all over it. It's a classic Russian hit—everything from the teeth and fingers to the Hudson River. And with you running into Oleg and Andrei at the gym yesterday—"

"It just seems suspect that Declan would ever introduce me to them." I paused, thinking back to the gym. "Well, they didn't exactly give me their names."

"You could be reading into that, but the fact that he's friends with these guys means he's probably connected to Alexander Konstantin."

"Declan mentioned making a deal with the Russians, but the Russian mafia wasn't the first thought that came to my mind when he said that." I gripped the steering wheel as the light changed. "Can Konstantin be the middle-man between Reid Enterprises and the Saudi deal? Is Konstantin even capable of creating that kind of connection in the Middle East?" Frustration pushed through me, knocking me off my game. It was a feeling I wasn't used to, and sure as hell didn't like.

"Konstantin could probably make the mayor of New York run in circles and sing damn opera if he wanted, but a deal with the Saudis?" He pulled his lips together in thought.

"This is getting complicated."

"Thank God I'm here to help you." He smirked at me and reached into his pocket and pulled out his black-rimmed glasses. "I've pulled up the rap sheets on Oleg and Andrei."

"And?"

"They've been in and out of jail for the last twelve years. But they rarely served longer than a few months. Most of the crimes were small. Just got out of jail recently, though. The both of them." Jake scratched his jaw. "Well, damn. I almost missed this. Nine and a half years ago, they were both accused of murder, but the case never made it to trial. Two people were killed at a club in the city —a bartender and Colin McGregor, the right-hand man of the McGregor crew, an Irish gang. The McGregors owned the bar, but —" He shifted in his seat and looked at me.

"What?" I pulled off to the side of the road, illegally parking so that I could focus.

"The club McGregor owned—you'll never guess who now owns it."

"I'm not great at guessing games."

"John Jackson and Declan Reid."

Everything went silent at that moment.

"Connor?" Jake snapped his fingers in front of my face.

"What's the name of the club?" I finally spoke, my voice breaking.

"The Wynn."

I rubbed my hands over my face. "The name of the bartender who was killed?"

"Jessie Scott."

21

OLIVIA

I WASN'T SURE WHAT TO DO, BUT I WAS PRETTY SURE ANDREI Belyakov was following me. When I saw him at the gym, I didn't think he recognized me, but the fact that he was tailing me must have meant that he, at least, had his suspicions.

But what could he prove?

I knew there was a chance I'd eventually come face to face with Andrei or Konstantin's nephew. They had only been out of jail since mid-April. The DA was always going after Konstantin and his crew, but he couldn't make the charges stick, or any sentences last longer than a year.

I ducked inside the subway train, popped in my earbuds, and pulled out my phone. I pretended to listen to music and read an eBook, hoping to seem unaware. Was it just a coincidence that Andrei was at the subway station? Boarding the same train as me?

I peeked up from my phone and glanced over my shoulder. I caught a glimpse of his large body, the tattoos spiraling down both his forearms. He was looking down at his phone and not at me. That was a good sign.

I hated Andrei, but it was Oleg who had pulled the trigger that night. Regardless of who took the shot, of course, Alexander

Konstantin was ultimately the one to blame. His marching orders had caused my sister's death.

I thought it would've been next to impossible to ever get on a case involving Konstantin, because of my past, but I had needed to do something. There were other men like him, and they had to be stopped. So as soon as I finished college, I applied to the FBI. When I discovered Blake, who I'd been sort-of dating, had been assigned to the case, I decided to stalk Konstantin and learn his behaviors and patterns.

I knew Konstantin was a boxing and MMA fan. He liked to party at clubs, particularly The Phoenix and out in Vegas. Loved gambling and women. When I realized there was a connection between Declan Reid and Konstantin, I presented my plan to Blake, but I struck a deal. Bring me in on the case for the information.

Okay, so I would've told him what I'd discovered even if he'd said no, but I had to try. I wanted to bring Konstantin down more than anything. And I thought if we targeted Declan we might have a chance at getting Konstantin. Then the skies opened with mercy on me as an admin position became available at Reid Enterprises, turning my idea into a reality.

Although Blake begrudgingly had agreed to my plan, he wanted my past to remain a secret from Sean, the only other member on the team. Blake had insisted to the director that our team needed to be small, to prevent any leaks. Too many people were on Konstantin's payroll—we had to be careful. No one other than our team and the director knew it.

At first, all I could think about was my chance to bring down Konstantin, the king of Brighton Beach, the man who'd caused Jessie's death. But as I got to know Declan more, I had hoped I'd be able to drag his ass to hell, too. I couldn't stand the man.

The doors to the subway opened, and when I looked up, Andrei was gone. I hadn't noticed where he got off. Perhaps his presence had only been a coincidence. I also didn't look anything like I did at the gym yesterday. I was dressed for work in a fitted gray skirt with silk blouse, and my hair was flat ironed, pin straight. Yesterday I had been a sweaty, make-up free mess.

I decided to stay on and ride the subway a little longer, varying up my routine. After exiting the subway, I hopped in a cab.

As the taxi pulled onto the Brooklyn Bridge, I peered at the bridge out the window, unable to take my eyes off the object as it loomed over the East River, linking the two boroughs.

My gaze pinned on its granite towers, and the web of wires and steel cables that poked the sky, arching and slanting in perfect symmetry to hold everything together. The bridge was secure. Stable.

I had to dislodge my heart from my throat when Connor had once told me about his escapades—one of them included bungee jumping off a bridge.

I caught a glimpse of the man I once knew when Connor dropped his guard with me this morning. He was definitely harder now. Steely. But if you cut through the many layers of Connor Matthews, you'd find the same twenty-two-year-old guy I'd met and fallen in love with.

Or thought I loved. I'd spent the last decade convincing myself I never really loved him after he abandoned me. But at this point, I had to call bullshit. We'd been in love. I just don't know how we went from love to him running off to join the Iraq War.

It was still difficult for me to picture fun loving Connor shooting a weapon. Killing someone.

"Here," the driver shouted, awakening me from my daze.

"I had to shower and get dressed for work before I came. Sorry," I said to Blake once I'd made it to our meeting place.

He shut the door behind me and followed me into the living room. I could feel his gaze on me, and when I turned around, I discovered I was right. He looked up from my legs and met my eyes. "We need to end this and soon."

Blake had been fine with the slow pace of the investigation up until recently, and now it appeared he'd lost his patience. I had to assume the fact that terrorists were now involved was the reason. "You talk to your friend in D.C.? Is Homeland or the CIA aware of the situation?"

"They're up to date. They'll be sending in reinforcements soon and specialists to help track the flow of weapons. Hopefully, we can take down some terrorist cells while bringing down the entire Russian New York mob."

Yeah, I just needed to figure out how to do it without hurting Connor. "I had a run-in with Andrei Belyakov and Oleg Konstantin yesterday." I squeezed my eyes shut, not wanting to see the reaction that would spring to his face.

His hand was on my arm and his breath on my face when I opened my eyes. "What?" His blue eyes grew dark, his pupils expanding.

I pulled my arm free from his grip and turned my back. "You have any coffee?" I escaped to the small kitchen, where the coffee pot was full and warm. Thankfully, Blake was like me—he drank coffee at all hours of the day.

"Olivia." He crossed his arms and leaned his hip against the counter in the kitchen, standing a few feet away while I made myself a cup.

"They were at the gym yesterday. I don't think they recognized me."

"Why didn't you tell me?"

"Because I was afraid you'd pull me from the case." I sipped my coffee and attempted to act nonchalant. Ha. Not possible.

"Damn right I'd take you off the case!" His arms dropped to his sides, and he shook his head. "Shit, Olivia. What if they made you?"

I knew I should also mention spotting Andrei at the subway, but I couldn't bring myself to do it. We were too close to bringing down Konstantin and Declan. If we could connect Konstantin to terrorism—to treason—no way he'd be able to wriggle out of that one.

"You were the one who identified them at the police station after your sister's murder."

"They didn't see me then. I was behind glass. And the case was never brought to trial, so they don't know me." Somehow, the case had been dropped due to police negligence. But I knew that was straight BS.

"They saw you at the club. You told me you charged Oleg like a damn bull and hit him in the chest, after what happened to your sister." He closed the gap between us, and I set my coffee down on the counter.

"Olivia." His hand touched my forearm. "This is exactly why I should never have agreed to let you on the case."

I started to shake my head like some bobblehead doll. "I was barely twenty when that happened. It was ages ago, and he didn't get a great look at me then. We were in a dark club. The second I ran up to him, the cops were on the place, and he took off."

"Yeah, missing his chance to kill you."

"We're getting close, Blake." I pulled my eyes up to meet his blue ones. "I'm actually glad Andrei and Oleg are out of jail. Now we can make sure they rot away for good when they're arrested." Not just on another one of their bullshit pseudo-sentences.

Blake stared at me, his eyes cold. I touched the counter with both hands, bracing myself. "If you're worried about Connor, don't be. He's a big boy. He can handle himself."

"How am I supposed to ensure the deal happens smoothly while also staying away from Connor like you ordered?" I pushed my hair to my back, frustration spearing me, my nerves wreaking havoc on my organs.

"I doubt Connor will bring his friend to the club, right? Regardless of what you think Connor's doing, he won't bring an FBI agent to The Phoenix." He shoved his fingers through his blonde hair and wrinkled his nose at me. "Make sure he's at the club tonight and agrees to sell the weapon to Declan. We can't waste any more time, especially now that Andrei and Oleg are in the mix."

* * *

Connor

I PULLED INTO MY FATHER'S PARKING GARAGE AND TURNED OFF THE engine. My brain was still spinning full throttle. Resting my hands on the steering wheel, I peeked at Jake from the corner of my eye. He was busy reading something on his phone.

"This is a bit hard to believe, don't you think?" Jake looked up from his phone, but my head now had that feeling of being at extreme altitudes, where your ears have a persistent, low-pitched ring inside. I couldn't think straight.

"Olivia would've been about twenty when her sister died. Would she have put such a long-term plot into place?"

Jake slipped his phone into his pocket and shifted to better look at me. "Anger doesn't have an expiration date. Maybe she stumbled upon the chance to go after these men while working for Declan."

I was shaking my head without realizing it. "No. Olivia's way too smart. There's no way any of this is a coincidence. She knows about Declan's connection to that club. She brought it up when we grabbed a bite to eat recently." I shut my eyes, trying to remember our conversation. Her olive skin had gone almost ghost white after she'd mentioned that the club where we'd first met was now owned by Declan. She'd been thinking about her sister—I just hadn't known about her sister's murder at the time.

"What?"

"I'm betting that Olivia has been after Andrei and Oleg for a while, but they've been protected by Konstantin or in and out of prison. She's on a revenge mission, and she targeted Declan to get to the mob." My eyes popped open, and I was sure the color was draining from my face.

Olivia was going to get herself killed. I knew if anyone had ever hurt Mason, I'd have done the same thing. But I would've been too impatient to wait for the right time to attack, like she clearly had. I'd want to ring my hands around the bastards' necks at the first chance.

Olivia could fight, though, and she was capable of firing a weapon without flinching. She'd been preparing, but there was no way Olivia could go up against Konstantin and his men. They'd crush her as soon as they found out who she really was.

"You're that sure Olivia is on a revenge mission?"

I reached for the door handle. "Hell, yes." I slid out of my Jeep.

"Why hasn't she been honest with you?"

I swung the door to the building open. "Maybe she thinks she can't trust me. She's worried I'll break her cover." I was afraid to tell her the truth, myself. I couldn't blame her, given the past we shared.

"You think she's doing this alone?" he asked as we entered the lobby.

"If she is, she's not alone anymore," I answered before my jaw clenched.

Jake held his hand out in front of me, stopping me a few feet away from the security desk. "We've been in these situations more times than I'd like to count."

My face pinched together. "Shit, I know. It's crazy."

"Alexander Konstantin," he said in a low voice as an elderly couple walked past us. "He's been chased by every federal agency, and they've all failed."

"*You've* never tried catching him, though, right?"

Jake grinned. "Hell, no. If I had tried, he'd be behind bars right now." He slapped me on the back.

This was what I needed. "Then let's take the son of a bitch down."

"Can I help you two gentlemen?" The security guard approached us. His appearance was a bit more Kris Kringle than an intimidating guard, with his white beard and hair, warm eyes, and full belly.

"My father lived here. Edward Matthews." I reached into my pocket and offered him identification before showing him the key to my father's home.

The man's face went long. "I'm so sorry for your loss. He was a good man."

Good man—my father? He must have had him confused with someone else, because my dad had never been kind to anyone in his life, unless it benefited him. "I haven't been to his home since he passed away."

The man nodded. "Of course."

"Do you know who found his body?" Jake asked, and both the security guard and I turned to face him. It was a little embarrassing that I didn't know the answer. I never asked Mason or the lawyer. My father never even made it to a hospital; he'd been pronounced dead by the medics in his house.

The security guard scratched his beard, and an awkwardness grew apparent in the lines of his leathered, aged skin. "His maid. I can't remember her name. Hold on, I'll check the list." The guard left us and walked over to his desk.

"We should have a talk with the maid and see if she knows anything," Jake suggested.

I crossed the lobby and approached the desk and pressed my palms to the counter. "Excuse me, sir? Can I get a list of all the approved visitors for my father? And do you keep a record of when people visit?"

The guard looked up from his computer screen. "We don't keep a record of visits, and for some reason, my computer is acting up. I'll try and get you the list when you come back down. My apologies."

"All right." I started to turn but stopped. "Sir, did you happen to notice anything out of the ordinary around the time of my father's death?"

The security guard clasped his hands together and brought them to his abdomen, and his eyes twitched a little. "I thought your father died of natural causes?"

"He did," Jake assured him, knowing we didn't want to ring any alarms. Even an aging security guard could be a potential spy. "Excuse us." Jake nudged me in the side with his elbow. "We should go up."

I gave the guard one last look and followed Jake over to the set of elevators. Once inside, I pressed the button for the thirty-fifth floor.

"I think that's the tenth time your phone has rang since you met me at the airport. You ever going to answer it?"

"It's just work."

"I take it this running-a-business thing isn't all that fascinating to you." Jake angled his head at me and fought back a smile. "You going to go back to your old life when Mason takes over the company?"

"If there's a company left for Mason to take over." I released the pent up air I held in my lungs. "I'm just glad I'm the one handling this and not Mason. Guess everything happens for a reason." God, Olivia would be alone in all of this if I wasn't involved. I had despised her for so long, and now . . .? I shirked off the thought of her in danger. The weight of the situation would crush me if I allowed it to hang. But what choice did I have? Our lives were now wrapped up in the same tragedy.

"Mason can handle himself, by the way. He's not just your kid brother, anymore," Jake commented as the doors opened.

The two penthouses sat on the top floor of the building. "3510." I motioned to the door with my head. "Mason can take care of himself. I know." I needed to stop treating him like he couldn't hold his own. He was a decorated officer in the Marine Corps, now.

"Has anyone been here since he passed?" Jake asked as I opened the door. He whistled as we entered the home.

We walked into the foyer, and my eyes darted to the ceiling. Light poked through the impressive domed ceiling of stained glass and bounced off the large mirror by the front door. We walked down a long hall, on what I assumed were marbled floors—I was never an expert at decorating—and we found our way to the living area. Olivia's apartment could fit inside the living room. "This place makes Michael's pad in Charlotte look small."

"Did he sell it yet?" Jake asked as he stuffed his hands in his pockets and looked out the wall of windows.

"I think so." I moved past the modern leather furniture, which couldn't have possibly been picked out by my father, and joined him at the window. "Nice view." I studied the tree tops of Central Park, which waved in the distance.

"It's a good thing your father's place is higher up than the buildings across the way. Anyone can see inside." He glanced at me over his shoulder.

"That's what these are for." I pointed up, and his eye caught sight of a long silver box that looked more like a steel beam than the hiding place for electronic blinds.

"You think you could get used to this life?"

I folded my arms and stared out the window. There were benefits to money, but I made a decent living doing what I enjoyed, and that type of money suited me just fine. I peeked over my shoulder at the lavish home—this kind of money was unnecessary, in my opinion. "You know me," I finally answered and looked at Jake. "I'd do better in a tent in the Amazon than here."

He laughed. "Sure. I can see that. But you grew up in New York. In this lifestyle, right?" He opened his hands palms up.

"People change."

He half-grunted. "I hear that."

"What we saw in the Middle East. What I've done . . ." I thought back to my recent case. Saving the girl in Mexico.

Keeping a family safe in Johannesburg, and before that, helping my friend Aiden's now-girlfriend. The list went on and on—a litany of moments that had severely altered my view on what really mattered.

"We should get started." I left the living room before Jake could speak and made my way up the black metal spiral staircase in search of the master bedroom. "Checking for his pills," I hollered out as I reached the top floor.

"I'll try and find the name and number of his maid," Jake shouted back.

I stopped just inside the entrance to the bedroom, and my hands dropped to my sides like dead weight. I cocked my head and stared at the canvases on the wall. Photos of Mason and I were displayed as works of art in a collage-style pattern above my father's four-poster bed headboard.

Black and white images. Mason and I laughing. Playing. Graduating high school. College.

What the hell? This wasn't like my father. He wasn't a sentimental person—he was cold, hard, calculating. He had been brutally honest with Mason and me as we grew up, always knocking us—okay, more often me—down for any mistakes. I'd strike out in Little League, and he'd yell at me. If I didn't make straight A's on one report card, I'd hear his wrath.

I couldn't ever do anything right. And he thought he was so damn perfect. It wasn't him that screwed up the marriage with my mother, after all. She'd been the cheater, the bad parent.

I swallowed and folded my arms, just staring at the images.

"Connor?"

I took a step back and turned around. "Huh?"

"I found a magnet on the fridge for a maid's service. I'm assuming it's the one he used."

"We should call," I said and pushed open the double doors that led to the master bath.

"Damn," was all Jake said when he entered the bathroom, which had enough open space to serve as a dancefloor.

There wasn't a medicine cabinet, so I started opening drawers. One drawer rattled as I opened it, three bottles rolling toward me. I picked them up and studied them. "Niacin, Lipitor, and Aspirin." I handed the half-empty bottles to Jake. "Like you said, they're probably legit, but we should have them analyzed, just in case."

I started to shut the door, but paused and pulled it back open. I picked up my father's hairbrush and cocked my head.

"What?" Jake shoved the bottles in his pants pockets and eyed the brush.

"Last time I checked, my father didn't have long, brown hair."

"Was your father seeing someone?"

"Looks that way. We really need that visitor list." I went downstairs and scoured the kitchen for a bag. We could run a DNA test on the hair.

After another long hour, Jake and I had managed to scavenge the entire place. We hadn't found anything out of the ordinary. If my father had information on Declan, Konstantin, or anyone else for that matter, it wasn't here.

Either my father didn't trust to keep information in his home, or someone had scraped the place clean. Probably the same someone who had him killed.

"You ready to call the maid?" Jake dialed the number on the magnet as we stood in the foyer. He pushed the speakerphone button, and the ringing echoed along the tall walls.

"Maids of Manhattan. This is Sarah, speaking."

"Hi, Sarah. I am trying to get ahold of whoever cleaned my father's place. Edward Matthews."

She didn't respond, but I knew she was still on the line. I could hear her breathing. "I—I worked for him." A muffled noise, and she said, "I'm so sorry for your loss."

"Was it you who found Edward's body?" I asked as Jake's brown eyes focused on mine.

"Yes. I found him," she answered with a shaky voice. "I'm so sorry," she said again.

"Sarah, I need to ask you a few questions. Is that okay?"

Her young voice sounded through the line, "Yeah."

"How long did you work for my father?"

"I only started cleaning for him a few months ago."

"Did you ever notice anything unusual? Or see him with anyone?"

"Um." She was hesitating. Why?

"Sarah?" I looked down at the phone.

"I only spoke with Mr. Matthews twice. Once when hired and one other time." Another pause. I was getting irritated. "I cleaned his place twice a week during the day. Once I was listening to music, and I had my headphones on, so I didn't hear anything when I first got there. I was in the process of carrying all my supplies in when I saw Mr. Matthews come into the living room. He wasn't wearing a shirt. Only dress pants, and a woman followed in after him, dressed in a robe."

My lips parted, but after finding the hair in the brush, I wasn't too surprised to hear about a woman. "What happened?"

"Mr. Matthews yelled for me to get out and come back the next day. I hurried away, and I didn't see him again until two weeks later when I discovered his body. I found him when I showed up Tuesday morning, the seventeenth. I heard the medics say he'd passed away the night before judging by, um, rig-a-mort-or-something." She released a loud breath; the sound crackled through the phone.

"What'd the woman look like?" I asked.

"Young. Brunette. Pretty. But I'd seen her before."

I exchanged looks with Jake, hoping for an ID.

"Your father had me meet him at his office when he first interviewed and hired me for the cleaning position, and she was there. I believe the woman worked there."

A pretty brunette from Matthews Tech. Had my father seriously been having an affair with Lauren Tate? God, no. I looked down at the floor, unable to think straight. I gripped my hair, pulling at it as he wrapped up the call.

"You okay?"

"I need to get out of here." I tossed the key to Jake to lock up and hurried out of the place before my pain suffocated me.

Jake caught up with me outside the elevator. "Any idea who she was talking about?"

I cursed beneath my breath. "Lauren Tate."

"You've got to be kidding me," he answered, a bit of Southern twang creeping into his voice.

We stepped into the elevator, and I pressed my hands to the mirrored back wall. "I wish I was kidding."

"You think he was sleeping with her?"

"She was in his robe," I said in a low voice while looking at Jake via the mirror. "God, the woman has come on to me, too." Chills rushed up my spine.

"Wow. I guess you were right about her. Women don't usually sleep with men three times their age unless they're after something."

"Yeah, and I'm thinking it wasn't his money." If only it were that simple. "I can't confront her about it. It'll just tip her and Declan off."

"Try and relax. I know this is hard to deal with, but we'll figure it out. I got your back."

We re-approached the security desk, but the man we'd spoken to previously was gone. "Excuse me?" I asked the younger gentleman sitting behind the computer screen. "Where's the guy who was here earlier?"

"He called me to come in for him. Said he wasn't feeling well." The younger guard straightened the lapels of his black jacket. "What can I do for you?"

I explained who I was and asked him for the visitor list. As he started tapping at the keys, I also asked if we could access video feeds of the cameras in the lobby.

"I'd have to talk to my supervisor, but I'm pretty sure that will require a warrant."

Damn.

"That's interesting," the guard said, looking up at me.

"What?" I folded my arms and studied the man.

"The visitor list of your father's is gone."

22

CONNOR

"WHEN I GET OUT OF HERE, I'M CALLING UP MY OLD GIRLFRIEND and proposing."

That's what my friend Jim said during my third year in the Marines. We had been sitting inside a crumbled building in Baghdad, which had been severely destroyed at the height of the Iraq War. The barely-there scrap of a roof was the only thing protecting us from the harsh rays of the sun.

My team had been sent in for ground support during a CIA op, which involved taking down one of the ringleaders of al Qaeda. My buddy and I had remained on lookout a hundred meters away as the black boot operatives had charged the building.

"Really? Why?" I shut one eye and focused through my scope.

"Because I should never have let her go to begin with—she was the one. Second chances are far and few between," he had answered. As I'd thought about what he'd said, my mind pulled up images of Olivia. For one long minute, a future with Olivia took root in my brain.

Then blood had sprayed my face.

I had pulled my friend against me and away from the window, holding my hand over his throat to stop the bleeding. When I'd realized there was no point, that he was gone, a fit of rage had consumed me. I grabbed my rifle and found the sniper peering out from a distant building.

Gunfire from inside the building that the CIA ops had entered popped loud in my ears as I shot the man. His body rocked back as my bullet smacked into his skull.

After the mission was complete, I went back for my friend. My body shook as I knelt over him. He'd never have his second chance, and I hadn't thought it possible to have mine. I thought the world wasn't big enough for Olivia and me to coexist.

But after being with Olivia again, I wondered if there'd ever be a world in which I could live without her.

"You find anything out?" Jake's voice shattered the memories of the past.

I chucked my keys on the entrance table and joined him in the living room of my rental home. "Here." I handed him a few files I had printed from my office computer and took a seat next to him on the couch.

He slipped his glasses on and flipped open the first manila folder before he shifted through the papers. "Financials?"

"As of last August, the company was in severe danger of either being bought out by a competitor or closing its doors. Declan and Lauren were correct when they told me the company would have been in serious trouble without the Saudi deal." I pinched the bridge of my nose. "The contract with the Saudis is directly with the Saudi Arabian government. It's legit, but Declan helped Matthews Tech win the bid."

"Which is corporate bribery—or espionage, if you will—but nothing earth-shattering." Jake looked up from the file. "This fits with Konstantin's MO."

"What do you mean?"

"Konstantin preys on financially weak businesses. Reid Enterprises was on the brink of collapsing when Declan took over. Konstantin stepped in and helped out, but only because Declan had something he wanted. I'm sure Konstantin uses Declan's clubs to launder money, sell drugs, and so forth. And the cargo shipments to and from the Middle East and abroad . . . Konstantin probably smuggles goods in them every once in a while," Jake explained.

"You think they targeted Matthews Tech because it was failing? They saw an opportunity to get into bed with a weapons and defense manufacturer?"

Jake nodded. "They needed to offer your father something big."

"There have also been ten sales transactions between Reid Enterprises and Matthews Tech," I admitted. "The last four of the shipments correlate with Tyson's flights abroad." I stood up and gripped the back of my neck with both hands. "I'm just wondering how Konstantin or Declan discovered my father opened the box to begin with."

"Andrei and Oleg were following him. Konstantin must have suspected something."

"How do you know?"

"I was scrubbing traffic cam footage and spotted Andrei and Oleg just outside Capital James Bank the day your father died. See here." He zoomed onto the video. I moved to the coffee table and leaned in toward the laptop. The same two men I'd seen at the gym were standing a few feet away from the bank entrance. "When your dad left the bank, they followed after him on foot. But I only have them on camera for about a block."

A sharp pain pinched my core as I watched my dad on the last day he'd been alive. I stood erect and turned away from the screen, trying to force back the sudden emotions that choked me.

"Both Andrei and Oleg were released from jail a few weeks before this. Konstantin didn't waste any time." Jake stood up and folded his arms across his chest, his brown eyes on me.

"You think they killed my dad, or did Lauren? She would've had the easiest access to his pill bottles." I still couldn't believe I was having a conversation about who killed my father.

"I'd bet it was Andrei and Oleg. We need to talk to the guard and access the video feeds from the lobby of your father's home. I can't get a warrant since this isn't an official investigation. I'll just have to access the security cameras the same way I did the bank and traffic cameras."

"Which is how?"

"Illegally."

"Takes being a criminal to catch one, huh?" I was surprised at my ability to joke at such a time. Then my thoughts shifted to Olivia. She was knee deep in all of this.

"What do you think we should do?" Jake walked over to the window and looked down onto the busy street, ten stories below.

"I'll have Declan set up a meeting with his associates—Konstantin will be there—then we'll get the safe deposit box open, and take them all down."

"And how do you propose we do that?" He spun around to face me as he jabbed his hands through his dirty blonde hair.

My lips twitched, and I smiled. "I think I have an idea."

23

OLIVIA

I DIDN'T KNOW FOR SURE IF CONNOR WAS COMING TO THE CLUB tonight, not until Declan had pulled me into his office.

I tapped my fingers on the bar and looked up at Bobby, who pressed his hands on the counter in front of me and angled his head to the side. "What's up, Olivia? You haven't been yourself lately."

The understatement of the year. "I'm just stressed. Working a lot." I averted my gaze to my hands. I had to raise my voice as the bass thumped louder.

Bobby reached across the bar and patted me on the shoulder. "You need to relieve some of that stress. Want to box tomorrow?"

Yes, but there was too much going on. "Customers," I said while nodding my head toward the two glamazon women who'd bellied up to the bar.

Bobby shot me a half smile and went to take the women's orders.

A new favorite song of mine blared through the speakers, and the remix had my shoulders instantly moving. The perfect tone of the man's voice sailed through the air, and I closed my eyes, not even fighting the heat that spread through my body as it raised the memory of Connor and me in bed.

Music was one of the most powerful memory delivery systems, which is why, up until recently, I'd steered clear of any music that would remind me of Connor, of Jessie, the baby . . . of everything I'd lost. But maybe I had been wrong to avoid it. It made me feel like a shot of adrenaline was zipping from limb to limb, opening my body.

Connor and I had never done drugs. We knew people who took pills at clubs or raves, but Connor was more raw and potent than any small white tablet could ever be. "You're my drug, Liv," he had whispered into my ear when we were at a club, dancing alongside the Mediterranean in Barcelona. After our time in Italy, we'd extended the trip by a week to pop over to Spain. We even spent a few days in Ibiza. It had been the best two weeks of my life.

I opened my eyes when a pair of hands touched both my bare shoulders. A ribbon of silky heat rushed through my body at his touch. I knew those hands. I wanted them on me. Everywhere.

"Connor," I said his name without turning around.

"How'd you know?"

I shut my eyes to his deep voice, remembering how he'd lain in my bed this morning. Exposed. So damn erotic. "How could I forget the way your hands feel on me?"

His warm breath was on my ear as he said, "Remember Ibiza?"

So the song had sent him up memory lane, as well. With my eyes still shut, I nodded. Unable to move. To breathe. A fire had started in my belly, and I wasn't sure if I'd ever be able to put it out.

We'd made love on the beach while the waves ate away at the sand.

I choked back the emotions that began to erode the happy memory—that was the night we'd gotten pregnant. I was almost positive. We hadn't been safe that night.

I was pretty sure the same thought sped to his mind, because his hands slipped free from my shoulders. I opened my eyes and stood up, turning to face him.

His hands were tucked in the pockets of his black slacks, and his chest moved slowly beneath a dark T-shirt. "We need to talk, Olivia. But first, I need a word with Declan."

Oh God, I didn't know what to do. I wanted to stop him, but I knew what it would mean if I did. "He's waiting for you," I said, instead. "Come on." I caught sight of Bobby stealing a glimpse of me, and I forced a smile.

"What time will you be done with work?"

"I can leave around one," I answered as we made our way down the hall.

"We can leave together?"

I wondered what he wanted to talk about. Did he regret what we had done? I wanted to regret it, but I couldn't bring myself to. The moments I'd spent in Connor's arms had silenced the pain.

"Connor." Declan popped out of his seat and motioned for us to enter. He was alone in his office, and I took notice of the fact that the two cages were missing. Did he finally decide to redecorate? Thank God.

Connor looked at me for a brief second, and there was something in his eyes—distress, maybe? I shut the door and followed him in.

Declan was standing in front of his desk with his arm extended. "Good to see you. We finally ready to make things official between our two companies?"

Connor rubbed a hand over his cheek before reaching into his pocket. "Here." He handed over a folded piece of paper.

That wasn't the contract. What was it? A rubbery nervousness had taken hold of my legs. I sat in the chair near where Declan and Connor stood and pressed my hands atop the skirt of my cream-colored dress.

Declan touched the black stubble on his jaw and stared down at the image in his hand. "I don't understand." He looked over at Connor.

"That's a shot of my father exiting the Capital James Bank in Manhattan. My father opened a safe deposit box the day he died." Connor rubbed his hands together before folding his arms across his chest.

What was going on? I straightened in my seat, gripping the arms of the chair, trying to steel myself.

Declan cocked his head.

"I think my father had planned on going to the Feds or blackmailing you. He clearly never had the chance, since he died of a heart attack."

Declan's mouth opened, and then he snapped it shut. He turned and walked around to sit in his chair. "Why would your father go to the Feds?" he said at last. "Or blackmail me?"

Connor remained standing. "More than likely, he planned on blackmailing you for a better business deal. My dad was a bit of a prick. I looked into the company's financials. You were right when you told me Mathews Tech was in trouble. If Lauren hadn't presented him with the Saudi opportunity—"

"Lauren? You're kidding, right? The only reason your old man hired her was for what was beneath her skirt. I came to your father with the deal—she's just benefiting from it."

I tried not to appear too eager about the details of the exchange, but my surprise over Connor's words had my eyes widening. I released my grip on the chair when I realized my knuckles were whitening.

"Okay, well, fine—had *you* not brought the deal to Matthews Tech, the doors would be closed now. But I'm guessing the way the contract was secured was illegal. And not just in a corporate bribery sort of way."

Declan's lips pinched together as he placed his clasped hands on his desk.

"Which is why I believe my father planned on screwing you.

Maybe he wanted to back out of the deal—hell, I don't know his intentions, but I think that there's something in that bank that could be detrimental to you."

What was he getting at? My mind raced, seeking the insight that would keep me one step ahead.

"I don't have access to the box—he didn't leave me the key. Guess he didn't trust me, either. I can have the court open it, though." Connor's arms remained crossed, his stance firm. "I'll give you whatever is in that box once it's opened. I don't need to see it."

"Why are you telling me this?" Declan was leaning back in his chair now, his hands on his stomach. He didn't look like he had a care in the world.

"I want to make this deal with a clean conscience. I don't want any lies or secrets hanging in the air. But I would like to make money. A lot of it."

"I thought you weren't planning on staying in charge?" Declan challenged.

Connor shrugged. "What can I say? Being rich has rubbed off on me. I'm not in the mood to give it up, yet."

Declan looked over at me, his dark eyes like knives. He didn't say a word.

"If you have the paperwork, I'm ready to sign. But as I mentioned, I don't want any secrets. I need to meet who I'm working with—*really* working with."

"That can be arranged." Declan's eyes switched to thin slits as his attention shifted back to Connor. "Tomorrow night. I'll let you know the location. But my associates will want proof of the weapon. Can you bring the prototype?"

Oh God, it was happening. The meeting. But I couldn't end the operation yet—I needed to track an actual shipment of weapons. And, apparently, I needed to get my hands on the box at Capital James Bank.

Had Edward Matthews been murdered? Connor must be

suspicious. How could he go through with this, especially knowing what he did?

"I'll get it," Connor coolly responded.

Declan was on his feet now. "Olivia, you can leave us alone for now."

No!

I nodded, and my knees trembled as I stood. Connor faced me, the muscle in his jaw ticking. What was his game?

"Save me a dance?" Connor asked.

What? Was he kidding? "Sure," I forced.

* * *

Connor

I SEARCHED THE CLUB FOR OLIVIA, BUT THE BARTENDER TOLD ME she was in her office. I went back down the hall I'd traveled before to get to Declan's, and kept going until I found her room. Her door was open and she was sitting behind her desk, staring at her laptop.

"Connor." She looked up from the screen, and her lips straightened. "Hi."

I shut the door behind me and moved to her desk. Her office wasn't nearly as large as Declan's. It was minimalistic, with two floor lamps and two black leather chairs parked in front of her desk. One picture donned the wall behind her: the club's logo, the phoenix rising from the flames.

I had tried so hard to forget Olivia, but how does anyone forget a woman like her? And she'd had my baby in her . . . But this wasn't the time to be thinking of that.

"We should talk."

Olivia was up on her feet and fast. "Not here," she said in a hushed voice.

Of course not. I looked down at my watch. It was half past twelve.

She stopped in front of me. Her eyes, a swirl of green and brown, locked on to mine. The neckline of her tight dress plunged low, offering me a swell of her soft flesh, and I had the urge to touch her collarbone and dip my hands lower.

"Let's dance." I needed to hold her. Move with her like we used too.

"I don't know," she said in a small voice as she looked down at the floor.

When I reached for her hand, our fingers lacing, she didn't protest. We moved down the hall, passing Declan's closed office door, and stepped out into the club, weaving through people and pushing through the cryogenic smoke.

The music hammered the room, sending vibrations through my body from head to toe.

Olivia led me up the spiral staircase, and with each step, my desire for her increased. My blood was pumping hard as we made our way to a more dimly lit dance area.

When she turned to face me, her eyes pinned me and my hand shot to her hip. I pulled her tight against me, and her lips touched mine. My cock grew painfully hard as my fingers slipped up under the silk of her dress.

I had to stop myself. I didn't want to draw another man's attention to her unfucking believable body.

But her hands were on mine, pulling them back until I was cupping her ass—over her dress, of course. Her command—the raw need of her gesture—had me so turned on that I thought I'd lose my mind.

We weren't dancing. Our bodies were grinding against each other. "We need to get the hell out of here," I said after tearing my lips from hers.

My eyes focused on her swollen pink lips, and I pulled her back to me without thinking. My tongue slammed hard inside her mouth, taking what was mine. What I'd been missing for years.

Breathless, she pulled away. "Connor," she said with a moan.

"Let's go." She held my hand again as we fought through the crowd. We rushed out onto the street, and I practically shoved my ticket at the valet.

With the New York buildings as a backdrop, I held her in my arms as we waited for my Jeep. I realized there was no turning back. How could there ever be? I'd never get enough of Olivia Scott—or Olivia Taylor, whatever she was calling herself.

She didn't know it, yet, but I would be her greatest ally in her revenge. And I wouldn't stop until I took down the damn Russian mob boss. I'd kill him with my bare hands if I had to. I'd lay him at Olivia's feet.

And when it was done, maybe—just maybe—we could roll around in the sand in Ibiza again.

24

OLIVIA

I'D LOST MY MIND. IT WAS OFFICIAL.

The man who had taken off and left me alone in the hospital after the loss of our baby was now someone I craved and wanted more than I wanted my revenge. How was that possible?

He moved his hand to my thigh, reaching for the silk of my panties. How was he going to drive a stick shift and—*oh God* . . .

His fingers slipped beneath the fabric, and he teased me with his touch. Then, just as quickly, his hand was back on the stick shift. "You're driving me crazy," he announced in a throaty voice.

"You're the one torturing me," I cried, shifting uncomfortably in the seat. My mind begged for a distraction. "I can't believe you still have this Jeep. You don't make enough money to buy a new car?" We'd made love in this car so many times.

"Despite some painful memories," I noticed his face grow hard for a brief moment, "I couldn't bring myself to get rid of it. It's in good shape. It was parked in a garage while I was in the Marines. And I'm always traveling around the world, so I rarely use it."

"Still, maybe it's time to upgrade," I teased.

He glanced at me out of the corner of his eye, and when he

spoke his voice was spiked with a serious dose of sexy deliciousness. "When I like something, I never let it go."

A flash of heat traveled back up my thighs, and I had to look out the window. My desire for him was at odds with the pain that lacerated me—the memory of him doing just the opposite of his promise. Of him leaving me.

I gulped and attempted to force the teeter-tottering of my emotions away.

The streets bustled with life, despite the late hour, and I blew out a breath as I stared out the window. Connor weaved in and out of cars, driving like the Jeep was a Ferrari. The sudden image of a shiny red rollercoaster popped into my mind as we neared my apartment.

I'd been on coasters before, despite a fear of heights, and I had become almost obsessed with them in the last ten years. I needed the feeling they gave.

As the coaster ascends the first steep arch, adrenaline pumps through you. The jerking motion propels you up, your stomach plays a game of kickball, and you wonder, *What am I thinking?* Then there's the moment of free fall. The wind slams in your face as you swoop down, the blood rushes to your ears, and you scream. It's hard not to when your body is faced with the terror of death.

But the rush . . . for those two minutes, you are more alive than ever.

Connor had once given me that rush. But unlike the roller coaster, he hadn't brought me safe back to earth. He'd crushed me, left me broken and alone. Until I felt like a shattered version of my former self.

I'd faced my fears after him. I sought out the tallest, most intense rides on the East Coast. I kicked my fear of height's ass. I even climbed that damn dangling rope in the gym at Quantico. And a surge of adrenaline and confidence wrapped me in a warm embrace with each little victory. But no amount of energy that coursed through my veins ever came close to manifesting the feeling that two little minutes with Connor Matthews once gave me.

I covered my face with my hands.

"What's wrong?" He parallel parked outside my building. "Olivia, are you okay?"

My shoulders flinched, and my eyes landed on his. "I'm fine."

Connor's hand was on top of mine, and I stared down at it, blinking a few times. "Let's go." I pulled my hand free and went for my buckle.

He offered me the gift of silence as we made our way to my apartment, but the tension mounted with each step we took. My body betrayed me as I ached to be touched by him again.

Once inside, I dropped my purse and keys to the floor and spun to face him. I wasn't sure if I wanted to scream at him or shove my hands in his hair.

"Olivia." He grazed his knuckles across my cheek. "You ready to talk?" Gone was any hint of sexuality.

I lowered my head and took a step back, and his hand fell to his side. "About?"

"I think you know what about." He angled his head as his brows pulled together, belying the heated moments we'd shared at the club and in the car.

"Did you sign the contract?" I sputtered.

"I did." He brushed past me and entered the living room.

"Do you think they murdered your father?" I whispered.

I shouldn't have asked that.

He jabbed his hands through his hair, messing it up, and shook his head. "Does it matter?"

Of course it mattered. How could he ask me that? "Connor, if Declan had anything to do with your dad's death, how can you join forces with him? Your dad was a horrible man, but he didn't deserve to die." I rubbed my arms, not sure what I was attempting, or why.

The crease in his forehead deepened, and he observed me like he would a hurt animal, whimpering on the ground for help. "Olivia."

"If your dad was murdered because of his relations with Reid Enterprises, how do you know that you're not next?" Okay, so I was breaking the rules, but I had to. "You're smarter than that."

"I thought you wanted me to work with Declan. You've been pushing that, right? I mean, sometimes you gave me pause, but for the most part you've encouraged me to meet with him." He stepped around the coffee table and closed in on me. "Am I mistaken?"

I gritted my teeth and tried to hold back the truth.

"Liv."

My desire to protect him was too strong. "You can't do this, Connor. Please, don't do this," I pleaded, surprised by the desperation in my voice.

In one quick movement, I was back in Connor's arms, and he was kissing me. Stealing the breath from me.

My hands pressed against his chest, and I pulled back to look up at him.

"I was beginning to worry you didn't care." His heart pounded beneath my palms as he stared down at me.

My head spun as I wondered how much he knew.

He leaned in and whispered into my ear, "If you go after Konstantin alone, you're going to get yourself killed."

Konstantin. He knew. Oh my God, how did he know? "What are you talking about?"

"Stop, Liv. Stop lying." He stepped away from me and walked into my kitchen. I assumed he was getting a drink to cool himself off.

When he returned with two beers, I took a bottle from him and braced it with both hands like a lifeline.

"Why didn't you tell me that the men responsible for Jessie's death were in league with Declan?" He brought the beer to his lips and crossed the room to the bay window. "Shit, Olivia. Is this really your plan—to infiltrate the Russian mafia? If anyone discovers who you are, you'll end up in the damn Hudson."

Defeated, my eyes widened, and I set the bottle on the coffee table. "How long have you known?"

"Today. I've been trying to put all the pieces together." He turned to face me. "I think my dad was suspicious of Declan and had his driver look into Reid Enterprises. After my dad opened the safe deposit box, he died, and his driver was killed and dumped in the river. Typical Russian hit." He blinked a few times as if in disbelief at the sound of his words. "Can you imagine what they'd do to you if they found out who you are?"

"I can handle myself." I moved away from him, unable to look at him any longer.

"Revenge is a dangerous game. I don't know how you've managed to pull this off, or what made you think you could take down Alexander Konstantin, but you can't do it alone." Connor's jaw ticked. He expected to protect *me*? It was absurd. I'd been dancing around with the idea of how I'd keep him out of jail.

I twisted back around, my eyes burning, my hands fisting at my sides. "You signed the contract! You made a deal with the bastard. Why?"

He dragged his hands down his face, holding them at his chin for a moment. "Olivia." He paused, his eyes on me, "I did it for you."

"What?" I blanched. "What are you talking about?"

Connor took a seat on the couch, set his bottle on the table, and looked up at me. "Declan needed to trust me, so I gave him a reason to. Now he not only trusts me, but he's set up the meeting with Konstantin." He rolled his shoulders back, loosening his apparent tension. "If I don't do the deal with Declan, we won't be able to capture the SOBs."

Oh my God. This was what I had wanted. And I had told Blake that Connor could help us. Thank God he had figured it out for himself.

Well, some of it.

Connor still didn't know who I really worked for. Did it matter? I felt queasy as I contemplated shedding my cover.

"How long have you been plotting? What do you know?"

I grabbed my drink, allowing the liquid to cool my insides as I swallowed. Holding the bottle to my chest, I studied Connor, wondering what to say. Should I keep the truth buried? Would he be safer in the dark?

Probably not. He was already a part of this, and now he was offering me a chance to catch everyone. Was it fate that Connor had walked back into my life right when I needed him?

"Connor." I took a step closer to the couch, and my eyes drifted to his thighs, the hard muscles evident even beneath the thin black pants he wore. "When Jessie died, I almost died with her. It was too much to handle."

He leaned back into the couch, but his face remained expressionless.

I sank onto the couch next to him but kept a few inches between us. I shifted to face him, but my hands trembled in my lap.

His hands came down over mine, grounding me. "When the men who killed Jessie were dismissed on some crazy technicality —basically, Konstantin paid someone off—it fired me up." I shut my eyes, and his grip tightened. "I was so angry. I made it my mission in life to take Konstantin down."

"You're patient. I wouldn't have been able to wait." His hand was now on my forearm, and his fingers ran up and down my skin. It was comforting to have someone in my corner, after all this time. Blake and Sean had my back, but this was different. "How does Declan fit into all of this?"

"I learned of their connection when studying Konstantin. He bailed out Reid Enterprises three years ago. He revived Declan's businesses, including The Phoenix and The Wynn, Jessie's club —*our* club." My lungs filled with air as I tried to calm myself, but I caught a scent of Connor's cologne, and it left me lightheaded.

"And?" His eyes claimed mine.

"Declan partnered with that Russian fighter John Jackson, who is a member of Konstantin's close circle of scumbags. Konstantin ponied up money for all of his clubs and restaurants, including the newest one in Vegas. So, I decided to go after Konstantin from a different route, through Declan."

"Wow. This is nuts, Liv." He smoothed a hand across his jaw. "I had my friend Ben look into Declan, but he came up empty."

I sorted through the file cabinet of facts that I had tucked away in my brain. "Konstantin is a silent investor in all of Declan's clubs. Under the table money. The only one on the books is the fighter." I rolled my neck, tension torturing my body. "There's a reason why Ben couldn't find anything. Konstantin keeps his associations under lock and key."

"But you figured it out?" His head tilted and brows slanted. "Why'd you keep me in the dark so long?" He removed his hands from me and stood back up.

"I didn't know if I could trust you. We weren't on the best of terms until the other night, so I . . . held back."

His shoulder blades pinched together, and he massaged the back of his neck. "You warned me tonight, because—what? We slept together? If we hadn't, would you have kept me in the dark and let me go down with Declan and Konstantin? Or worse, let me find out when it was too late, when Konstantin had already pegged you . . ."

I realized it wasn't rage. He was worried about me. "Connor, I'm so sorry." At least I was apologizing about something I'd actually done this time.

Facing me now, there was a familiar glint in his eye. "Let me take care of Declan. And Konstantin. I have a friend in the FBI who came to help me. It's not an official investigation, but I think it's safer to take these guys down off the books."

FBI. The three letters I was still keeping from him, and I wasn't sure why.

"You never know who Konstantin has in his pocket. Let my friend and I do this. Quit your job. Go somewhere safe until this blows over. I have friends who can protect you."

I laughed. Not a real laugh—a sarcastic, are-you-kidding-me, slightly hysterical laugh. I stood up until we were standing just inches apart. "Even if I wanted to run, Konstantin would find me. He'd make me disappear. The only reason I didn't wind up in the Hudson after Jessie died is because the case never made it to trial. If it had, I would have vanished. You and I both know that."

Connor wrapped his large hands over my forearms and leaned in close. "Then what the hell are you thinking, getting involved in this? Do you have a death wish?"

Yes.

Maybe.

I was an FBI agent, but that didn't mean I was immune to Konstantin. I hadn't thought about what would happen once I captured him, but now I knew he was making deals with terrorists. Perhaps Homeland and the CIA could put Konstantin in some dark cell and throw away the key. I wanted an island of scorpions, snakes, and other creepy crawly things reserved for him.

He'd gotten off the hook when he had my sister murdered, but a man who dealt with terrorists? That was treason.

My lips twitched at the thought.

"Olivia?" Connor snapped my attention back.

"What?" I couldn't help but shriek as I channeled the rage that had curled up inside me for so many long years.

"I'm not going to lose you again." The deep timber of his voice shook me.

It took me a moment to process his words. "You left me, Connor," I said slowly. "Remember? There's nothing to lose." A red hot flare of anger burst through my system, and I stepped back, but he imprisoned me with his gaze.

His mouth tightened and his breath hitched as the sweet spell of lust blustered down my neck, diving deep into my stomach.

I almost lost my footing as he came at me full throttle. I stumbled back, and he pinned me against the window with his body. His hands held my face as he pulled my lips against his.

An intense heat lit my core with the familiar spike of adrenaline.

He nipped at my lip, pulled back, and his green eyes bore into me. "Do you want me to stop?" he said in a half-groan, half-growl.

I felt his hard length strained by the fabric of his slacks, and instead of vocalizing my answer, my hand slipped down to touch him. He dropped his hands to hold my waist and leaned into me. He nuzzled my neck as I unzipped his pants and tucked my hand inside, working through the opening of his boxers.

"Liv." My name was a moan on his lips as he lightly bit my bare shoulder.

His hands were on my back now, working fast at my zipper.

I wasn't sure how we had ended up here again, but we were both burning with need.

"The window," he whispered. "I'd prefer to keep your incredible body to myself."

I released my hold, and he fastened his fingers with mine, tugging me to my bedroom. My unzipped dress fell into a puddle at my feet.

He stood in front of me. "You're so damn beautiful."

I was down to a nude demi bra, panties, and high heels only; my confidence was supercharged beneath his heated gaze. I pushed my thick hair off my shoulders, and it settled at the small of my back.

He closed the gap between us, and I fisted his shirt with my hand and pulled him to me. The back of my thighs brushed up against my bed, and my lips locked with his for a long kiss.

He braced me with one hand, and his fingers dipped inside my panties. "You're still wet," he said before his lips traveled to my neck. His fingers torched my skin as he graced my sensitive area with slow movements. Gripping his shoulders, I clung to his body, fighting the pull of impending orgasm.

"Not yet." A smile teased his lips, and he gently nudged me to have a seat on the bed. I lifted my foot, prepared to remove my heels, but he placed a hand over mine, stopping me. "Keep them on."

His heavy-lidded eyes drew me in. My heart fluttered, beating like a bird's wings against the cage. I wanted to rip my bra and panties from my body and bask beneath his stare. "Fuck me, Connor."

He removed his T-shirt, then freed himself of the rest. There was something so raw and carnal about Connor standing naked before me, his cock hard in his hand. "Olivia."

"Yeah?"

"I want to make you mine again."

* * *

Connor

"Wн—"

I didn't let her finish. I kissed away her words and held her hard against me, needing her more now than ever before.

The storm of emotions that had funneled inside me, circling round and damn round, making me Goddamn dizzy at times, had been unleashed tonight.

I. Needed. Her.

It was as simple as that.

There was no way I'd run this time. I wouldn't get it wrong again.

How had I spent almost ten years hating the one person on earth who knew me better than anyone? I'd been an idiot to think of her as a youthful fling, as a mistake of lust. She was the only woman I'd ever loved.

My hands wandered over her body before shifting her back onto the bed. I wanted to touch her everywhere, to feel every part of her. The need clawed at me from the inside.

"Take off your panties and bra." I stood over her, watching her perfect, tight body obey. Her eyes were focused on my chest, and they barreled down my body and drifted back up again.

Then, wearing only her heels, she was propped up on her elbows, waiting for me.

I touched her ankle and leaned in over her, tracing my fingers up her legs before grasping her hips. She gasped as I flipped her over and onto her stomach.

Her back arched and her firm, perfect ass called out to me. "Fuck." I got into the bed next to her, running my hand down her back. Then my hands slipped under her and to her deliciously wet center.

I repositioned myself so that my mouth could find where my hand had been.

She was gripping the comforter; her face buried as she jerked and started to move in rhythm with my flickering tongue.

She rocked into her release, and I savored the moment before gently rolling her back over. Her pink nipples were erect; my body was hard and aching for her.

"My turn." She started to sit up, but I shook my head and motioned for her to lie back down.

"I'm not nearly through yet. I plan on making you come until you're begging for me to stop." I knelt over her once again, teasing her nipple with one hand while sucking the other.

Her hand tore through my hair, and wild Olivia was back again, writhing beneath me.

An hour later, her sweet voice filled my ears as we both lay, breathless, on our backs. "You've gotten better with age."

I glanced over at her out of the corner of my eye. "So I didn't do it for you back then, huh?" I joked.

"You didn't do number five on the menu, then," she teased, and her eyes lit as her lips curved into a mischievous smile.

Italy. God love her. "Men get better with age. Women, on the other hand . . ."

She slapped my chest. "Don't you dare finish."

I smoothed a hand over my jaw and pinched my brows together. "Be careful."

"What? Why?"

I reached for her hand and slid it beneath the covers. "Your bossiness turns me on."

"Do your batteries ever run out?" Her fingers traveled up to my chest, and I pressed my palm over her hand.

"I hope not. I need the energy to keep up with you."

"I learned from the best."

My jaw tightened, and I couldn't help but grimace. Ten years of absence meant other men had the chance to—*stop!* I left her. I was the idiot.

I'd hoped to wait until the Declan issue was resolved, but we were getting so close. We had to discuss why I left, because I knew —hoped—that I'd been wrong.

But if I was wrong, how could an apology ever make up for it?

"Olivia, I want to talk about the baby." Silence greeted me. "Olivia?"

A light sound escaped from her nose. She was sleeping.

I squeezed my eyes shut, wondering how we would face the harsh light of the day. Would I be able to convince her that she was in way over her head with Declan and Konstantin?

Not when she'd spent nine years masterminding this plan to take down the Russian king of New York.

If my plan worked, though, it would all be over soon.

And if it didn't work, well, we might all end up dead.

I tried sleeping, but the stress and worry ate at me, keeping my eyelids parted for the few hours until dawn. I brushed my lips over her shoulder and pulled her close to me.

"Mm. Connor." Her eyes slowly opened, and she blinked a few times. "You're still here."

"Of course I'm still here."

"So it wasn't a dream?" Her eyes closed and she pulled tight against me, her cheek pressing against my chest.

"The sex?" I laughed.

"No." She forced her eyes back open. "The part where you know the truth? You know who I am."

I kissed the top of her head. "I know, Liv. And I'm going to help you. Don't worry."

Before she could respond, she jolted at what sounded like an animal dying from the other room.

"What the hell is that?"

She scowled. "It's the sound I assigned to Declan on my phone for when he texts me. High-pitched and annoying." She shifted away from me, pushed off the covers, and got up out of bed. "Wonder what he wants this early."

I watched her walk naked, her long tan legs carrying her to the other room. Not a hint of modesty. What a woman.

"What is it?" I stood up when she came back into the room, her face long and concern pinching the corners of her eyes.

"He needs to see me."

"No," I snapped.

She set her phone on top of her dresser and opened a drawer. I couldn't take my eyes off her as she stepped into a pair of pink silk underwear.

I just wanted to take them back off, pull her into bed, and pretend we were the only people who existed.

"Connor." She snapped on her matching pink bra and came at me. "I have to go. I can't raise any red flags by not meeting him."

"Let me handle this."

Her head lowered, and she stared down at my hand, which was now holding hers. "You can help me Connor, but I'm involved."

Of course. I knew I'd never change her mind. "Fine." At least she was willing to let me help.

"There's more we should talk about. Where will you be after I meet with Declan?" Stress and worry pulled at her smooth skin, and her mouth went tight.

I groaned, wishing I could lift her worries away. "Chasing some leads. Call me when you're done, and we can get together." My knuckles grazed her cheek, and she leaned into my touch. "We'll get through this."

Her body shuddered against me. "When this is over, things might be rough for a while. I'm not sure if we'll be able to—" She silenced herself.

I knew what she wanted to say, and I didn't want to hear it. "One day at a time, Liv." A lung full of air. Another deep breath. "One day at a time," I repeated.

25

CONNOR

"A text would've been nice, man. I had to track your phone to make sure you weren't in the bottom of the river." Jake waved his hand in the air in front of me.

"You tracked my phone?" Shock popped through my words. "For real?"

"Of course." A devious grin spread across his face. "While you were doing . . . whatever it was you were doing . . . I managed to get some results."

I fought back a smile and joined him in my kitchen.

"You want to change your clothes first?" His brow arched as he put on his glasses.

I glanced down at my wrinkled clothes, which still smelled of flowers and vanilla. I probably should've changed, because if I continued to inhale Olivia's sweet scent, I'd get distracted by thoughts of her.

"Dude."

"What?" I poured a mug of coffee and crossed the room to the bar top, which doubled as my kitchen table. "What is this?"

Jake handed me his iPad. "Andrei and Oleg in the lobby of

your father's home on May sixteenth. An hour after your father left the bank."

"Where was my dad?"

"He was there. I caught him and Tyson on the cameras just outside the building ten minutes before Andrei and Oleg showed up. They were arguing, and he handed Tyson something. Probably the envelopes."

"Shit." He probably knew he was about to die.

"How did Andrei and Oleg get up to my dad's place?"

Jake grimaced. "That grandfather security guard." Jake paused the video footage and expanded the image with his fingers, zooming in on the men as they talked to the security guard.

I rubbed a hand through my hair and set my black coffee down. "Shit."

"We should have a word with him."

I nodded. "So these guys killed my father, not Lauren. I'm assuming they didn't switch his pills, then."

"Most likely injected him with something to induce the heart attack." Jake reached for the iPad and steadied his eyes on mine. "I'm sorry. Since no one found him until the next day, he didn't have a chance."

"But there was obviously no sign of struggle. The medics would have noticed if the place was wrecked." I sank on a barstool and scratched my head, thinking.

"Which means he knew them. Maybe even opened the door and let them in."

Wow. "I'm still not sure if Lauren's off the hook. She's hiding something."

"I don't know, Connor. I did some more digging on her." He tapped at his iPad again and set it before me.

"After I saw that video footage, it made me curious about Lauren's involvement. I tried something I didn't try before."

"Which was?"

"Google and social media."

I almost laughed, but none of this was funny. "What'd you find out?" I glanced down at the screen. Images of Lauren on the arms of various men. A widowed Congressman, a rich oil tycoon, and a wall street millionaire. All with two things in common: they were old and rich.

"I tapped into her Instagram and Facebook accounts and discovered pictures with these guys. Looks like she has a thing for older men with deep pockets. She's been dating powerful men since she was nineteen."

"So my dad hired her for her looks, and they hooked up? I find that hard to believe." I pressed my hands to my face and released what sounded like a growl. Frustration tore at me, making my skin itch.

"She's not innocent by any means. I think she's a career opportunist. She landed internships with all three men she dated before your father—well, I should say she worked as an intern before she dated those men. I'm sure she was more than eager for the deal with Reid Enterprises—it would make your father even richer and give her better job security, at the least."

I pushed back to my feet as nervous energy spiraled around the cords of my muscles. "What about the accent?" I shook my head. "No, she has to be involved with Declan."

"Hell, I'm sure she was sleeping with him, but there's an explanation for that, too."

I stopped wearing out the kitchen floor and leaned my back against the counter. "Enlighten me."

"Lauren was adopted."

My forehead scrunched as surprise billowed inside me.

"She was born in the Ukraine. She lost both of her parents when she was six. She lived in an orphanage for a year before she was adopted by a family in New York. I missed it before, because the records were sealed. I had to call in a favor."

I leaned forward, angling my head. "Who?"

"Ava."

Jesus. Ava was the girlfriend of my Irish-American friend, Aiden. She was brilliant, almost putting our intelligence genius friend, Michael Maddox to shame. "You had Ava hack into Lauren's records? She didn't mind?" My hands crossed over my chest.

Jake removed his glasses. "You didn't want me dragging Michael into this, but you didn't say anything about Aiden. And we both know Ava would do anything to help you. You were there for her not too long ago."

I exhaled a breath out of my nose and shut my eyes. I needed to think. "Lauren's embarrassed of her origins? So she hid her adoption and accent?" I could see that, I guess. "She's still not off the hook, in my mind." I opened my eyes and rubbed a hand over my jaw. "The deal's happening with Declan tonight. I should be meeting Konstantin."

"You're just now telling me that?" He flashed me his white teeth. "Guess he took the bait."

"And he wants me to bring the EMF gun, of course. I'm still waiting for him to let me know the location of the meet."

"We have a lot to do, then. I also want to swing by the security guard's home. And I'm still working on your father's personal laptop and files."

I'd brought my father's laptop home from the office yesterday, although I hadn't expected he'd find anything of help. It was worth a shot. "All right. Well, let me shower and we'll get going. We need to stop at my office first, though."

As I hopped into the shower, a slow pull of dread buried deep inside me. I needed to call Olivia. Was she okay? I couldn't stand the idea that she was with Declan right now.

* * *

Olivia

"Is Sean back yet?" I was sitting in my Audi in the parking garage near the boxing gym.

"Still in D.C.," Blake answered, a pinch of annoyance in his voice.

"The deal is going to happen tonight. You should alert Homeland."

"Connor made the deal?" I could almost picture Blake's lips curving into a grin with glee.

I wasn't sure how much I wanted to tell him. I knew how he felt about me telling Connor the truth, but he needed to know that Connor was on our side. I didn't want Connor winding up arrested in all of this.

My stomach turned at the thought. "He made the deal, but—"

"I don't want to hear it, Liv."

I leaned back against my seat. "We can talk later. Declan wants to see me right now." I powered off my phone before he could respond. I was tempted to add Blake to my shit list, although he'd rank well below Konstantin and Declan. I wasn't sure if he was being jealous, or was just out for blood.

I no longer cared if Blake disagreed with my decision, I didn't want any lies wedged between Connor and I. I wanted to erase the pain of my past, rather than bury it. Something buried could be dug up again.

I massaged my neck, trying to rid myself of the sharp, stabbing pain that greeted my spine. After allowing myself a few moments of silence coupled with delicious images of Connor naked, I exited the Audi.

I rubbed my arms as a chill rocked my body. I wasn't cold. The sun was finally blasting its warm heat after several days of rain. The fat raindrops that had been splattering across the city on and off all week had served as a reminder to me that I was in the middle of a storm.

With the sun out today, and the sky a canvas of miles of blue— I wondered if it was a sign that the end was near.

I stopped outside the frosted glass doors of the gym and read the sign. "What the hell?" Since when was the gym closed on a Friday?

I blew out a breath and dialed up Declan. "I'm here," I said when he answered. "But the gym's closed."

"Use the side entrance," he brusquely responded before hanging up.

I stalked down the busy street with slow steps and rounded the corner into the alley. The passageway was narrow, and the smell of tuna and something rotten blasted my senses as I closed the gap between me and the door.

My hand touched the doorknob, but I had to force myself to turn it. My body grew tense as concern flickered through me. *Don't go in.*

But I had nothing to worry about, right?

I swung open the door and moved inside the empty boxing gym.

"Glad you could make it." I heard Declan before I saw him.

I stiffened as his tall, lithe body entered the room. The fluorescent lights above me turned on as he moved closer. I remained still, just inside the door.

It wasn't too late. I could turn and run.

He was dressed in black sweats and nothing else, his naked chest and rippled flesh serving as a reminder that, no matter how tough I was, it would only take one strong punch from him to take me down.

"What's up, Declan?" I crossed my arms over my yellow T-shirt, irritation and anxiety spearing me.

He kept walking until he was within arm's reach. His dark eyes caged me in his gaze, and I took a shaky breath.

The back of his hand brushed against my cheek, and my knuckles whitened at my sides. My jaw clenched, but my eyes grew still under his spell. I couldn't say anything as he touched the pad of his thumb to his own lips.

He whispered, "I called to collect my raincheck."

I shook myself free of my daze. "What?"

He took a step back, allowing me room to breathe.

"You promised me a fight."

"Oh." *Ohh* . . . "Now?" I gulped. No one knew I was here. I'd thought we were meeting at The Phoenix, and when he'd texted me to come to the gym, I'd assumed it would be full of people.

"Change." There was a sharp bite to his word that made it an order, rather than a request. I didn't appreciate commands, but I also didn't want to piss off Declan. I was too close to ending this.

I glanced down at my jeans and sandals.

"You keep clothes in the locker room, right?" He sensed my hesitation.

Shit. "Yes." I gathered my strength to speak again. "Is there a reason you feel like throwing punches at me right now?" I slipped a smile to my face, forcing myself back into the role I'd been playing for so long.

My dark hair whirled around to my back, and I straightened as he turned away from me. I watched the angel wings on his back as he crossed the room, which housed one professional-sized boxing ring and two small, side-fighting rings. "I also wanted to talk to you about business, and I thought we could make it more interesting."

"Sure. I'll just change."

"You can leave your purse here. I don't want you getting the urge to play around with your phone." His eyes darted to mine once I glanced over my shoulder at him. "I don't have much time."

My heart raced, but I obeyed and dropped my purse on the closest bench.

As I made my way out to the main gym, all of my training screamed: *He knows something. Get the hell out!*

I couldn't leave, though. I couldn't risk everything I'd worked so hard for, just because my inner voice was a coward.

My eyes landed on the main entrance just as I pressed against the locker room door. The main door required a key to enter or exit when it was locked. The only way out was the way in which I had come. Even if I wanted to run, I couldn't.

A lungful of air, which poisoned my nose with the pungent smell of feet and sweat, did nothing to calm me as I pushed inside.

I peeled the clothes from my body and grabbed the set of extra gym clothes I kept on hand. My hands trembled as I dressed in tight black pants, a white tank top, and pink sneakers.

I'd been wanting to hit Declan in the face since the day we met. I'd never forget the first time I interviewed with him. I attempted to use sex appeal in order to get the notorious playboy to hire me. I would never stoop so low as to use my appearance to get a job, but to maintain my cover was another thing entirely.

With a resume perfected by the FBI, I had carried myself with confidence into Declan's office. "I'm Olivia Taylor, your next assistant," were the first words that fell from my mouth. "I throw a killer left hook, work a minimum of ten hours a day, and I do what it takes to get the job done. You need me."

Declan had looked up from his computer screen to find me standing just inside his office. His eyes traveled from my silk blouse down to the hem of my tight black skirt, and lower. The way his eyes burned my flesh—the devious thoughts I knew lurked beneath the surface—blossomed in me an instant distaste. I had meant what I said about the left hook, but then I wanted to add, "I'd love to use it on you now."

His lips had twitched, and his smooth, deep voice skated over my skin, giving me the chills. "You're hired, Miss Taylor."

I'd been in shock, but when he explained I was the most qualified candidate, I thanked God the FBI had done wonders with my resume.

"You can do this," I whispered to myself, studying my image in the mirror. I swept my hair into a ponytail, cleared my mind, and moved with slow steps back to the boxing area.

As I opened the door, my heart stopped.

Andrei and Oleg were standing next to Declan, and they were staring right at me. The dynamic murderous duo. I thought about turning around and attempting an escape.

My eyes darted to the side door, through which I had entered. Could I make it in time if I sprinted?

"Olivia, I invited two buddies of mine here, as well."

"Good to see you again," Oleg's deep Russian voice carried heavy across the room and splattered against me like paint.

What did he mean? Good to see me after meeting for the first time this week, or good to see me again as in, "I killed your sister, and I recognize you."

"Hi." That was all I could muster. I realized I was standing just in front of the double doors. A statue.

"I mentioned to Oleg and Andrei, here, that you like to spar," Declan said as I finally started to move.

Oleg and Andrei's eyes remained on mine as I approached. Oleg was taller and more muscular than Declan. He had bleached blonde, spiky hair and red, gold, and black ink scrawling from his fingers up to his throat and hairline. Religious tattoos, no less. His sharp nose twitched, and his faded blue eyes widened as I stopped in front of him.

Andrei was practically a mirror image of Oleg, but with brown hair.

"Why's the gym closed?" I ignored his earlier comment.

"I have business here today." Declan pulled himself up into the fighting ring.

"What kind of business?" I asked, unable to stop myself.

Declan motioned for Andrei to join him. "Are you two fighting?" I asked.

"No, you two are."

Andrei crossed his arms and smirked at me.

"Andrei's never fought a woman before. He doesn't believe a woman can take him on." Declan smiled at me. The man had the nerve to smirk! A spark roared to life. I moved past Andrei and ducked under the rope. "You really want at me first?" I tried to make light, despite the anger that barreled inside me.

"I'll take it easy on you, sweetheart," Andrei said. He removed his T-shirt to reveal even more tattoos. His chest was a shrine to Catholic holy figures.

I was pretty sure that even such devotion couldn't save his soul.

Declan grabbed two sets of gloves and tossed a pair at both Andrei and me.

My eyes locked on to Andrei's, and I raised my gloved fists in the air. Goosebumps traveled across my skin as we squared off. Was this happening? How far would it go?

Andrei lunged at me, and I bobbed out of the way. He was strong, but I was fast. I danced around his punches, tossing a few of my own.

"Enough," Declan said on approach after only five or so minutes. "Is that really all you have?" He angled his head at me and held out his hand to Andrei, requesting the gloves.

"Andrei might've taken it easy on you because you're a woman, but I'm for equal opportunity." Declan sneered.

My mind flashed to Jessie and my hand bunched into a fist at my side.

"Time to pay up. I'm ready to cash in on that rain check," Declan said in a low voice before moving with fast feet right at me.

I didn't have time to react as his fist connected with my jaw. My head slammed back, and the floor was no longer under my feet.

I struggled to stand, but couldn't pull myself up. My vision was blurry as Declan hovered over me.

"We're just getting started, Olivia *Scott*."

26

CONNOR

I EXITED THE CAPITAL JAMES BANK AND GLANCED AT THE FAMOUS bull of Wall Street as I jumped into my Jeep.

"Is it done?" Jake asked from behind the wheel, before shifting gears and joining the rush of cars on the street.

"Yeah. I'll have to swing back by the office later when everyone's gone. But the plan should work." I hoped it would, at least.

"You hear from Olivia yet?" he asked a few blocks later, just as we passed the sushi restaurant Olivia and I had eaten at—well, almost eaten at.

I reached into my pocket for my phone. "No. I've called her five times now. I'm getting worried."

"I'm sure she's just tied up with Declan."

Tied up? An image of Olivia in bondage and Declan, the damn devil, wielding some sort of flogger popped into my mind. Bile rose at the thought. "You think the guard will be home?" I needed to snuff the disgusting image from my mind before I crushed the phone in my palm.

"The other guard said he didn't work again until Saturday. I'm not sure if it will do us any good, but I'd like to see how much he knows before you walk into the shark tank tonight."

"You think he's on Konstantin's payroll?"

"I don't know, but the man is an accessory to murder. Regardless."

Murder. My father, Tyson, Olivia's sister . . . It was all too damn much.

And I still hadn't shed a tear. What was wrong with me? Were my tear ducts broken, or had I hardened into some steely inanimate object, incapable of tears?

I hadn't cried since my friend was murdered in Iraq. I should've done better recon. I shouldn't have missed the insurgent.

"You all right, man?"

"Just thinking about Jim."

Surprise flickered across his face as he tightened his grip on the wheel. "Jim Kazanski?" Jake had been on a different mission than me, but he knew Jim.

We all knew Jim. Funny-as-hell Jim.

"Why are you thinking about him?"

"I don't know." I pinched the bridge of my nose and shut my eyes.

His hand was on my shoulder as he stopped at a light. "It wasn't your fault." His voice was thick and threaded with emotion. "I told Jenny what you said."

My eyes popped open. "What?"

He removed his hand when the light changed. "I know you thought she couldn't handle it, but I would want to know if I had been her. I didn't want to tell you at the time—I knew how bad you felt after losing him."

"You told her Jim was going to propose?"

Jake nodded as I studied his profile, his eyes on the road. "Jim said if anything ever happened to him, he wanted me to look out for her."

I lowered my head. "Fuck." A tangle of emotions pulled at me, but my eyes remained clear.

"I have no intention of delivering any message to your ex, F.Y.I." Jake parked the Jeep. "You don't get to die on me."

I looked up at my friend. He was the oldest of all my friends—close to thirty-five—and I always felt he had assumed the role of older brother as if a few years made any difference at this age. Still, it was nice knowing I had someone like him in my corner.

"We're going to take down the Russian mob, Denzel-style. No worries."

A smile tugged at my lips. I couldn't help it. "Denzel-style, huh?"

"You know that movie where he took down the Russian mob—like all of it—with a flick of his wrist? We can do that. No problem." He started for the door. "Hell, we should study that movie so we can learn a few things."

"I'm not sure about you, but I don't need to learn a damn thing," I joked, allowing his cheerfulness to comfort the sick swell of emotions in my stomach. "We could teach him a few things, though."

Jake came around next to me after hopping out of the Jeep. "Sure, buddy. And I'm Arnold."

I glared at him. "More like Eastwood, dude."

He smoothed a hand over his face and drew his lips into a straight line as he narrowed his eyes, giving me his infamous Eastwood impression. "'Ever notice how you come across somebody once in a while you shouldn't have messed with? That's me,'" he quoted in a low, deep voice.

Reality slapped me in the face as we entered the apartment building. "Come on, man. We have a Russian mob to take down and a girl to save." It felt good to be my old, carefree self. But I wasn't sure if that was who I needed to be right now. Being pissed off would more than likely get me or someone else killed, though. I couldn't be off my game, either way.

Not when it came to Olivia's life on the line.

Jake's fist tapped the door of the security guard's home, which sat on the first floor of an older building. The graffiti on the walls and the overpowering odor of urine led me to believe this man hadn't saved up for retirement when he was younger.

He'd be a prime target for the Russian mob. Money could buy a lot of things: food, utilities, people . . .

"Who is it?" The old mans' voice called out from behind the door.

Jake swooped his FBI badge up in front of the peephole. I wasn't sure if it was dangerous to be waving that around, but at this point, I wasn't sure if it mattered. The deal with Declan was tonight, and after that, all the cards would be on the table.

The door slowly creaked open. The man's brows rose and fell as he studied us. "You two," was all he said.

The smell of cigars jabbed me in the face as he spoke, and I had to stop myself from choking at the stench. "We need a word." Jake entered the man's apartment without an invitation, practically forcing the older man to step back and out of the way.

We made our way down the narrow hallway and into the living room of the dimly lit apartment. A large flat screen TV dominated the wall, surrounded by one small sofa and an oversized, brown leather reclining chair.

The man reached for the cigar in the ashtray next to the chair, and he lowered the volume on the golf tournament that was playing on the TV.

Great. This man had helped criminals in order to chill at home and watch golf on the big screen. I wanted to shout that he'd helped murder my father, but I bit my tongue.

Jake shoved his FBI badge in his pocket. "Why'd you lie to us when we met with you the other day?"

The man inhaled and blew cigar smoke off to the side, seeming nothing like the Santa Claus lookalike we'd encountered before.

"Why'd *you* lie? You didn't mention you were FBI," he spoke after a beat.

"That wasn't pertinent at the time," Jake answered. "You deleted Edward Matthew's visitor list from the computer. Why?"

The man's eyes flitted to mine for a brief moment. I shoved my hands in my pockets, letting my FBI friend work his magic.

"I have no idea what you're talking about." He pushed the cigar back into his mouth.

"How much did the Russian mob pay you to make that list disappear?"

"Russian mob?" The cigar slipped free from his lips. "What are you talking about?"

"The two men you allowed up into Edward Matthew's home are members of the Russian mafia." Jake crossed his arms.

The man rubbed a hand over his white beard, put out his cigar in the ashtray and sank into his reclining chair. "Listen, they were on the list." He held up his hands in front of him as I glowered at him. "Your father," he looked at me, "put them on the approved list back in April."

That was when they'd been released from prison, according to Jake. "If he put them on the list, why were you so quick to erase it?" I challenged, but attempted to maintain my cool.

"Because he took them off a few weeks later, right before he— um . . ." He frowned at me. "They told me they needed to talk with him, that it was important. They paid me to let them go up." He snaked a hand around to the back of his neck. "I thought that you might discover they were removed from the list but allowed access. I didn't want to get in trouble."

So my father had the sense to take those murderers off the list. But why would he let them into his home?

"There has to be more to this story." I shook my head. "What is it you're not telling us?" I removed my hands from my pockets and braced the arms of his chair, leaning in, my face close to his stinking, cigar-infused breath. "Tell me, dammit."

The man stared up at me with apologetic eyes. I started to open my mouth, but my phone was vibrating. Olivia?

Jolting upright, I dug into my pocket and clutched my phone. "What the hell?"

"What is it?" Jake came over to me.

"Olivia just texted that she's boarding a plane for Vegas."

"Why's she going to Vegas?" Jake looked at me, the lines of his face pulling together in worry.

I quickly dialed up her number, needing the answer myself. "Voicemail." I redialed a few times, only to be greeted by the sweet sound of her voice asking me to leave a message. "She must already be on the plane."

"Why would Declan send her to Vegas?"

"I don't know. Maybe it's better she's not here when this all goes down, but I still don't like the idea of her being out there. Alone."

"Are we through?" the man interrupted us.

"You got my father killed, asshole. It will never be through."

His mouth opened, but he didn't speak. He covered his face with his hands, and I didn't stick around to see what else he might have had to say. "I need to make a call."

Once outside, I checked the recent flights out of New York to Vegas and dialed up my friend Ben.

"Hey, man. I'm sorry I haven't been any help," he responded after one ring.

"You can be of help now."

"Sure. What can I do?"

"Remember Olivia from the club?" I asked, finding that my hand had clenched into a ball at my side.

"Of course."

"She's on her way to Vegas, and I need you to keep an eye out for her. Make sure she stays safe. She should be at The Phoenix tonight." I wasn't sure why Declan wanted her in Vegas when the meeting was a few hours away, but at least I knew she wouldn't be caught in the crossfire.

"She in danger?"

God, I hoped not. "Maybe. Just watch out for her, okay?" My voice broke.

* * *

Olivia

A MIDNIGHT BLACKNESS GREETED ME. I SQUINTED A FEW TIMES and moved my hands around in front of me, trying to figure out where I was.

My skull was going to explode. Something hard brushed against the fingers of my outstretched hand.

A blinding light flashed on a moment later, and a moan escaped my lips.

"You're awake, I see." Declan's voice sounded like an echo, surrounding and teasing me.

I still couldn't see. I closed one eye and squinted out the other. A sharp and sore throb in my jaw, which shot straight up my cheek and to my forehead, had me closing my one good eye again.

What had he done to me?

"Where am I?" I slurred a little, realizing my bottom lip was swollen and cut. Forcing my one eye open again, I tried to focus on what was before me.

Bars. The other cage wasn't too far away.

Jesus. I wanted to cry, but I was too proud. And the pain would be terrible. He must have knocked me out cold.

"You're exactly where you should be," Declan responded, and I could almost make out his silhouette. I had to snap my eyes shut again.

"Why are you doing this?" I grumbled.

My brain scrambled to make sense of everything, but there was only one answer: Andrei or Oleg had alerted Declan to who I was. Of course, he might not know I was FBI. He might just think I'm on a revenge mission, like Connor did . . . But did it matter? He had me in a Goddamn cage.

"Olivia Scott, my sweet assistant. You know exactly why." The sound of his voice chilled my body.

I pressed up against the cool bars of the cage. With my one eye open, I caught sight of Declan with his hands casually hidden inside his pockets.

He was wearing a dark suit, as though he was about to broker a deal. *Oh God, with Connor.*

"I don't know what you're talking about," I slipped the words out before softly moaning at the pain that wreaked havoc on my face. "I promise."

He cocked his head at me, and I tried to make out my surroundings. I could hear noise from above, maybe. I wasn't sure. Fighting against the ringing in my ears, I listened.

Were we in the basement of a club? There was concrete flooring, cement walls, and pipes trailing above my head in the exposed ceiling. It was a vast space. My nose wasn't working great, but it felt cool, damp, and had a bit of a musty smell. Yes, it had to be a basement.

Was it The Phoenix? I'd never been down below before. It couldn't be late enough for the club to be open already, could it? How long had I been unconscious?

"What time is it? Where am I?"

Declan removed his hands from his pockets, pressed one palm to the outside of the cage and smirked at me. Damn bastard. "You've been curious about these cages, and now you know. They're reserved for naughty girls like you."

I glanced down in the direction of Declan's gaze. My tank top was spray-painted in my own blood—probably from my lips. I rolled my tongue over my teeth, checking for any missing ones.

Thank God, they appeared to be intact. Of course, what did that matter? I would probably never make it out alive. Especially if Konstantin had anything to do with it.

"Declan, please."

He took a step back and folded his arms. "You have no idea who you're dealing with, Liv." His dark brown eyes bore into me as if he was attempting to collect my soul. "Who killed Jessie, anyway—was it Andrei or Oleg? They couldn't even remember who had pulled the trigger." He casually scratched the back of his neck, but I knew he was goading me.

He crouched down so we were at eye level and he gripped the bars, pressing his face close to the metal. "You learn anything interesting while spying on me?" His voice was low, a seductive whisper of darkness, attempting to rope me in.

I wouldn't give him the satisfaction.

"FBI agent Olivia Scott. It's so nice to finally meet the real you."

My lungs expanded, needling my ribs, and I released a long, slow breath. The thin glimmer of hope disappeared. He knew the truth; there'd be no way out.

He shifted back to a standing position but kept his eyes on me. "You seem surprised. I can tell by the look in your," he paused and grinned, "one good eye."

Asshole. "I don't know what you think you know, but I won't tell you a damn thing."

He snickered while he popped open a button on his blazer and crossed his arms. "You actually think you have anything valuable to say to me?" He flashed his teeth.

How'd he find out? Andrei and Oleg wouldn't have been able to figure out I was FBI, right?

"People know where I am. They'll come looking for me." Blake. Connor. One of them would find me. They had no idea where I was, but they would look.

I had to cling to that hope, at least.

Declan pulled a phone with a metallic case from his pocket, a phone I assumed to be mine. "I told your boyfriend that you were needed in Vegas. I didn't want him worrying about you."

Connor. So, Declan didn't know about Blake? "Connor's not involved in this. I promise." My desperate plea to save him was probably wasted breath, but I had to try. "We reconnected. It's just sex with him." God, I hated saying that to Declan, but I'd do anything to keep Connor safe.

Declan's lips twisted into another sinister smile. "I'm fully aware of your relationship with Connor. In fact, I supported it."

What in the hell was he talking about? I was tired of playing his mind games. "What do you want from me?" I shouted, and then flinched.

"You're just a tool, Olivia. Don't get too excited."

"A tool for what?" The words sprang free from my lips as I rose to my feet.

"You're tough." He circled the cage, and my head shifted each direction to maintain contact with him as he moved. "But you're not tough enough, or smart enough, to go up against me. Or the Russian mafia. Everyone who has tried has failed."

He stopped in front of me, and I clung to the bars, dying to break free and knock the glorified sneer from his face. He thought he had won, but I couldn't—wouldn't give up. "I managed to fool you for a pretty long time, don't you think?" I responded, knowing I shouldn't taunt him, but unable to stop myself.

"You think I didn't know? Or that your sudden promotion had to do with your fantastic ass, I mean, your managerial skills?" His breath was on my face; my skin crawled at his words.

"Someone will find me. Konstantin might think he's untouchable, but you aren't." I took a shaky step back.

He reached for the knot at his tie and tightened it while peering up at me from hooded eyes. "Oh, you mean your boss?" His long fingers blazed down his tie before he tucked it inside his suit jacket and clasped the button of his blazer once again. "Blake?" He scoffed

Fear melted my insides, turning me into nothing more than liquid. The floor dropped beneath me. "What happened to him?" I choked.

"Why don't you ask him yourself?"

27

CONNOR

I GLANCED DOWN AT THE STEEL CASE THAT HOUSED THE EMF GUN. When I dropped by the office, I had dismissed all employees, demanding they take a long weekend for all of their hard work. It hadn't been easy to get those go-getters to leave work early, but I had no choice. I couldn't exactly waltz out of the building with the technology and go unnoticed.

I didn't take the gun then, though. I waited and went back once the office was cleared out. I couldn't risk raising any red flags if anyone saw me with the case. CEO or not, it could cause problems.

"I need to talk to you before you go," Jake hollered as I stood by the front door, prepared to leave.

I checked my watch. It was quarter of eleven. "The meeting is in forty-five minutes. Did you find something?" Our plan was set. I thought we were good to go.

"I just found something on your father's computer. Or, I should say, in the cloud." Of course—the proverbial cloud of data that floated above our heads.

"What'd you find?" I went into the kitchen, where he was sitting in front of my father's computer.

"He erased some files from his computer and his tablet, but the information was still stored in the cloud." He tapped at a few buttons. "Look at these photos. Look at the dates."

I zoomed in, pressing my fingers against the touchscreen, and my hand fell to my side. "This is a picture of Mason in uniform—in the Middle East, no less." I observed Jake, my body growing hot, my heart rate kicking up. "The picture was taken last September. He was stationed in Saudi Arabia at the time."

I released a strangled breath and looked at the next photo. It was of me, standing in front of my friend Michael Maddox's brownstone.

"Your mother is in the next image. Also taken in September."

"Was my dad spying on us?"

"Tell me, why would he have a picture of Olivia?"

Olivia was jogging at the Constitution Gardens in D.C.—it must have been before she'd started working for Declan. "What the hell?"

"There's more—"

My ringing phone stopped him. "It's Ben," I said after pulling the phone from my pocket. "Hey. Everything okay?"

There was a moment of silence on the line. Then, "Olivia's not in Vegas."

I braced my hand on the back of the barstool as my feet staggered back. "What do you mean?" My heart started to thunder in my chest.

Jake looked at me and raised his hand in the air.

"She wasn't at the club. I checked with my buddy who works security at the casino where her club is, and he said she never checked in. Actually, she didn't have any type of reservation."

Ben's words shook me, stealing my breath as nervousness ripped through my body like a tidal wave. I couldn't respond. My mind was racing with possibilities, and the only one that made sense was that she was in serious trouble.

"I don't have any contacts at the airport, so I don't know if she ever flew to Vegas. I'm sorry."

I wasn't sure what to say, so I muttered, "Thank you," and hung up without thinking. "Olivia didn't make it to the hotel in Vegas."

"You think that text wasn't from her then? Or did she lie?"

"Why would she lie?" She lied about a lot of things, but I hardly believed she'd make up a trip to Vegas.

"Well, the thing is—I know Olivia," Jake said slowly. My hand lifted from the barstool and my fingers curved into a fist at my side as I braced myself for whatever news Jake was about to deliver.

"I recognized her from the picture." He scrubbed a hand over his jaw. "I didn't know your ex was Olivia Scott. She's FBI."

"You must be mistaken." There was no hesitation. "*That* she would have told me. Right?" We came clean with each other. Why would she withhold that information from me?

"She was a student of mine at Quantico. When I realized who she was, I checked the FBI database. She's currently on assignment in New York under the leadership of Blake Manning. The details of her case are classified, though."

I couldn't wrap my head around it. A lot of things were making more sense, now. But still—the FBI?

"That explains why someone was asking me about you."

"Isn't this a conflict of interest?" I folded my arms across my chest, still not sure if I could believe what he was telling me. Olivia, an FBI agent? "Konstantin's guys killed her sister. Surely the FBI wouldn't allow Olivia to work on a case involving Konstantin."

Jake half shrugged. "When you sign up with the FBI, they learn everything about you. Hell, they use polygraph tests on us. They interview family members. They probably even know she once dated you."

"Wait." I held my hand out in front of me. "Really?"

"Yeah. They know all my dirty laundry." He grimaced.

"She's in danger, Jake. Declan must know, and he probably has her." The color drained from my face. "Are they going to use her to get to me?"

"Shit. I hope not."

"None of this explains why my father had surveillance photos of me, Mason, Olivia—hell, even my mother."

"We'd better figure it out and quick because you have to meet with Declan soon."

"If anything happened to Olivia . . ." I couldn't finish my thought. My blood heated as I sank to the barstool, my mind clambering to make sense of it all.

"We'll get your girl back, Connor."

* * *

Olivia

I KNEW MY ONE EYE WAS SWOLLEN, AND MY "GOOD" EYE HURT, SO it took me a minute to decide whether my eyes were playing tricks on me.

He moved across the large room, and I noticed an uptick in the beat of the music above. It wasn't The Phoenix, I realized. The Phoenix didn't play 90s throwback jams. So where was I?

When the man stopped in front of me, I squeezed my eye shut again. There was no way.

He was just a mirage. He had to be.

"You pummeled her face pretty bad."

I sucked in a breath at the sound of Blake's voice. What did it mean? No, I refused to accept it.

"She deserved it," Declan answered.

Blake's fingers curved around the bars, covering mine as my knuckles whitened. At his touch, I jerked my hands free and banged against the back of the six-foot tall, oval-shaped cage. The dark steel gleamed, taunting me, as I opened my one eye to look at him.

My boss. My mentor. My ex-lover.

My enemy?

Declan stood a few feet behind Blake, a look of satisfaction spreading across his face. He relished my shock.

"What's going on?" A whisper stole the words from my brain and delivered them to Blake.

Blake removed his hands from the bars and gripped the back of his neck with one hand. "I help Konstantin out whenever our interests align. I volunteered to be on the case when I heard they were going after him again." Blake's blue eyes were sharp on me.

A knife of betrayal impaled me, and I had to gather my strength. I thought it was luck that he'd landed the case—lucky for me so I could help lock the man up. "And how'd your interests align?"

Money?

"How long have you been on the take?" My cheeks grew warm, and my hands clawed at the fabric of my pants as anger gathered inside me.

Blake leaned his back against the empty cage and stared down at the floor, avoiding eye contact with me. Was he embarrassed by his deceit? Remorseful? Not that it mattered at this point. I groaned as I realized the sheer futility of it all. The man I'd been reporting to for the last nine months had been on the other team, all this time. All of my sacrifices had been for nothing.

"You wouldn't understand, Olivia. Things aren't always so black and white."

"FBI." I raised one hand, then the other. "Criminals. Pretty clear cut to me." I forced myself to remain standing, even though my body begged to drop, to mourn my losses. "Well, until an FBI agent becomes a criminal." I shook my head in disgust. "So, I wasted the last nine months, for you to do—what? Destroy any evidence and report that Konstantin can't be taken down?"

Blake's eyes were finally on me, but it was Declan's voice in my ears. "Do you really think any of this is a coincidence, Olivia?" Declan came up next to Blake, eager to hammer me down.

My nostrils flared. "What do you mean?"

"Your idea to come after me set everything in motion. And now, I have you to thank for the fact that I'm thirty minutes away from finally getting my hands on the EMF gun. I'm about to become a billionaire." Declan toyed with the cuffs on his blazer. "You think that a job just happened to come open at my company in September when you pitched your idea to Blake? Or that your promotion had nothing to do with the fact that Edward Matthews was dead, and your ex-lover would be taking over the company?"

My lower lip trembled at his words. "Even the Russian mafia's not safe if terrorists attack New York again."

Declan angled his head and studied me. "What are you talking about?"

Blake pushed away from the cage and came near me. "She's—"

"I didn't tell you about the terrorists," Declan interrupted. "What's going on?" Declan was standing in front of Blake, his finger against Blake's muscled chest.

"Oh? He didn't tell you that we hacked your computer at the club? Maybe Blake was saving a little something in his back pocket to use against you." I tried to remain confident as I dealt with the two magnum-sized egos that held my fate in their hands.

"I had to. She ran the idea by Sean, and I couldn't say no, or it would look suspicious," Blake defended. "I didn't think Sean would uncover anything."

Blake was now the target of Declan's vicious stare. "Why didn't you tell me you found something?"

"I didn't have a chance." Blake cleared his throat. "Besides, you never told me the weapons from Matthews Tech were going to extremists in the Middle East."

Declan sniggered. "Would that have mattered?"

Blake shook his head. "But I might have demanded more cash."

Disappointment stabbed me. "I understand Declan's lack of morals, but Blake, you're a federal agent, what happened to you?" I couldn't allow myself to indulge in the sadness that attempted to strangle hold of me. I needed to stay strong. I had to get through this.

"Money goes a long way, sweet thing," Declan answered for him.

"Call me sweet thing one more time." I gripped the bars, wishing I had Hulk-like strength to tear them apart.

Declan ignored me, his focus on Blake. "I want whatever information you took from my computer." His deep voice grew loud in my ears. At least my hearing was fully functional again.

"Of course," Blake said, holding his hands up.

I tried to run through the last nine months in my mind, searching for signs I'd missed. "You really used me to try and get Connor to make the deal?" I cringed at the thought, but everything made sense now.

Both Blake and Declan had pushed me to get close to Connor —manipulating my past to their advantage. Even going so far as to scare me with Andrei and Oleg's presence. Blake had never been worried for my safety. Goddamn him. He should have been nominated for actor of the year. "How'd you know I wouldn't go behind your back and reveal the truth to Connor?"

"Of course you told Connor the truth." Declan guffawed. "Can you believe this one, Blake? She'll say anything." He pulled out his cell phone and tapped at the screen before his cold eyes focused back on me.

"I ordered her not to tell him, but I don't know. It doesn't matter anyway, right? You just need to get the weapon, and then we can finally be done with Matthews Tech."

Too many lies had been buried—it was time to reveal the truth. I scrounged up the energy deep inside to keep fighting. "Tell me one thing. Why me? I brought up the idea of using Declan, but you could have used the idea without me."

Blake didn't say anything, and I didn't know how to interpret his silence. Was he conflicted? I didn't want to care, but perhaps I could switch him back to the right side of the law somehow. "Blake, we had something special," I lied.

That was the wrong choice of words, apparently. Blake's blue eyes turned liquid cool. "You fucked Connor. Don't try and play me, Olivia." He shook his head and closed the gap between him and the cage.

I took a small step back, all that the cage would afford, and noticed for the first time the true evil inside the man I'd once called my superior. Men like him were worse than Konstantin and Declan. Because they seemed good on the outside. "Answer my question, Blake. Tell me why you decided to ruin my life," I said through gritted teeth, defiance blazing fast and furious through my body.

Declan shook his head. "Tell her, Blake. Tell her she's the reason why there's a pile of bodies."

I stared at Blake, confusion capturing my face. What sick game were they playing? If the bars weren't in between us, I'd grab him by his T-shirt and stab the son of a bitch. If only I had a knife. "What the hell are you talking about?" I growled.

"As much as I'd love to stay and chat, I have a meeting to attend." Declan was taunting me. He had no intention of telling me anything. He turned and started through the dimly lit basement. The music faded in and out above my head. And the second cage sat empty, waiting.

28

CONNOR

"I THOUGHT I WAS MEETING WITH YOUR ASSOCIATES." I HELD ON to the steel briefcase and studied the three men who stood in front of the boxing ring with folded arms. Were they supposed to be intimidating? "These are the men you're working with?" I asked in disbelief, eying Andrei and Oleg.

"They work for him," Declan answered.

I already knew he was referring to Konstantin, but where the hell was he? As Declan closed in on me, my eyes shot to his knuckles. They were red and swollen. He'd been in a fight recently, and my stomach shrank at the possibility of it being with Olivia. No, he wouldn't hit her. Would he?

Declan gestured to the men to approach me. "They need to check you for wires if you don't mind."

I lowered the case to the ground, reached into my pocket, and tossed Declan my phone. "It's off. And I'm not armed." I raised my hands up, allowing the men to scan me, and then pat me down.

"He's clear," Andrei said, nodding at Declan.

Declan slipped my phone into his pocket. "Is that the gun?" He started to reach for the case, but I lifted it and pulled it back.

"You can see the weapon when you meet your end of the deal," I snapped, my eyes narrowing on him.

He whipped a quick smile to his face, smoothing it on for the sake of appearances. But we both knew better. I could see it in his eyes. He knew I had no intention of handing him the gun.

"Where's Olivia?" I wanted to charge him, to have him feel the weight of my knuckles as I broke his nose.

Declan took a step back and glanced at Andrei out of the corner of his eye. "Vegas," he said while looking back at me. His lips flattened like the line on a heart rate monitor.

"Sure. And you're not working with Alexander Konstantin. And these men aren't hitmen."

He rubbed a hand over his jaw and held up a finger in front of me. "I've always liked your honesty. You're far more respectable than your father was."

"Is that why you killed him?"

"I have to say that I'm pleased we're done acting. I was growing tired of it. It's much easier when we just talk straight."

"How long have you known I had no intention of working with an asshole like yourself?" I stood my ground, and my fingers tightened on the handle.

"Oh. I knew long before you took over the company."

"Do you always do business deals by threatening potential partners? I'm not sure if my father would have cared if you killed my mother, to be honest, but Olivia? That has me curious. I've been struggling to figure out how you think she fits into the picture." I scratched my jaw but held firm in my stance. "Not unless you have inside information."

He turned away from me and waved his hand at the two Russians.

Andrei reached inside his blazer and produced a 9mm. The black barrel of the gun was a few feet away from me, but I didn't flinch. I'd been expecting it.

"Olivia's the reason you're here. Or I should say her past

connection with you is what made everything possible." He cocked his head, and I had to suppress my desire to attack. "Konstantin had been looking for a weapons company to make a deal, and when the Feds decided to go after him again, your little angel came up with a great plan to get to him through me." He shrugged his shoulders and moved closer. "When I discovered her connection to Matthews Tech, a failing, and struggling weapons company, the plan made itself."

I couldn't wait to rip the smug bastard's face off. Tension rippled through my body, and I was prepared to blast him, but I had to be patient. His arrogance was revealing. "So, you threatened my father into making a deal with you, huh? Promised to kill my brother or me?"

A disgusting grin smeared his face. "You'd be surprised."

"Why'd you kill him, though? He went behind your back to take you all down?" It was hard for me to believe. I'd thought my father was guilty of corporate bribery and hated the idea that he'd worked with such a snake. All this time, he'd been doing it not to save his company, but to save his family. "He knew he was going to die, didn't he? That's why he wrote those letters? He discovered that you found out what he and Tyson had been working on."

"Hell, he let my men right in the door. He refused to open the safe, but that was a bridge we could cross on another day." Declan checked his watch and looked back at me.

My father must have known Declan would come after Mason or me after he died, but he probably assumed I'd open his letter right away. What an idiot I had been.

Another thought crossed my mind, and I couldn't help but be curious. "So, tell me something. Why the games with me? Why not just pressure me the way you did my father?"

"We would have threatened you, but you didn't open the letter. You stuck the damn thing in your car!" He laughed. "So we developed a new idea—one that involved you making a deal with me, and Olivia pushing you to do it." Declan reached into his pocket. He waved a white envelope before me—*my* letter. "This was an interesting read."

"Oh yeah? If you give me the key, I'd be happy to open the box." I took a step closer to him, not the least bit intimidated by the goons. The briefcase would easily deflect a gunshot.

I hoped it wouldn't come to that, though. I needed information. Like where the hell was Olivia?

"I honestly don't care about the contents of that damn box. If you and Mason are out of the picture, there'll be nobody to open it. So it remains inconsequential, don't you think?"

Was the man threatening to go after my kid brother? He had no idea who the hell he was dealing with. "Where's Olivia?"

"Why on Earth would I tell you that?"

Standing in front of Declan now, I could feel his breath on my face. Neither of us would back down. "Take me to Olivia." My face was burning as rage consumed me.

"Why would I do that when you have the prototype here?" He nodded at the case I still clutched. "I had no intention of making any kind of deal with Matthews Tech. Just needed the prototype."

I shook my head, and a breath of air escaped from my lungs. I looked over at the assholes who'd killed my father, Tyson, and Jessie. I had every intention of making sure they either rotted in jail or in hell. I preferred the latter.

"You and I both know you'll never get your hands on it until I see Olivia," I responded as my eyes bore into him. "The case was designed by the best minds at MIT," I lied. "If the wrong code is entered and my voice doesn't activate the briefcase, then a chemical gas is released inside the case to erode and destroy the weapon."

He rolled his neck a little and sighed. "Fine. If you want to see your woman before she dies, then so be it. I made preparations just in case . . ." He motioned for Andrei and Oleg to follow.

His two goons trailed behind me as we made our way to a dark Lincoln Navigator. The fact that Declan made no attempt to blindfold me meant that he didn't anticipate I'd be leaving the next building alive.

"Don't take the normal route," Declan instructed Andrei, who was in the driver seat, his tattooed hand resting on the wheel. "I'm assuming your FBI pal is watching us."

I glanced at Oleg, who sat next to me. "No, he's not," I replied. Jake had other plans.

After about ten minutes of silence, as Andrei took turn after turn, Declan asked, "Do you love her?"

"Go to hell!" I rubbed my free hand against my jeans as my fingers wrapped tighter around the handle of the case. I couldn't wait to clobber the prick.

"I'm just curious how much you're willing to do for her. I had hoped you and Olivia would reconnect, but you made me a little nervous out in Vegas. I was worried you were too pissed, that I'd have to use your brother instead."

I kept my mouth shut, trying to put a temporary cap on my rage as it grew with each passing moment.

"Poor, star-crossed lovers." Declan laughed. "You two probably worked it all out between the sheets." He tapped my letter against his knee and peered at me from over his shoulder. "Your father sure was a grade-A asshole."

I had no clue what he was talking about.

Declan pulled a folded white sheet from the envelope and switched on the light above his seat. "Are you as bored as I am, Connor? Maybe this will cheer you up."

He fixed his gaze down on my father's fluid handwriting, a smirk lighting his cheek as he began to read, "Connor, I'm so sorry for everything. I can't imagine what you must be going through right now, but I chose you to carry this burden because I know you can handle it." Declan's high-pitched sing-song voice had my nerves on edge. "I'm going to die. Today or maybe tomorrow. It's my life or yours. And your brother's." Declan paused for a moment, his eyes reading me. Then he dived back in. "I'm dying with the hope that you'll live. I know that I can trust you to use this information to take down the bastards who have been threatening our family. Yadda yadda yadda, passcodes and security box numbers." He grinned and cleared his throat.

"I regret so many things in life, but none of them more than what I did to separate you and Olivia."

Oleg was staring at me now, and Andrei shot me a quick look in the rearview mirror. Repulsed, I looked away from everyone and out the window.

"Ready for more?" Declan loved every second of this. "Let me be very clear, son. Olivia Scott, your ex-girlfriend, did not have an abortion."

My gaze landed back on Declan, and the smile that met his eyes had me lunging at him.

Oleg was on me in an instant, pulling me back, and Andrei slammed on the brakes.

"Calm down, Connor," Oleg warned.

"Your father was a shitty guy—allowing you to believe all these years your girlfriend had an abortion when in fact she'd had a miscarriage."

Hearing the truth from Declan's tongue was more than I could stand. I started for him again, but the tip of Oleg's gun pressed against my temple.

I would be no good to Olivia if I were dead.

"Where was I?" Declan's brows slanted as he refocused on the letter.

I leaned back in my seat and placed my forehead in my hand, worried I'd lose my shit again hearing my father's words from Declan's mouth.

"The hospital called after Olivia lost the baby. You were at my house at the time, and I answered your phone when you weren't in the room. I went to the hospital, paid the bill, and told Olivia you wanted to end it. I'm so sorry I lied to you both, but at the time, I thought it was for the best."

"We're here," Andrei announced as we pulled into an alley.

Declan tucked the letter back into the envelope. "Guess you don't need to know the rest. Inconsequential now, don't you think?"

Olivia had a miscarriage. I wasn't surprised—not anymore. I'd started to suspect that my father had lied after Olivia and I had slept together the other night.

How could I have believed my father's lies, though? I'd loved Olivia so much, and yet, when he showed me the hospital paperwork and the bill . . .

"Connor?" Declan's voice was in my ear.

Andrei stood outside the open door, waiting for me.

I forced the memories from my mind, but when I saw where we were, I had to fight every damn part of me not to go after Declan again.

The blood rushed from my face as we made our way through the club where Olivia and I had first met, where Jessie had died.

I followed behind Declan, and Andrei and Oleg trailed closely behind me. We made our way to the back area down a set of stairs.

When I rounded the corner and saw Olivia, my entire body tensed up. I couldn't help but reel my arm back and pound my fist into Declan's face.

* * *

Olivia

"Connor," I cried out as Andrei, Oleg, and Blake drew their weapons.

Connor stormed Declan again. His face was beet red as he attacked him, his fists swinging.

"Back away from Declan or she dies," Andrei warned as he focused his weapon at me.

Connor faltered. His hands dropped to his sides.

Declan wound back his hand, and he struck a blow to the side of Connor's head. "You piece of shit," Declan rasped.

Connor ignored the pain. He charged across the room. "Olivia. Are you okay?" He pressed his palms to the cage and, for the first time, I felt safe. I knew Connor probably couldn't help me—he was down here with me now—but part of me had to believe we'd get out of this alive.

"I'm so sorry I dragged you into this mess." His fingers covered mine, and I leaned my head forward, pressing it against the metal.

"Get her out of here," Connor roared, spinning around to face Declan.

"Open the case." Declan touched the blood at his lip.

Andrei was behind him, holding a large metal briefcase. Was that the gun? Did Connor bring it with him? *Oh God.* Where was Konstantin?

"I'm not opening the case until you take her out of there," Connor demanded, stepping up to Declan.

Declan waved his hand at me like Connor's request was no big deal. It probably wasn't. We were outnumbered. Blake appeared by my side with a key.

The sound of the key in the lock was the sweetest noise. The second the door swung open, I dove at Blake, beating his chest. I ignored the pain shooting down the left side of my cheek as Blake gripped hold of my wrists. "You disgust me," I screamed in his face.

Connor's hands were on my hips a second later, pulling me free. I buried my face in his chest as he wrapped his arms around me. "I won't help you as long as you have her down here. She goes free or no deal."

I looked up to see Declan, Andrei, Oleg, and Blake standing side by side a few feet away. How were we going to get out of this? It didn't seem possible.

Declan removed his blazer and tossed it at Oleg. He started to roll his sleeves up to his elbows, exposing the cross and skull. "If you don't open the case, she dies."

Connor was staring at the men, his body trembling against my skin. But not from fear, I had to assume. He was pissed. He glanced down at me in his arms and pulled me closer.

Connor rattled off the numbers for the lock, and I flinched. Why would he do that? Once they had the weapon, they'd kill us. But the way his fingers blazed up and down my back, comforting me, meant he wasn't afraid.

"I thought you said it required voice activation and—" Declan said as the case popped open.

"I lied," Connor said in a low, calm voice, his eyes focused.

Declan held the gun in his hand, running his fingers over it. "A thing of beauty. I couldn't believe that Matthews Tech was manufacturing this gun. What good fortune. Of course, you didn't have the funds to make much headway on it. You would never have succeeded if we didn't land the Saudi deal." Declan approached Connor and me, holding the EMF gun in front of him, his team of idiots lining up behind him like a wall.

"So the deal had nothing to do with helping the company—it was all to expedite the development of the weapon, so you could steal it and produce it yourself?" I was floored.

"Smart, right? If Olivia hadn't pushed her boss to join the case, Konstantin and I would have teamed up with some other tech company, and we may never have had this weapon. So," Declan said, tilting his head and finding my one good eye, "thank you, Olivia."

Connor's heart was beating slow in his chest. That was a good sign, right? If it was racing, that meant he was nervous. He appeared calm. He was my rock, and I clung to him.

"It won't work." Connor took a step back, releasing his hold on me. "Go ahead. Try it out."

Declan studied the gun and played around with it. The muscles in his face grew taut, and he handed it over to Andrei. "What's wrong with it? I thought it was finished?"

"Oh, it is," Connor answered. "But it's useless without the chip. The chip has all of the technology in it." He raised his hands in the air, palms up. "No chip. No weapon."

Declan looked over at me and back at Connor. "Where's the chip?"

Connor pulled me close to him again. "You honestly thought I'd just show up and hand you the weapon? I knew you had Olivia."

Declan's eyes were on the concrete floor. "Are you prepared to die like your father—willing to exchange one life for another?" His dark eyes flashed as he reached behind his back and pulled out a handgun.

"Until Olivia's free, you'll never get the chip," Connor said smoothly as he wrapped an arm around my shoulder and tugged me closer. Shielding me.

Declan looked over at Andrei and Oleg. What was he thinking? My heart was thrashing wildly in my chest, and I wasn't sure if I could remember how to breathe. Different scenarios, each with alternate outcomes, played out in mind.

"What do you propose?" Declan clasped his hands in front of him and trained his eyes on Connor.

"You let Olivia go, and I get you the chip. But she comes with me, and I make sure she's released. Then the chip is yours."

"Where's the chip?" Declan asked in a low voice, hiding his anger behind a thin veil.

"At the bank," Connor replied, and I maneuvered around to his side, curious to read Declan's features.

"Might as well open your father's box while we're there." Declan pointed to the cages. "The bank opens at eight in the morning. We'll leave then. You'll be sleeping there for tonight."

Oh God, not again.

"You've got to be kidding." Connor shook his head.

"If you really want to swap your life for this woman, then get in the damn cage!" Declan's voice exploded throughout the room. The music above increased just in time to mask his shout.

"It's okay," I whispered.

"Olivia," Connor's voice was a plea as I willingly re-entered the cage. Blake moved past Connor and was quick to lock me back up. Glowering at him, I forced myself to ask, "Where's Sean?"

"Unfortunately, he has to die." Blake removed the key from the lock and stepped up next to the empty cage, which sat a few feet away from mine.

Connor stared at me behind bars. Then he lowered his head and moved inside the second small prison. There was no way I'd let Connor die for me, but I also knew Connor had no intention of doing that. Connor was never without a plan.

Blake locked Connor's cage and pressed his palms against the bars, staring at him. "Is her pussy really worth dying for? I sure as hell don't think so. And believe me, I know . . ."

Connor sprang forward, his hand reaching between the bars and grasping Blake by the throat. His eyes grew wide as his skin turned crimson.

Blake pushed away from the cage, breaking from Connor's grip and kneeled over, coughing.

"Come on—leave the two lovers alone. It's their last night together." Declan motioned for Andrei and Oleg to head toward the set of stairs that led out of the basement.

Blake re-approached the cage. "After you die, I'm going to fuck her again. And she's going to like it," he said in a low voice before Connor slammed one palm to the metal frame.

How could I not have known the kind of man he was? I knew he was dominant and controlling, but no—he was a fucking psychopath. I shrank against the back of the cage as Blake followed Declan up the stairs.

"So, you're FBI?"

I wasn't all that surprised that he knew. I just wish it had been me who told him. If only I hadn't listened to Blake, things could've been different right now. "I'm sorry. I wanted to tell you, but—"

Connor held up his hand and leaned against the back of the narrow cage. "You don't need to apologize. Trust me," he said in a low voice.

I didn't expect that. "My boss, Blake, he's on Konstantin's payroll."

Connor's eyes grew round. "Makes sense. I knew they had to have someone on the inside. There was no way they could have manipulated all this from the outside." He was surprisingly calm, and I hoped that meant he wasn't worried.

"I'm sorry about what he said to you." My face flushed with embarrassment.

"*That* was Blake?" I saw him swallow as his hands curled into fists at his sides. Yeah, I wanted a piece of the prick, too.

"He actually used my history with Konstantin. They chose your father's company to prey on because they thought they could use our relationship to their advantage." I wasn't sure if they were recording us, but they weren't about to learn anything new if they were.

Connor took a few breaths. "They threatened my father. Sent him photos of me, Mason, my mother, and even you. If he didn't work with Declan and make the Saudi deal, then they'd kill one or all of us."

"Me? Wow. They must have gotten their information mixed up. Your father wouldn't care about me." I was surprised to hear his father hadn't willingly entered the deal. I never liked the man, so it hadn't been a far stretch for me to imagine he'd partner with Declan to save his company. I guess I'd been wrong.

I never would have thought that my ex-boyfriend would somehow lead to all of this, but I guess it takes the mind of a criminal to think up such an absurd idea.

"My father felt guilty about you," Connor admitted after a few long minutes of silence.

"What? For calling me white trash and saying I was using you for your money?" I didn't mean to say that. This wasn't the time or the place, but my anger with his father ran so deep I couldn't hold myself back.

Connor's sun-kissed skin lightened. "He said that to you?" He held on to the bars and hung his head low. "Olivia, it's more than that."

I wasn't sure if I could handle any more revelations. I'd met my max for a lifetime.

"My father felt guilty because he lied to me about you."

My eyes remained on Connor's bowed head, but I couldn't speak.

"He came home from the hospital showing me paperwork for a D&C. An abortion. He said that you demanded he pay your hospital bill because you didn't have insurance. And he told me that he offered you money if you'd end things with me. Fifty-thousand." Connor looked up, and my hand was pressed to my chest. I couldn't breathe. "He was an arrogant prick. He had some PI research you, and he discovered that you lied to me about your age. I was furious with him, and we fought. I didn't believe it, but when I called the hospital to ask about you, the nurse said you weren't taking calls. She wouldn't tell me what happened to you, but when I said I was the father, she whispered into the phone that the baby was gone."

"I had a miscarriage, Connor. A D&C is performed after a miscarriage, not just for an abortion," I dragged the words from my mouth, almost choking on them. "How could you ever think that I would terminate the pregnancy?" I covered my face with my hands.

"Olivia, I'm so sorry. I was young and stupid. I should never have believed my father. I was just so angry about losing the baby, and when he told me about the money, and I saw his credit card on the hospital bill, I snapped. I took off, ignored your calls, and ended up in the Marines. I never gave the truth a chance," Connor's voice broke.

I looked up at him, pain striking me from so many angles. I felt like I was being punched all over again. "I didn't ask him to pay my bill. I refused, but he did it without my knowledge. And yes, he did offer me money if I'd leave you, but I said no. God, he hated me so much . . ." The man was worse than I'd ever thought.

All these years I'd hated Connor, and he despised me over a lie. "How could you believe him?" I whispered. "I was mourning the loss of our child. Alone and afraid." I sank to the floor, holding my knees to my chest; it felt like I was losing the baby all over again. Losing my sister all over again.

Everything was gone.

And I was alone.

"I'm so sorry."

"None of this matters right now." I shoveled the emotion somewhere deep inside, burying it.

"It does matter, Liv. I don't deserve your forgiveness."

I didn't want to talk about it anymore.

But I was stuck inside a cage, and a few minutes later, a thought occurred to me. "How'd you even find out the truth?"

"My father knew he was going to die. He left his lawyer with a letter in the hopes I could help bring down Declan and Konstantin, but I barely spoke to my father in the last ten years, since the baby . . . I had no desire to read what he had to say." He laughed bitterly. "If I had opened it, we wouldn't be here right now."

I rubbed my hands up and down my pants, trying to slow my heart as it fluttered furiously in my chest. I could finally begin to lift my bad eyelid, although it hurt like hell. "Connor?"

"Yeah?"

I wasn't sure what I planned to say, but I allowed my heart the freedom to take control of my brain. "I think we should put the past behind us. Don't you?"

His light green eyes focused on me, and I could see a glimmer of hope on his face. But I also saw his hesitation—or maybe it was guilt—as the muscles in his face tightened. "Just try and get some rest, Olivia."

At some point, I must have heeded his advice and fallen asleep. Because the next time my eyes flashed open, Declan was standing in front of me.

29

CONNOR

"She comes with us or no deal. I can't trust that you'll let her go once you have the chip."

"And how do I know it's the real chip?" Declan folded his arms across his white T-shirt.

"It'll be legit. Just don't kill me until you verify it. There are plenty of people you can threaten to hurt if I'm lying, right?" I was being sarcastic, but in part, it was true. Not that I needed to worry about that.

Blake opened Olivia's cage. I had to do my best to channel my anger elsewhere as he opened mine. I wasn't sure who I wanted to kill first. The list kept expanding.

"Do you think we'll be able to let Olivia live with what she knows?" Declan's lips twitched at the edges, but he didn't smile. "Is your FBI friend at the bank waiting? We walk inside, and a team of Feds surround us?" He circled me, his eyes darting back and forth between Olivia and I. "No, Olivia and I will go separately and wait close to the bank. And Andrei will go in the bank with you. You can get the chip and grab whatever your dad stashed in that safe deposit box." He stopped in front of me and smoothed a hand through his hair. "Once Andrei confirms you're back in the car, safe and driving, with the chip and information, I'll put Olivia on the phone, and she can verify when she's free."

My face pinched together, anger running through me red hot. "That wasn't the deal. Once Andrei and I park outside the bank, I need to hear from Olivia that she's safe. Then I'll go inside the bank."

Declan's lips pulled together as he shook his head.

"It's this plan or no deal," I promised. "There won't be any Feds at the bank—I wouldn't risk Olivia's life."

Declan studied me, contemplating my offer.

"Don't do it, Connor," Olivia cried out.

Her face was covered in purple and blue, and I wanted nothing more than to steal her away.

The sound of a safety being removed had my attention. Oleg's gun was pressed against Olivia's temple, and her eyes flashed shut. "Want me to just end her here and now?"

"I won't be far from the bank. If you screw me over on this, and your FBI friend rescues you," Declan said, edging closer to my face, "you can be sure that I'll hunt you down and torture Olivia right in front of you. And I won't stop there. I'll destroy everyone you care about."

"Konstantin wants the weapon today. We'd better get a move on." Oleg sounded impatient.

I moved to Olivia and touched her cheek with the back of my hand. I leaned forward and swept my hand through her hair. "We'll be together again. Don't worry. Maybe we'll even eat at our favorite restaurant."

Her eyes focused on mine, and she inhaled sharply.

"How romantic, Connor. You're about to die, and you're thinking about food." Declan handed me my father's envelope. "At least whisper something sexy in her ear. Not that you'll ever have the chance to follow through . . ."

My hand fell to my side, but I had trouble looking away from her.

"Come on, Olivia. You're going with Oleg and I. Blake, you can go with Andrei and Connor. If the FBI shows up, you know what to do."

"I'll take Connor back to Konstantin's place after. He's growing impatient," Andrei responded.

"Fine. I'll meet you there." Declan motioned for Olivia to join him, and my heart grew heavy in my chest. "How does it feel to be back in the club where your sister died?" he asked as he and Olivia headed to the stairs.

Olivia halted, and a strange sensation prickled my skin.

I knew he only intended to let her go for all of five minutes while I was in the bank. But I only needed five minutes.

"Now." Declan took her by the elbow and forced her to move. "You ready?"

I rolled my eyes at Blake before following him and Andrei up into the empty club. They had parked in the alley behind the club, in a white Range Rover.

"I wouldn't fucking touch me," I said while spinning toward Blake, my chest heaving up and down after he attempted to push me into the back of the vehicle.

"I don't know what she sees in you." Blake slipped on his shades. "The people women will do for money."

My hands shot out, bunching Blake's T-shirt, and I brought my face close to his. "I'd advise you never to mention Olivia in my presence again. I don't give a fuck if you have a gun. I'll rip your face off," I growled. The idea of Blake and Olivia in bed together crashed into my mind, and I had to do all I could not to twist Blake around and push him up against the car, to ram my fist into his smug jaw.

Blake jerked free as Andrei came around next to us. "You guys have problem?" his voice thick with the accent of his mother tongue.

Blake took his sunglasses back off and shook his shirt as though my touch had left him infected.

"Let's roll." Andrei motioned for us to get in the car. He appeared to be the most civil of the animals I'd been forced to deal with in the last twelve hours. Not like that was saying much.

I reached into my back pocket for my father's envelope and held it in my hands as we drove. The letter was gone from the envelope—Declan had left only the key and passcode to the safe deposit box. Of course Declan would take it. I still couldn't believe the lie my father had told me about Olivia. Life would have been so different if he hadn't ripped my insides out.

But I was angrier with myself. I should never have believed it. Olivia had called me several times when I left New York, but I sent her to voicemail each time, before finally chucking my phone altogether. She hadn't believed my father's lie—not until I never showed up again.

I didn't deserve her. But I'd give anything for another chance. Of course, we needed to survive this first.

"We're here." Andrei slid into a parking spot across the street from the bank. He picked up his cell phone and called Declan. "We're at the bank."

"Have Olivia call from her phone." I waited with impatience for Andrei's phone to ring.

A few torturous minutes later, Andrei placed Olivia on speakerphone. "I'm getting out of the car now."

"Are you okay? Where's Declan?" The envelope crunched in my hand as worry gripped me.

"He's still in the car. But Oleg got out. He's watching me as I walk."

The busy street bustled behind her voice as she moved. "Connor, I'm worried about you," she said breathily.

"I'll be fine. Just put some distance between yourself and them. And keep your phone on. I'll call you once I'm out of the bank."

"That's enough." Blake grabbed the phone from Andrei's hand and ended the call. "Let's get this over with."

I ignored my shooting desire to snuff the light out of Blake and got out of the car. "It'll look a bit strange with both of you going in with me." I cocked a brow and folded my arms.

"I'll go with him," Andrei said. He motioned for Blake to get back in the car.

"I don't like this." Blake swung the car door open and got behind the wheel.

"How much are they paying you to betray our country?" I asked, and Blake glowered at me before slamming the door in my face.

"Guess not enough," Andrei said with a grin. He saw my surprise and shrugged. "Hate cops. Even dirty ones."

"I couldn't agree more." We dodged cars as we rushed across the street, up the stairs, and to the entrance of the bank.

"I'd like to open two of my safe deposit boxes," I said to one of the bank managers after I approached her. I gave her the box numbers and my ID, and she began tapping at her computer screen.

"Let me get the keys. I'll be right back." The woman disappeared down a hall of the massive bank, which featured a golden dome ceiling that reminded me of an old Catholic cathedral.

"Let's make this quick." Andrei remained by my side as his gaze darted around the room.

I spotted the woman coming back with the keys, and she escorted us down a different hall to a closed steel door.

Once inside, she brought us to the first box, the one in which the chip was inside—not the real chip to the EMF gun, of course. But Andrei wouldn't know the difference. The banker and I stuck our keys in at the same time. Then I entered my passcode, and we both turned our keys.

The box popped out, and I retrieved the chip.

Andrei held his hand out, and I handed the chip over to him. A smile of satisfaction met his lips as the banker and I made our way over to the next box. We repeated the same procedure, and I held my breath as the box popped open, not sure what I'd find inside.

Thank God.

I reached for the USB and held it in the palm of my hand. This time, when Andrei requested it, I shook my head. His jaw went tight, but he couldn't argue with me and raise suspicion.

"Thank you, ma'am." We left the room and started for the bank exit, but someone bumped smack into me.

"Sorry, man," an Irish voice filled the air.

"Watch where you're going," I grumbled before Andrei and I made our way out of the bank.

"Where is it?" Andrei barked out the second the doors were shut behind us.

I stopped at the top of the cement stairs that led out to the busy street. "Get Olivia back on the phone. I'll give you the USB as soon as I know Olivia's still okay." I retracted my arm from his reach. "You don't want to make a scene. There's a cop car parked across the street and the bank security guard is just inside."

Andrei rubbed his hand over his jaw and his eyes darkened. He released a breath through his nose and reached for his phone. "Here."

"Hello?" Olivia answered after the first ring.

"Are you okay?"

"So far, so good. What's going to happen now?" she asked, making no attempt to veil the fear in her voice.

"Everything will be okay, Olivia. I prom—" Andrei snatched the phone from my hand and hung up.

"Time to go." He held out his hand for the USB.

I handed it to him, but I didn't follow as he started for the Rover. "Andrei?"

"What?" His "W's" came out sounding like a "V" every time he spoke.

"Was it you or Oleg who killed Olivia's sister that night at the club?"

He walked back up the few steps he had climbed down and

faced me. "I don't remember. If me, it was accident, though. I don't make habit of killing women."

That was a surprise. Hell, I almost believed him.

"Oleg, on other hand—he don't mind." His thick accent poured over me, and I wondered if he was telling the truth. "Why you ask?"

"Just wondering who I need to kill." I shrugged at him and started down the steps.

* * *

Olivia

I WASN'T SURE IF OLEG WAS FOLLOWING ME. IT HAD BEEN AWHILE since I saw him, so I was beginning to believe Declan had other plans for me. For some reason, he wanted me to feel safe. Then he'd come after me when I didn't expect it. There was no way he would just let me go.

Maybe it was Blake who would come after me. He had the most to lose if I ever opened my mouth.

I stopped in front of the sushi restaurant that Connor and I loved. It was early in the morning, so it was closed, but I had to believe Connor had meant for me to come there.

"Olivia."

I spun around. "Jake," I cried in surprise. A flood of relief slammed into me, and it took me a moment to comprehend the fact that I'd be okay.

He came from out of the shadows of a nearby store. "Come on. We don't have much time."

"Where's Connor?"

He took my hand, and we moved down the busy street. "He'll be needing our help."

"Why didn't he just escape from the bank? You could have

helped him, or he could have gotten away, I'm sure." I gulped as he tore down the street, pulling me along with him.

"Sure, but you want to take down Konstantin, right?"

"Of course." I tried not to think of the worst case scenario—the one that resulted in Connor's death.

CONNOR

WE WERE AT BRIGHTON BEACH. THE BLUE SKY ALLOWED THE SUN to reflect off the water. The weather wasn't quite warm enough to dip into the ocean, but the typical crew of people who jogged the beach were already pounding the sand.

The strip club we were about to enter was a notorious hangout for the Russian mafia. The untouchable Konstantin had been known to hang out at almost every spot on the beach, with little care or concern about being pinched by the cops.

Given that he had FBI agents under his thumb, I could only imagine how many NYPD officers were making bank off of him, as well.

Andrei led the way inside the dimly lit club, which I assumed to be closed, and Blake followed after.

The smell of tobacco assaulted my senses and the swirl of smoke made me blink. The club was a cheap reproduction of the other gentleman's club that Konstantin owned in the meatpacking district. I'd only been to it once, by force, over ten years ago. That was before I'd ever met Olivia.

Alexander Konstantin sat on a red velvet couch, which was tucked away from the center dance stage. A Russian song was playing, a bartender was fixing coffee, and two women wearing only thongs and nothing else were on each side of Konstantin.

"This is him?" Konstantin was surprisingly fit. He was in his fifties and was well-built, with silvery gray hair, pockmarked skin, a bulbous nose, and flinty eyes.

He motioned for me to come closer as Declan entered the club from another door. Olivia wasn't with him, so I had to hope she was with Jake.

"Connor Matthews, it is so nice to meet you." Konstantin waved his hand and nodded at me. "Have a seat."

The metal case that held the EMF gun was beneath the table near Konstantin's legs.

"Here's the USB and chip." Andrei handed the two small objects to Konstantin.

"Your father didn't need to die, but he didn't give us much choice," Konstantin said while tossing the USB over to Declan. "Get my computer out of the office. I want to see what's on it."

The women on each side of Konstantin rubbed their hands against his white collared dress shirt. Their red nails ran up and down his chest, but their eyes were on me. "He's handsome, Alex," the blonde all but purred.

"Sorry. Not my type," I blurted, directing my attention to Konstantin.

"That's right. You have a thing for FBI agents, huh? It is like Romeo and Juliet. Two lovers who will both die." He smirked.

"Sir, should we test the weapon?" Oleg crouched down and reached for the gun.

"Now, on who do you propose we test it?" Konstantin pressed his palms to the table and his lips twitched.

"Sir, something's not right." Declan came into the room and set the laptop on the table in front of Konstantin.

The computer turned black and green HTML code began to scroll fast across the screen. "What the hell?" Konstantin shrieked.

I raised my hands, palms open, and lifted my shoulders. "Weird," I said before a smirk found my lips.

"What's happening?" Konstantin shoved the computer at me, and I caught it neatly in both hands.

"Just downloading every file that's on your hard drive. You don't have anything illegal on there, now do you?" I pushed to my feet, and Konstantin's men were on me in an instant. I wasn't sure how many weapons I had pointed at me.

Oleg popped open the case of the EMF gun and gripped the weapon in his hands. He studied it, trying to figure out how to lock the chip inside.

"Good luck with that," I said before winking at him.

"What the hell did you do?" Declan was at my side, his breath at my ear.

I rolled my shoulders back and cracked my neck. "What? You actually thought I came to this little party unprepared?"

"Kill him!" Konstantin shouted.

As Oleg moved in to take the kill, two canisters flew into the room, and he glanced in the direction of the sound. The lights went out as I bobbed away from Oleg's shot in the dark, and I twisted his arm around. I wanted nothing more than to kill the prick who'd stolen the life from Olivia's sister and my father, but the gas from the canisters began to fill the room.

As we both slumped to the ground, I released my grip.

* * *

Olivia

"Is it enough?" I asked Jake as he walked away from the team of federal agents who were swarming the strip club. My hands rubbed up and down the sides of my pants as I bit my lip. Jake had made a call to the FBI field office in New York after he and his friend tossed the gas into the club, effectively knocking everyone out—including Connor.

Connor was still asleep on one of the medic stretchers.

"I'd say it's more than enough to put every one of them behind bars. We might even be able to take out a few ISIS cells between the information Edward Matthews provided on the USB and everything on Konstantin's computer."

I dragged my hands over my face, feeling a true sense of relief for the first time since Jessie died. "Did you catch any heat?" I glanced over at the Irishman as he approached us.

"He's not your typical civilian." Jake grinned. "And I just told them this was all your idea, and you couldn't let anyone know because Blake was working with Declan and Konstantin."

If only that were true! "Any word on where my team member Sean is?"

"Not yet, but when Blake wakes up, we'll find out."

God, I hoped to hell he was still alive. Too much blood had already been shed.

"Thank you, Aiden," I said as he joined Jake and me in front of the club.

His sharp blue eyes focused on mine, and he patted my shoulder. "Happy I could help."

I was still amazed that Connor had the kind of friends who would swoop in to perform such dangerous feats. And at the last minute, too. Jake and Connor had called Aiden for help just last night. He had bumped into Connor at the bank, planted a tracking device on him while swapping out the USB with one loaded with software that would hack Konstantin's computer.

My lungs filled with air at the sight of Connor stepping out of the ambulance. He raked a hand through his hair and squinted in the sunlight as his eyes found me.

I charged over to him, and he met me half way, pulling me into his arms and nuzzling his face in my hair. "Connor," I cried.

"I was so damn worried about you," he said once he pulled away and touched my face with the back of his hand.

"Are you kidding? You're the one who came close to dying." I shook my head, and a smile skirted my lips. "Was it your idea to knock yourself out with gas?"

He started to laugh, but brought his hand to his mouth as a cough escaped, instead. "Of course." He wrapped his arm around my shoulder, and we walked with slow steps over to meet Aiden and Jake. "Looks like you met my friends."

"Ava sends her regards," Aiden said, slapping Connor on the back and shaking his head. "Michael was in L.A., or you know he would've been here." Aiden glanced at me and then back at Connor. "We have to stop meeting up like this. Could we please arrange a normal reunion? Maybe a bloody picnic?"

Connor coughed again as he laughed. "Hey, no one died at Michael and Kate's wedding. Well, almost. That one guy almost did when he got a little grabby with Kate."

"Lucky for me, Michael didn't want to get blood on his new bride," Aiden commented.

"You called it. I was sure he'd slug the guy. Lost ten dollars to you on that one," Jake added. "Although Connor and I knocked a little sense into him, later." He winked at me.

I touched my bad eye and forced a smile. Connor had a whole other life since we'd been together. We'd lost so much time because of a lie. But maybe it was supposed to be like this.

Maybe Connor and I had been too young, then.

But what about now?

Before I could think any more about that, Blake was walking out of the strip club, his hands cuffed behind his back. He was arguing with the two FBI agents who flanked his sides, but he stopped talking as he came close to me. His beady eyes drew into thin slits, and I swallowed at the sight of him.

When I charged, Connor was right behind me, his hand on my hip. "You son-of-a-bitch. You make me sick," I spat.

Blake jerked his head up and snickered at me. "You too, you bitch."

Connor moved in front of me, and his fist slammed hard into Blake's jaw.

I had wanted to stop him, to say something cliché like, "it's not worth it,"—but it really was . . . the sound of his knuckles connecting with Blake's face was almost sweet.

Blake lowered his head, and Connor turned to face me. "This is over, Liv. It's finally over." He rubbed my arms before touching the bruised skin by my eye. He leaned over and kissed the sensitive areas by my eye, cheek, and lips. "Everything'll be okay."

And I believed him.

31

CONNOR

"And you understand the position is temporary? If it works out, my brother might make you president or CFO. But for now, I need someone to run the company until he takes over."

The man pressed his hands on his lap and smiled. "I'd be more than happy to help out."

He was the tenth person I'd interviewed this week, and I was hoping he'd be the last. I'd hired a new director of sales and operation to replace Lauren earlier that morning. She'd been shocked when I canned her. Although she hadn't been in league with Declan or Konstantin, she had no qualms about the Saudi deal, even though she'd known it had been achieved through bribery . . . plus, she'd slept with my father. And, hell, I just didn't like her.

"As long as your background checks out, you're hired."

The man rose to his feet, shook my hand, and thanked me. We chatted a few more minutes before I had Elsa show him out.

"You sure this is what you want?" Elsa came into my room after the soon-to-be CEO was gone.

I leaned back in the chair and squeezed my eyes shut. It had been three and a half weeks since the showdown at the strip club.

Three and half weeks since I'd seen Olivia. I'd already accepted an interesting bodyguard case for a guy in Scotland, and I had no interest in staying at the office any longer.

I should've thought about the plan to hire a temp CEO a long time ago, but I would never have learned the truth about my father or been able to help Olivia.

It was still hard for me to believe my dad had died to save his family. I had yet to tell Mason—I was waiting until he came home. I hated lying to him, but I didn't want to distract him when he was fighting in the Middle East.

He'd kill me, though, once he discovered all that I'd withheld.

"Connor?"

Shit, I still hadn't spoken, had I? "I just can't be here anymore. I'm sorry, Elsa." I nodded at her, and she forced a tight-lipped smile before pulling the door closed.

I buried my face in my hands, pressing my elbows to my desk, and images of Olivia's haunting eyes and beautiful hair flooded my mind. We had agreed to give each other time. She had to wrap up the undercover operation and sort through the craziness of Blake's betrayal, and I needed to clean up the mess at Matthews Tech.

I had made the decision to hand over the EMF prototype to the military. It had no business being sold in the private sector. I had thought it would cost the company a fortune, but the government was so thankful that they awarded Matthews Tech with several new billion-dollar defense contracts.

I was doing my best to wait and let Olivia call me, but I wasn't sure how much longer I could hold out.

The buzzing of my cell phone had my head rising, and my pulse increased with the hope it was her.

The number was blocked.

"Hello?" I answered.

"Is this Connor Matthews?" a deep voice asked.

I straightened in my chair. "Yes." A slow unease built up inside me as I waited, tense, for the man to talk.

He cleared his throat. "You're listed as Mason Matthews's emergency contact."

I jumped to my feet, clutching my phone to my ear as the blood drained from my face.

"There was an explosion, and I'm afraid your brother was injured. He was flown to the Landstuhl Regional Medical Center in Kaiserslautern, Germany."

"How is he?" I pressed my hand to my desk, trying to steady myself. Worry stripped me to the core, and my nerves twisted like heated steel.

* * *

Olivia

MY HEELS CLICKED AS I WALKED DOWN THE EMPTY HALL. I WASN'T sure what I would say when I got there, but when I'd heard the news, I had to come.

Just breathe, I reminded myself as I rounded the corner and stopped just outside the room.

I tapped on the door, and after a couple seconds and a jolt that felt like a triple shot of espresso, the door opened.

Connor stood before me in jeans and a black tee, blinking. "Is that really you? I've been up for three days straight, so I'm just wondering if my eyes are playing tricks on me," he said in a throaty voice.

"Holy shit. Is that Olivia Scott? *The* Olivia?"

Connor's lips cracked into a smile. I dropped my small suitcase and rushed over to Mason's bed. "Thank God you're okay. I thought you were still—"

"Sleeping Beauty?" Mason rubbed a hand over his bruised face. "Hell no, some bomb's not going to take me out. But I'm beginning to wonder if it did some damage to my eyesight because I'm questioning whether you're real or not." I reached for Mason's hand and held it between my palms.

"I'm real. Promise." I smiled at him before peeking over my shoulder at Connor, who stood a foot behind me with folded arms. He'd grown a beard since I'd last saw him and he looked mentally and physically drained.

"He was in a coma for two days. Scared the shit out of me, but the doctors say he'll be okay. He's a tough SOB." Connor came up next to me. "I can't believe you flew all the way to Germany. How'd you know he was here?"

"Jake called me."

"Of course he did . . ."

I released Mason's hand and smoothed a smile to my face, but had to cover my mouth to try and stifle a yawn.

"Olivia, I appreciate you coming, but why don't you get some rest. I'm fine. Hell, better than fine. Look at me." Mason's gray eyes focused intently on me, and a devious smile teased his lips. "Why don't you check in at your hotel and get some sleep? Connor can drive you."

Mason had been a freshman in high school the last time I saw him, and now he was a Marine. It was crazy how time flew by.

"He looks good," I said as Connor tossed my bag into the backseat of the BMW.

"Thank God. I don't know what I would've done if—" His hand dropped to his lap, and he shifted to face me. "I'm sorry I wasn't there for you when Jessie . . ."

I reached out and touched his scruffy beard. "You don't need to do that, Connor. I'm here for you and Mason, and all that matters right now is that he's okay."

He studied me, his brows slanting and his lips slightly parting. I wasn't sure if he believed me—that, or guilt was weighing him down. "I missed you." I pulled my hand away from his face, but he caught my wrist and brought my fingers to his mouth, brushing my hand against his lips.

I shut my eyes to savor the blitz of heat that shot through my system at his simple touch. I didn't want to think about the mistakes of our past, anymore. Too much had happened, and I just wanted my "two minutes" with Connor. Only, I wanted them to last a lifetime.

"Does Mason know about what happened? With Declan? Konstantin?" My eyes fluttered open after he released my hand. "Your father?"

He turned away from me and started the car. "I told him this morning."

"Oh. How'd it go?"

"If he could've reached me, he would have smacked me in the back of the head for not opening my father's letter as soon as I got it." He gripped the stick shift as he pulled out onto the main road. "I've kicked myself every day since then."

"Thankfully, no one else got hurt." Blake had begrudgingly told the FBI where to find Sean. He had been tied up in a different facility owned by Reid Enterprises. Bruised, but alive. Thank God. "Everything happens for a reason. We took down the Russian mafia. Kind of crazy, right?"

He slipped me a sideways grin. "I just lent a hand. You did the hard work—all those months with Declan." He grimaced.

After a few minutes, he asked, "How's everything going?"

I stared down at Connor's hand on top of the stick shift and had the sudden desire to slip it between my thighs.

I looked away and out the window as we drove down the empty road, which was lined with trees and green rolling hills. "It's good. The FBI's working with Homeland, the DEA, and even the military. Konstantin's reach extends everywhere, and many people are involved." It was an intricate web, but it was unraveling fast for Konstantin.

"Are you staying in the FBI?"

I laced my fingers together on my lap and studied them as if my hands had all of the answers. "Not sure. I joined because I wanted revenge for my sister. I'm not sure if there's a place for me there anymore."

Connor's hand was on top of mine now. Warmth spread from my fingers down my arms and throughout my body.

"You can always join the road with me."

"Join the road? What happened to the company?"

He pulled up in front of the hotel. "I hired someone to manage it until Mason can take over."

I nodded. "Is Mason okay with that?"

"He yelled at me. A lot." Connor flashed me his white teeth. "But he'll get over it."

I rolled my tongue over my teeth, contemplating our future—what to say—but he went ahead and got out of the car. He grabbed my bag and tossed the keys to the valet. "Would you like your own room or . . .?" He reached for my hand and pulled me up against him.

We were standing in the middle of the lobby with people surrounding us, and of course, Connor didn't care. My breasts pushed against his hard chest, and he held me close to him.

His fingers combed through my hair before his hand cupped the back of my neck. "We can share," I whispered before I bit my lip. His eyes darkened, mirroring the lust I felt, which had percolated for the last month in his absence.

"Good answer." He yanked on my hand, hurried us out of the lobby and to our first floor room.

As soon as the light turned green on the lock, he scooped me into his arms.

He set me on the bed and stared down at me, his chest rising and falling. "I know you're tired, and so am I, but—"

I slipped my T-shirt over my head and tossed it to the floor. "I don't care. I want you."

He groaned and lunged onto the bed, his hand sliding under my back as he braced himself on top of me. His tongue met mine, and for the first time in my entire life, I felt at peace.

His lips traveled to my neck, and he teased me with his fingers as he pinched my nipple beneath my lace bra. "I'd never grow tired of this," he whispered into my ear, his breath creating a ripple of shivers throughout my body.

I arched my back and bucked my hips as he worked to remove my skinny jeans, which was no easy feat.

"Are these glued to your legs?" He pulled and tugged, and I couldn't help but laugh. "Finally," he said, tossing them over his shoulder before reaching for the button of his pants.

Perching myself up on my elbows, I watched as he stripped before me. His tan chest, defined abs, and—I wet my lips—rather incredible hard-on—had set my pulse racing. I unclipped my bra and tucked my thumbs under the line of my panties before pulling them down.

The white of his eyes were less visible as the beautiful green grew wider. A low growl escaped from his lips.

"I love you, Connor Matthews." The words came from my mouth before I realized I'd said them.

After staring down at me for what felt like forever, his mouth pressed to mine, which delivered an irresistible blow to my insides. My thighs tightened around where his hand shifted, and he had my body moving in rhythm with his touch. "I could do this forever," he said into my ear as my body shuddered from orgasm.

I jerked up against him as his hard cock filled my wet center, and I gripped his shoulders, trying to support myself as I cried with every thrust.

His eyes remained on mine as he moved, and I was captivated by him. "And I plan on doing it forever."

My hands wandered over his muscled biceps, which were flexed as he held his weight above me. "Connor," I cried out again as I felt the delicious ache between my legs stirring. "Yesssss . . ."

He lowered his head as his body convulsed a few minutes later, and he sank next to me and pulled me into his arms. "I love you,

Liv. I never stopped." He kissed the top of my head, and I drifted to sleep.

* * *

Connor

"Olivia?"

With closed eyes, I felt around the bed, finding it empty. Where was she?

I wasn't sure how long I'd been asleep, but I could have sworn I'd heard a door shut.

"Olivia?" Forcing my eyes open, I discovered the bedroom empty, and the bathroom door closed.

My legs felt like dead weight as I moved to the bathroom, desperate to get more sleep. I'd been awake for seventy-two hours before Olivia had arrived at the hospital, after all.

I still couldn't believe she'd flown to Germany to be there for Mason, for me.

I had been so wrong years ago, but I planned on spending the rest of our lives making it up to her. She was the woman I was meant to be with.

It was fate.

Jim's words were in my mind once as I reached for the doorknob. *Second chances are few and far between.*

And I was being given my second chance.

"Olivia, are you okay?" I tapped at the door and touched the round knob, but it was locked.

"Just a second, Connor," she responded in a strained voice.

"You okay?"

"Yeah. Hang on."

I heard the toilet flush. Then running water.

A couple minutes ticked by as I sat naked on the bed, waiting.

"Sorry." She opened the door and stood fully dressed in its frame.

"Why'd you get dressed? I wasn't done with you."

Her bottom lip tucked between her teeth and her eyes darted to the floor.

I was on my feet. At the sight of her, concern gripped hold of me. I touched her chin and guided her face up toward mine. "What is it, Liv?"

"Do you believe in second chances?" she asked in a soft voice.

Was she a mind reader? "You're here, aren't you?"

"I mean—" She reached into her pocket.

I studied what she held in the palm of her hand, and I dropped to my knees. For the first time since my friend died in Iraq, emotion pushed through me, and I allowed it to escape.

Olivia was in front of me, and I crushed her against me. "We're having a baby?" I choked out, reaching for the pregnancy test.

I stared down at the two stripes on the test and rubbed a hand over my face.

Her eyes welled with tears, and she nodded. "What do you think?" Her voice broke.

My thumb touched her cheeks, smoothing away the tears. "I think we'd better have a boy. Because I don't know how I'll ever handle a daughter of mine dating. If she looks anything like her mother . . ." I scrubbed a hand over my short beard.

She tilted her head back, and the sweetest sound filled my ears —her laughter. "I can see it now—the shotgun by the door." She shook her head at me as her lips opened into a broad smile. "I think you'd make a daughter proud."

ALSO BY BRITTNEY SAHIN

Want more Connor & Mason?

They make a guest appearance in the romantic mob suspense, *My Every Breath.*

Hidden Truths

The Safe Bet – Begin the series with the Man-of-Steel lookalike Michael Maddox.

Beyond the Chase - Fall for the sexy Irishman, Aiden O'Connor, in this romantic suspense.

Surviving the Fall – Jake Summers loses the last 12 years of his life in this action-packed romantic thriller.

The Final Goodbye - Ben Logan's book

Stealth Ops SEAL Series

Finding His Mark

Finding Justice

Finding the Fight

Finding Her Chance

Finding the Way Back

Becoming Us Series

Someone Like You - A former Navy SEAL. A father. And off-limits.

My Every Breath - Cade King has fallen for the wrong woman. She's the daughter of a hitman - and he's the target.

Dublin Nights

On the Edge - Travel to Dublin and get swept up in this romantic suspense starring an Irish businessman by day…and fighter by night.

On the Line - novella

Stand-alone (with a connection to _On the Edge_):

The Story of Us– Sports columnist Maggie Lane has 1 rule: never fall for a player. One mistaken kiss with Italian soccer star Marco Valenti changes everything…

CONNECT

Thank you for reading Olivia and Connor's story. If you loved the book, please take a quick moment to leave a review.

Sign up at brittneysahin.com to receive **exclusive excerpts** and **bonus material** for my novels, as well as take part in great **giveaways**, which include gift cards, signed paperbacks, and e-books by some of your favorite romance authors.

For more information:
www.brittneysahin.com
brittneysahin@emkomedia.net

Printed in Great Britain
by Amazon

36479585R00173